Rough and Deadly

Paula Williams

Read *Murder Served Cold*
the first in the series.

CROOKED
CAT

Copyright © 2019 by Paula Williams
Artwork: Adobe Stock © Dmitry Ersler
Design: soqoqo
Editors: Alice Cullerne-Bown
All rights reserved.

No part of this book may be used or reproduced in any manner
whatsoever without written permission of the author or Crooked Cat
Books except for brief quotations used for promotion or in reviews.
This is a work of fiction. Names, characters, and
incidents are used fictitiously.

First Black Line Cats Edition, Crooked Cat, 2019

Discover us online:
www.crookedcatbooks.com

Join us on facebook:
www.facebook.com/crookedcat

Tweet a photo of yourself holding
this book to **@crookedcatbooks**
and something nice will happen.

To my family, friends and neighbours who have all appeared in my stories at one time or another (although none of them are murderers - as far as I know).

But a special dedication goes to my husband who tries not to look too worried when I exclaim: "That would make a great place to hide a body!" and when my bedtime reading is my well-thumbed Crime Writers' Handbook, the one with the subtitle "Sixty five ways to kill your victim"….. my love, thanks and apologies to him.

Acknowledgements

My sincere thanks to Laurence and Steph at Crooked Cat Books for believing in me enough to take a chance on this, my second book with them. And to my fabulous editor, Alice Cullerne-Bown for her kindness and encouragement, not to mention her infinite patience over All Those Capital Letters I still seem to be Addicted To!

My thanks once again to the people of Somerset and those from my small village in particular for providing me with such a rich source of inspiration. Although it goes without saying, I only used them for the 'goodies'. The 'baddies' are complete figments of my over active imagination.

My thanks, too, goes to all those lovely readers who took a chance on my first book, *Murder Served Cold*, read it and left such lovely reviews. You've no idea how those kind words helped and encouraged me.

But the biggest thank you of all goes to you, the reader. Without you, none of this would be possible. My sincere and grateful thanks.

About the Author

Paula Williams has been writing since she was old enough to hold a pencil but she's been making up stories since she was old enough to speak, although her early attempts were more of the "It wasn't me, Mum, honest. It was him" genre.

Her first 'serious' effort was a pageant she wrote at the age of nine to celebrate St George's Day. Not only was she the writer, but producer, set designer and casting director, which was how she came to have the title role. She also bullied and blackmailed her three younger brothers into taking the supporting roles, something they still claim to be traumatised by.

Many years later, this pageant became the inspiration for her first publishable short story, Angels on Oil Drums, which she sold to the UK magazine Woman's Weekly. Since then she's had over four hundred short stories and serials published in the UK and overseas and has a number of novels in large print which are available in libraries.

Following the success of her first full length novel, Murder Served Cold, Paula has gone on to write a second in the series and is looking forward to writing many more. A proud member of both the Crime Writers' Association and the Romantic Novelists' Association, she also writes a monthly column, Ideas Store, for the UK writers' magazine, Writers' Forum and blogs at paulawilliamswriter.wordpress.com She can be found on her author page on Facebook at facebook.com/paulawilliams.author and on Twitter at @paulawilliams44

She has two grown up sons, two beautiful daughters-in-law and three gorgeous grandchildren. She lives in Somerset with her husband and a handsome rescue Dalmatian called Duke who is completely bonkers and appears frequently on her blog. (The dog, not the husband!)

Rough and Deadly

Chapter One

The barn door screeched like a soul in torment as Margot dragged it open and peered into the darkness. She gave a quick glance back at the still-empty yard and smiled. Great. She was here before him. Chance to go in and have a good look round before he tried covering things up.

The stupid man hadn't even bothered to lock the door. Yet another black mark against him. What sort of security was that? Anyone – including children – could just waltz in here and help themselves to the disgusting stuff.

She stepped inside, felt around for the light switch, then cursed as she caught a fingernail on the rough breeze block wall. That manicure had cost a fortune, too. She fumbled inside her bag for her phone to give herself some much-needed light.

"Damn it!" She tossed the completely dead phone back into her bag. She was sure she'd charged the wretched thing this morning. She hoped John hadn't been trying to call her. He'd kill her if he found she'd let her phone die again. He got really uptight if he couldn't get in touch with her while he was away.

It was quite sweet, really, the way he worried about her. Still, she'd make a point of charging the phone the minute she got home.

She took a deep breath, then wished she hadn't as the stench of decay filled her nostrils and hit the back of her throat.

"Get a grip, Margot," she told herself sternly. It was a cider farm, after all. The sickly, cloying odour was just rotting apples, nothing more sinister. Even so, she wouldn't be sorry to get back into the fresh air again. The smell was getting deep into the pit of her stomach.

Gradually her eyes became accustomed to the dim light. She could make out the outline of two large vats against the far wall. That must be where the cider was kept during the fermentation process. Next to that was a cluttered bench where, she imagined, the bottling process took place. Not a hand basin nor a sterilising unit was anywhere to be seen, as far as she could make out.

She knelt down and felt the floor. Her fingers slid across the soft, dust-laden surface. Either it hadn't been swept in years or, even worse, it was just compacted earth. Once again, she cursed her dead phone but she'd seen – and smelt – enough to confirm that her suspicions had been correct.

Even in this poor light, she could see the place was a hygiene horror scene. The Environmental Health department would shut the place down in a heartbeat. And not before time.

She stiffened at a sound in the farthest, darkest corner, behind one of the vats.

"Mr Compton? Is that you?" she called. But there was no reply. As she moved, she heard a scuffling, not big enough to be human. Then silence.

Rats! It had to be. She'd heard stories about how cider makers would throw dead rats into the cider vats to speed the fermentation process. She was never sure if this was actually true, or if it was yet another story the regulars of the Winchmoor Arms told her to wind her up.

But having now seen and smelt this place, she could well imagine Abe Compton taking part in such a disgusting and unhygienic process.

"Rough cider, this be the proper stuff, this be," he'd said, in the thick, Somerset accent that she had difficulty following. His round, red face beamed with pride as he went on. "Not that fizzy lemonade they do sell in them gastric pubs and clubs. You should try some, missus. 'Twould put hairs on your chest."

Try it? She wouldn't even use the stuff to unblock her drains. As for his foolish wife, advising her to serve it to her dinner guests – well, she'd set her straight on that.

"I wouldn't be seen dead drinking it," she'd said. And she'd meant every word.

She glanced down at her slim gold watch. By angling it

towards the sliver of light from the partly open door, she could see it was ten past seven. Where was the wretched man? How dare he keep her waiting? According to the message on her answerphone, he'd particularly wanted her to be here no later than 7 o'clock. The cheek. And now he didn't even have the courtesy to be on time.

Well, she'd given him long enough, and now he'd missed his chance. Tomorrow she'd be contacting the Environmental Health Officer to make an official complaint about the place. She hadn't been that bothered when he was making the cider for his own consumption. It was none of her business if he chose to poison himself. But now he'd persuaded that foolish woman in the Winchmoor Arms to stock it and sell it on to unsuspecting members of the public, that was a different matter entirely. She'd been planning to give him fair warning about cleaning up his act. But it was too late now.

Somebody had to do something. And that somebody was her. As the newest member of Much Winchmoor parish council, it was her civic duty. And it would earn her some much-needed Brownie points with the other councillors.

Of course, she hadn't actually been elected yet, but that, she'd been assured, was a mere formality.

She'd told John she was going to a meeting of the Floral Arts Society tonight. She'd always been a great believer that what you don't know can't hurt you.

She'd seen enough and turned back towards the open door, looking forward to getting back into the fresh air. But as she moved towards it, the door closed, plunging the place into total darkness.

"Mr Compton? Is that you?" she called again. Completely disorientated by the pitch black, she strained her ears for sounds of movement. "For pity's sake, man, put the light on. I can't see a thing. It's as dark as the grave in here."

She heard a sound behind her. A footstep. A rustle of fabric. A waterproof coat maybe? Then a sudden swish of movement. A rush of air. Then no more.

No more light. No more movement.

Only darkness. As black and as permanent as the grave

itself.

Margot Duckett-Trimble would never see, hear or feel anything. Ever again.

Saturday evening, six days earlier

"OK. Let me get this right," I said, trying hard to keep my cool. "You're standing me up on a Saturday night? For a sheep?"

On the other end of the phone, I heard Will sigh. And I didn't need to see his face to know he'd be wearing his favourite, long-suffering expression.

"Oh, for pity's sake, Katie, you're such a drama queen. Of course I'm not standing you up."

"Oh no? I have tickets for the Bad Cowboys in concert, the hottest gig in town and one that I've been looking forward to forever. Then you tell me, half an hour before we're due to leave, that you can't make it. What do you call that, if it's not being stood up?"

"I call it earning a living," he said, all quiet and po-faced. Believe me, Will can be very po-faced when the mood takes him. "And, what's more to the point, I also call it animal welfare. I've got a couple of young ewes who are looking a bit panicky. They're due to lamb at any moment and I'd rather not leave them. I could meet you in the pub later for a quick pint, if all goes well."

"Forget it," I said waspishly. "A quick pint and a packet of prawn cocktail crisps is not my idea of a fun Saturday night. And I'm quite capable of going to a concert on my own, Will Manning. I don't need you to escort me."

"Oh really? And how are you getting there? Your Mum's lending you her car, is she? Only, if I remember right, the last time you borrowed it, you managed to wrap it around a metal gate while attempting a three – or was it a ten? – point turn. And as I further recall she said she'd never let you borrow it again."

"I didn't wrap it around a gate. It was only a little dent and I—" I began, but he cut in.

"Sorry, Katie. Got to go. Don't go doing any more ten point turns, will you?"

"Don't call me Katie…" I said, but he'd already gone.

"Problems?" Mum asked.

I nodded. "Mum, I don't suppose I could borrow your car, could I?"

…

Monday morning

Have you ever had one of those days that start bad and get progressively worse? Saturday was one of those. I worked freelance for the local newspaper, *The Dintscombe Chronicle*, which meant I got to do all the rubbish jobs that the staff reporters didn't want to do. That was how I came to be covering the Longmoor Parva Fun Dog Show (at least that's what it said on the poster) in the afternoon.

Only the fun, if there ever was any, stopped when the heavens opened in the middle of the grand parade and turned the playing fields into a quagmire. After which I had to cycle home, all five miles of it, in the driving rain.

This was followed by Will and his no-show in the evening. Days didn't get any worse than that. Or so I thought, until I reached the Monday from hell.

Being stood up for a pregnant sheep is not funny. But being up to my armpits in perm lotion while a gaggle of old ladies wittered and giggled about it like I wasn't in the room, is about as un-funny as a banana skin on a tightrope.

I vowed it was the last time I'd let myself get strong-armed by my mum (the Cheryl of Chez Cheryl, *'Your hair, our care, perms a speciality'*) into working in her salon.

"It's no good, Katie," she'd said over breakfast that morning. "You'll have to help out. I'm booked solid because of the funeral. How Sandra could do this to me, today of all days, I don't know."

She shuddered as she forced down a second spoonful of prune and bran compote. This was her latest wonder diet, where the only food you were allowed was so disgusting you never wanted to eat anything ever again.

"You should have some," she mumbled as she struggled to swallow. "Much better for you than chocolate Hobnobs."

I didn't think it would go down well if I pointed out that she was the one who couldn't fit into last year's clothes, not me.

"As for poor Maurice..." She gave up and pushed the bowl away with a sigh. "Can you imagine how he must feel? His wife running off with a chiropodist called Clint? At her age, too."

Sandra is Mum's assistant, sixty going on ninety and a martyr to her feet, or so she'd have us believe. And yes, I should have known better than to make 'corny' jokes about Sandra knowing her 'bunions' and how Maurice should have put his 'foot' down. Mum doesn't have much of a sense of humour on a Monday morning, when she's faced with a full appointment book and no assistant. Particularly when all she's had for breakfast is a couple of spoonfuls of prune and bran compote.

Chez Cheryl is Much Winchmoor's top hairdressing establishment, or so it says on the sign on our gate. Although that isn't quite as impressive as it sounds, seeing as it's Much Winchmoor's only hairdressing establishment and is established in our front room (*closed Mondays, Wednesdays and Sundays, special rates for OAPs*).

But it wasn't closed that Monday, more's the pity. Because that afternoon there was a funeral in the village and if there's one thing this place enjoys, it's a good funeral. Everyone was going, hence the stampede to get their hair done. "As a mark of respect to dear old Albert," was how they put it.

There'd be more nice tight curls at Albert's send-off than in the poodle section at Crufts, or the Longmoor Parva Fun Dog Show. All courtesy of Chez Cheryl.

"But Mum," I protested, "I'm busy today. I've got my write-up on the Dog Show to do for the Chronicle, and then I was going job hunting. I've found this new recruitment agency which looks promising."

"That's what you said about the last one, and the best they could come up with was a shelf stacker in a supermarket twenty miles away," she said. "So for now, you don't have to go job hunting because this one's found you. I'll pay you the going rate. And when the rush dies down I'll see if I can do something to tone down your hair colour." She gave a puzzled frown as she peered at my hair. "What shade did you say you used? It's not anything I recognise."

It wouldn't be. I hadn't exactly intended to end up with purple hair. But I'd been experimenting with some of Mum's colours, mixing a bit of this and a bit of that, and although I'd been aiming for a slightly more subtle shade of aubergine, I quite liked the way it had turned out and thought it looked cool with my short, spiky cut.

The other thing I liked about it was that Will would absolutely hate it. Which would serve him right.

Mum stood up, patted her own neatly trimmed curls and glanced up at the kitchen clock. "Right then. I'll see you in the salon in ten minutes," she said, even though I couldn't remember actually agreeing to do it. "And make sure you're wearing something decent that doesn't show everything you've got. How you don't catch pneumonia beats me."

How about that? My mother telling me what to do, wear and eat, like I was six years old. She'd be checking my homework next.

But I was twenty-four, with a degree in Media Studies. Fifteen months ago I'd had a life – and a head full of dreams of how that life was going to turn out.

I'd had this really ace flat, not too far from Bristol city centre, perfect for hitting the clubs and bars, which I did most weekends. I'd had a job I loved as dogsbody with a local radio station, and a long term relationship with this dead gorgeous bloke who looked like a young Brad Pitt.

Oh yes, and I'd had a cool name back then, too. Everyone called me Kat.

Now, I was back home living with my mum and dad

and sleeping in the same small bedroom I'd had since I was a little kid. All the mates I used to know were either married, had moved away, or both. I had debts the size of Manchester and I'd have to live to be a hundred and twenty-seven before I finished paying off my overdraft.

And no one remembered to call me Kat instead of Katie. No matter how many times I asked them to.

I kept reminding Mum and Dad when they moaned on about how they were victims of the boomerang generation (that's me, apparently) that I wasn't exactly back home by choice.

But my long term relationship turned into even longer term financial difficulties when my Ratface boyfriend dumped me and ran off, not only with my ex-best friend, but the car that was half mine, and my signed photograph of David Tennant as Dr Who.

Then, a week later, my dream job turned into a nightmare when I had the 'we're having to let you go' and 'this is hurting me more than it's hurting you' talk from my about-to-be ex-boss at the radio station.

In no time at all, the strain of keeping up the rent on the ace, not-quite city centre flat I'd shared with Ratface, while I tried in vain to find another job, led to financial meltdown.

After which I'd been forced to go back to my parents, with my tail as firmly between my legs as the dogs at Saturday afternoon's rain soaked not-much-fun dog show.

I'd been back in Much Winchmoor for just over a year now. And if jobs in a buzzy city centre are hard to find, in a back-of-beyond Somerset village they are rarer than hens' teeth. Especially without the half a car that I used to own.

Mum was very sympathetic and was in no hurry for me to move out. And why would she be? She had a live-in helper in the salon whenever she needed one. But Dad was always dropping hints about how it was time for me to be moving on.

In the past year I'd been dumped twice (initially for my

ex-best friend and, more recently, for a pregnant sheep), sacked twice (once from the radio station and I'd still prefer not to think about the second one) and now my Dad wanted my room for a snooker table.

Even when I began to think that maybe, just maybe, I had something going with Will, this guy I've known forever and who I used to think of as a brother until my feelings towards him turned decidedly un-sisterly, what did he do after standing me up?

Nothing.

No phone call. No text. Nothing.

And yes, I knew he was a farmer, and that he was in the middle of lambing. But there I was, last Saturday night, all glammed up in this dead cool sparkly top and my best pair of jeans that I hadn't worn since the Ratface era, watching the Eurovision Song Contest with Mum and Dad. Because, of course, Mum didn't lend me her car. And even if she had, I didn't really fancy going to the concert on my own, whatever I might have said to Will.

Much Winchmoor? Not-Much Winchmoor, more like it. This village is buried so far in the depths of Somerset even the postman has to use SatNav to find us.

Back when I went to primary school here, Much Winchmoor had four farms, a post office-cum-general store, a butcher, a pub and, of course, Chez Cheryl. Now the school was on borrowed time, there were no shops and there was only one farm. Or two if you counted Abe Compton's cider farm, which I didn't because his cider was disgusting stuff that addled your brain and turned your knees inside out.

The High Street's higgledy-piggledy houses with their tiny windows and wonky rooflines were mostly all holiday cottages now, with names like 'The Old Post Office', 'The Old Forge', 'The Old Bakehouse' and, before long no doubt, 'The Old Village Pub' – although The Winchmoor Arms had enjoyed a brief but ghoulish surge in trade recently.

"Where did you say Sandra was today?" Olive

Shrewton's question jerked me back to the Monday from hell, where thankfully they'd finished with my love life and were now picking over the mystery of Sandra's absence. "She'll be that upset when she hears Clint the chiropodist has upped and gone. She reckons it's only his magic fingers that do keep her going."

I had to hurriedly turn my snort of laughter into a cough, which wasn't difficult as I was rinsing off her perm lotion at the time and the fumes were hitting the back of my throat. Conscious of Mum's eyes boring into me, I refrained from commenting that Clint's magic fingers must have kept Sandra going a bit too well, seeing as how she'd skipped off to Torquay with him. Mum had sworn me to secrecy, although goodness knows why. Trying to keep a secret in Much Winchmoor is about as futile as attempting to keep a ferret in a paper bag.

"Olive's ready for you now, Mum," I said, but as I did so, Mum's phone rang. She took it out of her pocket, frowned, then answered it.

"Look, I can't talk at the moment," she said in such a snippy voice I thought the person on the other end of the line must be trying to sell her a stair lift or maybe one of those walk-in baths. "I'm up to my eyes here at the moment," she went on. "Can I call you back?"

No stair lift or bath salesman, then. But whoever it was had got right under her skin, as her cheeks burned scarlet the way they always did when she was annoyed.

Every ear in the room strained to hear what was being said on the other end of the line but Mum pressed the phone closer and turned her back. She listened for a while then said, "Oh no, I'm sorry to hear that." Even though she sounded anything but sorry.

Another slightly shorter listen. More ear-straining around the room. Then she said: "Yes, yes. I can understand you're upset. No. No, that will be fine. Of course. Bye."

"Everything ok?" I asked.

"Yes, of course," Mum said with a very unconvincing

attempt at a nonchalant shrug. "Just one of those wretched nuisance calls."

Needless to say no-one in the room bought that line. After all, you don't offer to call nuisance callers back, do you? But it was obvious Mum had decided that whatever it was, she didn't want it discussed by the massed members of the Much Winchmoor Grumble and Gossip Group.

"Bring Olive across, will you, Katie? I'll be ready for her in a second."

Olive's wet hair made her look like a gone-to-seed dandelion that had got caught in the rain. Her soft grey eyes shone with curiosity as she prepared to quiz Mum about the phone call. I wrapped her in a towel and was leading her across to the chair in front of the mirror when the salon door crashed open.

The most irritating woman in Much Winchmoor stood there. The Monday from hell had just got a whole heap worse.

Chapter Two

A stick-thin woman with sleek blonde hair swept in, on a drift of expensive perfume. It was Margot Duckett-Trimble, our very own lady of the manor. Even though she was an incomer (you have to live in the place at least twenty years to be otherwise) she swanned about Much Winchmoor like she owned the place, which, come to think of it, she did. Or at least, a significant chunk of it.

Although, strictly speaking, it was her husband John (who was 'something big in the City,' as she was always at pains to point out) who probably signed the cheques.

Since the Duckett-Trimbles moved into Winchmoor Manor three years ago, every time one of the houses in the village came up for sale, particularly the little higgledy-piggledy cottages that overlooked the village pond, John would snaffle it up for Margot to turn into one of her 'darling little holiday homes'. Including the one that used to belong to my gran, something that caused a fair amount of bad feeling in the village, not to mention long, angry silences between my mum and dad.

"Cheryl," Margot announced like she was auditioning for the part of Lady Macbeth. "I'm desperate. My car is refusing to start. And the wretched taxi firm can't get a car out to me in time."

Mum looked confused. "I'm sorry. But I make a habit of not lending my car out. Not since a certain person—"

"Merciful heavens, I don't want to borrow your car." Margot looked horrified at the idea. "I was on my way to Bath to have my hair done. John's bringing a group of important businessmen for dinner this evening and my hair's a frightful mess. I was in a bit of a panic, but then I thought you could probably fit me in."

Her satin-smooth blonde bob didn't appear to have a single strand out of place. But what did I know?

"Oh, I see," Mum said. "Well, I'm sorry but I'm really busy this morning. I've already got Olive here waiting—"

Margot Duckface, as she's known locally, looked down her long beaky nose at Mum's four customers, all in various stages of the perm process.

"You're Julie's grandmother, aren't you?" She inclined her head regally towards Olive.

Olive nodded, and I swear if she hadn't been trussed up like an oven-ready turkey she'd have bobbed a quick curtsey.

"Julie's such a sweetie," Margot purred. "Always so grateful for the few hours light cleaning I find for her up at the Manor, especially now they have another little mouth to feed. She often says she doesn't know how they'd manage if it wasn't for the money I pay her. I don't suppose you'd mind…?"

I couldn't believe it. The wretched woman was only expecting Olive to give up her position in the queue to her, like we were still back in the Dark Ages when villagers tugged their forelocks and knew their place.

"Bless you, my dear, I'm in no rush," Olive said placidly. "I'm sure young Katie here will fetch me a cup of tea – two sugars and a chocolate biscuit, please, Katie – while I'm waiting. You carry on."

"Thank you, Olive," Mum, relieved, turned to Margot. "I'll be two minutes finishing Millie, then I'll be right with you, if you'd care to take a seat in the Reception area."

Margot pouted, then glanced at her slim gold wristwatch and shrugged. With a rustle of silk she arranged herself on one of the spindly chairs that, along with a wobbly glass-topped coffee table holding a few dog eared copies of *Hello!* and *Somerset Life*, made up Chez Cheryl's Reception area.

Margot smiled graciously at the two women waiting there, then at the room in general.

"I trust you're all going to vote in next week's parish council elections?" she intoned, in a voice that put me in mind of Maggie Smith's dowager countess in Downton Abbey.

"Suffragettes died for your right to do so, remember."

The two women said of course they would, while Millie Compton nodded so vigorously, she almost had Mum's styling comb up her nose.

"I'll be there, Mrs Duckett-Trimble," Millie twittered. "We need another woman on the parish council since poor Marjorie passed on."

In case you're wondering, poor Marjorie Hampton didn't 'pass on' of her own free will. She was helped on her way by a murdering maniac who was now doing time for her killing.

"Can I count on your votes, ladies?" asked Margot.

She had been on the campaign trail for weeks. There was one seat up for grabs and two candidates. But talk about having to choose between a rock and a hard place. Will's lunatic sheep dog, Tam, would have been in with a fair shout of getting elected if she'd chosen to stand.

With her high and mighty ways, Margot Duckface was as popular in Much Winchmoor as a bluebottle in a cake shop, while the other candidate, Fiona Crabshaw, was equally disliked on account of being married to Gruesome Gerald. He'd been a local councillor for years but was 'invited' to resign his seat on the District Council last year when he'd been 'almost' involved (as in, not proven) in an iffy land deal.

It wasn't Fiona's fault, of course, but the voters of Much Winchmoor were a cautious lot and were not keen on having another Councillor Crabshaw in the village.

Millie Compton, however, had no reservations about where to cast her vote. She was well pleased with her cauliflower-tight perm and, as Mum was making out the bill, she turned to Margot.

"You can count on my vote, Mrs Duckett-Trimble," she simpered, then added in a low, hesitant voice. "I-I couldn't help overhearing as how you're having visitors up at the Manor tonight."

"A business dinner," Margot yawned, as her elegantly manicured hands flicked through *Hello!* and she pretended to be fascinated by a picture of some celeb's new garden shed. "A terrible bore, of course, but it's the price you have to pay when your husband's something big in the City."

"Oh, I know," agreed Millie, who didn't know because the only thing her husband was big in was making a nuisance of himself when he got trolleyed. "My Abe's cider's ever so good this year. The best yet, he says. It goes down a treat with the tourists in the Winchmoor Arms. 'Tis a proper taste of Somerset, they do say. So I wondered if you'd like some for your visitors? Foreigners, I hear they are."

Margot's finely drawn eyebrows shot up. "I intend calling on your husband soon about his cider."

Millie glowed with pride while the rest of us gaped like a nest of baby starlings. Abe's HeadBender cider was as rough as rough cider could get, and not for the faint hearted. Only a couple of nights earlier there'd been talk among the Winchmoor Arms regulars about how many rats and other livestock unlucky enough to wander into his barn ended up in the vats.

Abe's cider, they reckoned, could strip the flesh of a piece of meat quicker than a shoal of piranhas.

But Millie's glow vanished abruptly as Margot went on: "I've heard worrying reports about his poor hygiene practices and have strongly advised Mary not to sell it in the pub any more. The poor woman has enough problems running the place single-handed without risking prosecution for poisoning her customers."

"But my Abe wouldn't—"

"It's people like your Abe who give not only Much Winchmoor, but our entire glorious county of Somerset, a bad name. When tourists ask for a glass of 'scrumpy', they mean the nice sparkling stuff they advertise on TV. Not that rough, cloudy muck that looks like washing-up water and tastes like battery acid. As for my guests," she shuddered dramatically. "I wouldn't be seen dead drinking it, least of all offering it to them."

There was one of those horrible silences, like the time on the school bus when Will dared me to say this dead rude word. And I was the only person on the bus who didn't know what it meant. Nor how very rude it was.

17

Poor little Millie stood there, her face scarlet, her newly permed head bobbing up and down like the little nodding dog in the back of my grandad's hatchback.

"I-I just thought... so sorry to have troubled you..." she muttered as she fumbled in her big squashy bag. "I'm sorry, Cheryl, my purse is in here somewhere. If I can just—"

"It's ok, Mum. I'll sort it." I put myself between Millie and the others in the salon to shield her from their not entirely sympathetic eyes. There were many women in Much Winchmoor with very good reason not to approve of Abe Compton's HeadBender cider and its after-effects.

"So what's it to be?" Mum asked Margot. "Something off the fringe, maybe? It is a little on the heavy side, isn't it?"

"Good Lord, no." Margot jumped like a startled thoroughbred. "Jean-Christophe would have a fit if I let anyone other than him near my hair with a pair of scissors. A shampoo and blow-dry will be fine. You can do blow-dries, I assume?"

Mum clamped her lips tightly together and those little red spots appeared in her cheeks again. She led Margot across to the basins and shampooed her, more's the pity. I'd been looking forward to sending trickles of icy water down that long, elegant neck and seeing if I could get a dollop of shampoo to land smack on the end of that beaky nose.

Half an hour later, Mum was just putting the finishing touches to Margot's sleek bob, and Olive was happily munching her way through her third chocolate Hobnob, when the front door crashed opened again. A vision in bubblegum pink Lycra with a cascade of strawberry blonde hair (think Dolly Parton without the frontage) stood there, with enough jangling bracelets to sink the Titanic.

Now, when I said earlier that Margot Duckett-Trimble was the most annoying woman in the village, that was before I was aware my Aunty Tanya was in the vicinity. She was married to Dad's brother, Uncle Richard, and hated being called Aunty Tanya. Said it made her feel old and frumpy.

Which was precisely why I called out, "Hi, Aunty Tanya."

She turned to me, her eyes cold and hard. "It's you, Katie.

For a moment I didn't recognise you."

She raked me with her hyper-critical gaze, taking in my ripped jeans and the horrible pink gingham tabard Mum insisted I wore in the salon, before resting finally on my hair.

She turned to Mum, her face a study in false concern. "Oh my goodness, Cheryl. Did you have a rogue batch of colour? Still, at least it was Katie, and not one of the paying customers."

"Katie's hair's none of my doing," Mum said sharply, as a small wave of barely suppressed laughter rippled around the salon. "But heavens, Tanya, you must have flown to have got here so quickly. I wasn't expecting you until lunch time."

The mystery of Mum's 'nuisance' caller was solved. So, too, was the change in her mood since taking it. Dad and his brother Richard were what Gran Latcham used to describe as 'chalk and cheese.' So, too, were their wives.

Relations between Mum and Tanya had always been a bit strained, although there was a time a year or so back when it looked as if they were about to get more friendly when they had a girlie weekend away together in Brighton or somewhere. I can't remember exactly. But it didn't come to anything and things were now as edgy between them as they'd always been.

So what was Tanya doing here? And why?

"I was just outside Dintscombe when I phoned," Tanya explained. "I left at the crack of dawn. Couldn't stay in that house another minute. Do you know what he—?"

"Why don't you go on through to the living room and you can tell me all about it later?" Mum cut in, as the air in the salon crackled with curiosity. "Katie will bring you a cup of coffee and we can have a proper talk when I've finished here, which won't be long."

She then turned her attention back to Margot Duckface who was reaching in her expensive designer bag, making sure the distinctive Mulberry logo was in full view, as always, while she did so.

"How much do I owe you, then, Cheryl?" Margot asked as Tanya was about to squeeze past her.

"Excuse me…" Tanya began, then gave an exclamation of

surprise. "Oh, hello. Fancy seeing you here."

Margot frowned at her. "I'm sorry? I think you're mistaking me for someone else."

Tanya's cheeks flushed pink beneath her spray tan. "Oh yes, yes. Of course I am. I do apologise. Just for a minute there, I thought you were – never mind. You can't be her." She glanced around the salon and, although she didn't quite add, 'not in a place like this,' it was quite clear that was what she was thinking. "My mistake. I'm so sorry."

Margot gave a condescending smile. "Don't worry about it. It happens all the time. People say I look very much like the lady who reads the news on ITV. But I wouldn't know, as I'm strictly BBC myself."

She reminded everyone not to forget polling day, then swept out like she'd just done us all a huge favour by honouring us with her presence. A collective sigh of relief rippled around the salon like a Mexican wave.

"That woman is so damn rude…"

"Katie," Mum cut in sternly. "We don't pass comments on the customers, do we?"

Well, she might not. But Olive and the other members of the Much Winchmoor Grumble and Gossip Group had no such scruples.

"Stuck-up cow," Olive muttered. "Poor Millie. I know my sister's all sorts of a fool, not least for marrying Abe Compton, but there was no call to rip into her like that – even though Abe's cider is the best paint stripper outside of B&Q. But our Julie could tell you a thing or two about Lady High and Mighty Duckface, you know. For all her hooty-tooty ways, she's no better than she should be."

"Really?" I asked, but at a warning glare from Mum I decided a change of conversational direction was called for. "So – um – how is Jules?"

Although Jules and I been best mates at school and vowed to stay BFFs (that's best friends forever), as you do, we had drifted apart after I left home to go to uni. And when I came back last year, it was kind of hard to take up where we'd left off. She'd changed in the five years I'd been away and so, of course, had I.

She'd had her second baby three months ago now and, apart from visiting her just after the baby was born, I hadn't really seen that much of her since. I'm not very good at talking to or about babies, so Jules and I tended stay in touch mainly through Facebook and occasional texts.

But, to be honest, the other reason I'd been, well, not exactly avoiding her but not going out of my way to meet up either, was that whenever we did, she'd end up giving me the third degree about me and Will.

Not that there *was* any me and Will at that moment. Not after Saturday night and the deafening silence ever since. I'd texted him a couple of times but, as usual, he'd ignored me. Well, this time I wasn't going to go chasing after him.

"Our Julie? Up to her eyeballs in debt and nappies, that's how she is," Olive was saying. "And that useless husband of hers can't hold a job down for five minutes. But she'd love to see you, though, Katie. You two used to be such pals, didn't you?"

"I'll pop in and see her soon. I'm a bit tied up at the moment, what with helping Mum out in here and trying to find a job."

"Still no luck, then?" She clucked sympathetically. "D'you know, I might be able to help you there. It's only temporary, mind, but one of my neighbours is in a bit of a fix. She's broken her ankle and can't do very much for herself at the moment. So she's been paying someone come in once a day to help out. But now her carer's had to go off to look after her own daughter who's expecting twins any day. She's a nice, friendly little body."

Horribly aware that everyone in the Salon, including Mum, was settling down for another in-depth discussion of my job prospects, or lack thereof, I made yet another conversational swerve.

"It's good to have nice, friendly neighbours," I murmured.

"Friendly?" Olive gave a bark of laughter. "I'm not talking about Elsie Flintlock. It's Millicent Lydiard, her carer, who's the friendly one. Oh no, my dear, I don't think you could call

Elsie friendly. Not even on a good day. And since her ankle, she doesn't have too many of those."

I could well believe it. Elsie and I had crossed swords before. She had a tongue sharp enough to cut shoe leather and an opinion on everything from the world economic crisis to the required number of biscuits in a packet of Cheddars. Not to mention an encyclopaedic knowledge of who'd said what to whom and why.

Times were hard and I was desperate for a job. But look after an crabby old lady with an attitude problem?

Thanks, but no thanks. I wasn't that desperate.

Chapter Three

By the time Mum and I had finished off the last of the perms and sent them on their way in good time to get a decent seat at the funeral, Tanya was on her third cup of coffee and the last of the chocolate Hobnobs.

"Sorry, Cheryl." She held up the empty packet as we came into the kitchen. "But you know what I'm like when I'm upset. The original emotional eater, that's me. It'll be Richard's fault if I end up as fat as a house. I swear I've put on two pounds already today. Look at me. I shan't be able to see my toes soon."

If she had put on two pounds, it was hard to see where they'd ended up. Tanya's skin was stretched that tightly over her skinny frame, there wasn't room for an ounce of fat, let alone two pounds of the stuff. And it certainly hadn't landed on her hips and thighs. Had it done so, her pink Lycra leggings, which clung like a second skin, would have burst open like overfilled sausages.

It was obvious she was expecting either Mum or me to tell her not to worry, that she looked lovely and slim and didn't need to think about dieting. But neither of us said a word.

"I'll just pop up and change my shoes," Mum said, not even appearing to notice how Tanya bristled at her lack of response. "My feet are killing me this morning."

There was an awkward pause after Mum left the room. My stomach rumbled at the sight of the empty packet of biscuits. I'd been looking forward to one of those all morning. I put it in the bin and asked if she'd like more coffee.

"There's some of Mum's prune and bran compote from this morning if you're still hungry," I added with a grin.

"She's not still on one of her crazy diets, is she?" Tanya's patronising smile set my teeth on edge and made me wish I hadn't mentioned it. "I'm sorry to say this, Katie, but it doesn't look as if they're working, does it?"

"Well, I think…"

But Tanya was not interested in what I thought and steamrollered on, as if I hadn't spoken. "Cheryl was such a tiny little thing when we did our training together all those years ago, you know. She was much smaller than me then, but now look at us." She stretched out one pink Lycra-ed leg and flexed her tiny but well-defined calf muscle. "Of course, I do have the advantage of a personal trainer and I spend hours in the gym. We should all work at looking our best, you know, Katie."

"Dad likes Mum just as she is and that's the main thing," I murmured, as I tried to control the urge to strangle her, or at least wipe the self-satisfied smirk off her face.

She sniffed. "Yes, but then, Terry always was easily pleased. Unlike his brother." Her face darkened. "Still, I suppose it's all too easy to let yourself go when you live out here in the sticks, like your mother does. How she can spend her days giving perms to a load of doddery old ladies is quite beyond me. It would drive me to distraction."

It was beyond me, too. But there was no way I was going to let her know that.

"Aunty Tanya…" I began, but before I could think of something that would annoy her as much as she was annoying me, Mum came back. She was wearing a pair of pink, fluffy slippers that she'd had for as long as I could remember. Tanya's finely-drawn eyebrows rose at the sight of them.

"Still keeping up with the latest fashions, I see, Cheryl," she murmured. "Just as well you didn't bring them to Bournemouth with you, wasn't it?" She turned to me. "Your Mum and I had a trip to Bournemouth a while back, didn't we, Cheryl? You should have seen her then, Katie. Not a shabby old slipper in sight, I can tell you. In fact, we—"

"Katie," Mum cut across Tanya's reminiscences. "Didn't I hear you say you'd call in and see if you could be any help to Elsie Flintlock?"

"No. I—"

24

"Yes, I thought you did. Off you go, then. I'll see you later."

"But I've got my piece to do for the paper," I protested, as she all but elbowed me towards the door. "The new editor's a stickler for deadlines."

"A newspaper?" Tanya's overdrawn eyebrows shot up. "Glad to see your expensive university education wasn't completely wasted after all, Katie. Last I heard you were working behind a bar. So which paper is it? *The Times?*" She gave a tinkle of laughter as she added: "Or the local freebie?"

"Somewhere between the two," I said. "I'm freelance at the moment but there's a chance of a staff job…"

"In the meantime, there's a definite chance of a job in the village going begging," Mum said as she handed me a letter and gave it a significant tap. "This came in the morning post for you. And I don't need to remind you, young lady, a job's a job after all, and you can't afford to be choosy."

It was a letter from my bank. I didn't need to open it to know what it was about. I stuffed it in my pocket and headed for the door. As I reached it, I turned back to say I wouldn't be long and was shocked at the expression on my mother's face as she and Tanya faced each other across the room.

If, as they say, looks could kill, I half expected that when I got back I'd find Tanya stretched out cold on our kitchen floor.

***

Crabshaw Crescent is a cluster of old people's bungalows, named in honour of our since-dishonoured Councillor, Gerald Crabshaw. Or Gruesome Gerald, as I preferred to call him.

I'd been standing on the doorstep of Number Six for so long I began to wonder if Olive had got it wrong, and Elsie Flintlock wasn't housebound at all but had gone to Arthur's funeral, along with the rest of the village.

Relieved, I turned to walk away. At least I could tell Mum I'd tried. However, before I reached the front gate, the bungalow door opened and a woman with scarecrow hair and a face like she was chewing a wasp peered out. She was wearing a Homer Simpson slipper on one foot, a plaster cast on the other and was leaning heavily on a walking frame.

"I'm not buying," she snapped and went to close the door.

"I'm not selling," I said quickly. "It's Kat, Elsie. Olive said you need someone to help out while your ankle gets better and I wondered—"

"Kat?" she cut in. "What sort of daft name is that? And it's Mrs Flintlock to you. I don't hold with all this Christian name stuff. It's not respectful. And if you – get back!" she suddenly yelled. "Now."

I jumped back, startled. There had to be something more wrong with her than a mere broken ankle. Elsie could be pretty feisty, not to mention downright rude. But this was something else.

"I'm sorry to have troubled…"

I got no further. I was too busy leaping out of the way as, snapping and snarling like the hell-hound itself, something small, brown and angry shot between the legs of Elsie's walking frame and hurtled towards me. I'm not keen on dogs at the best of times and didn't fancy hanging around to find out if this one's bite was worse than its bark.

"Prescott! Get back. Now," Elsie roared in a voice loud enough to have stopped a jumbo jet in mid take-off. But the dog ignored her – and me, too, thank goodness – and streaked off down the path between the bungalows like a heat-seeking missile.

"Shall I go after him?" I asked.

"No point. The little ratbag will be half way to Dintscombe by now. Well, don't stand there letting the heat out, girl. It's ok for you youngsters, with money to burn on your binge drinking and fancy phones. Us poor pensioners have to be more careful with our pittance that we worked hard all our lives for. Come along in, and be sure to wipe your feet."

I wiped my feet then followed her into a small, overheated room that was dominated by a large flat screen television in one corner. A high-backed chair and footstool was placed in front of the window while the far wall was covered in photographs of what I assumed to be the same boy, sometimes grinning, but more often glaring at the camera. They'd obviously been taken at various stages of his school career.

"Your little dog. He's, erm…" I tried to find something good to say about the animal but couldn't, so I gave up.

"Prescott's a loud-mouthed, out of control little hooligan," Elsie said. "But he's company. At least, he is when I can manage to keep him in. He needs his daily walk and is going stir-crazy without it."

"I'm good at dog walking." You see what getting snarky letters from the bank can do, when you're desperate for money? I didn't even like dogs, particularly this one. And I was being slightly economical with the truth about being good at dog walking. But I did used to take Gran Latcham's elderly Labrador for a sedate amble around the block when Gran became too ill to do so. "And I can do other things as well, like cleaning and…"

"Hah! I've placed you now. You're Cheryl's girl, Katie." She looked at me critically. "Not that anyone would know from the state of your hair. Not a very good advert for your mum's salon, are you?"

"Mum doesn't do my hair."

"I can see that," she sniffed. "Did you know there's a very pretty young blonde vet just joined the Dintscombe Veterinary Practice?" she went on, while I struggled to work out where the abrupt turn in the conversation was leading.

"Er, no. Our cat Cedric is very fit for his age and we don't have call to go to the vet very often."

Her sharp blue eyes glinted as she peered at me. "That's as maybe. I'm just telling you this for your own good. Because from what I hear, you and Will Manning haven't been getting on so well lately. And you know what they say about gentlemen preferring blondes? It applies to farmers, too. Especially when the alternative is someone with hair the colour of a well-pickled beetroot."

I felt a pang of sympathy for Posh, Britney and the Royals. The Much Winchmoor Grumble and Gossip Group was as relentless as any paparazzo. And this particular member, whose hair was like an unravelling Brillo pad and who was therefore in no position to criticise mine, was the worst of the lot.

I was about to say that I wasn't actually after a job when the crackle of the letter in my pocket reminded me how beggars with an Manchester-sized overdraft can't be choosers.

"So you're after a job again, are you?" she went on while I was still trying not to think about pretty blonde vets or bank managers. "I thought you were working for *The Chronicle* now?"

"Well, yes, I am. But it's freelance and..."

"I can't pay you much and it's only until Millicent Lydiard's back – even though she's a wittering fool who chirps about the place like a mad canary. Do you chirp?"

"I don't..."

"Good," she cut in again. Conversation with Elsie, I'd discovered long ago, was a strictly one-way process. "So, are you going to stand about like a spare part, or get me a cup of tea? Strong with two sugars, please."

"You're offering me the job? But I haven't said I'll..."

"I'll let you know when you've made the tea. And I like it in a bone china cup with matching saucer. You'll find them in the top cupboard."

She didn't let me know. Instead she drank the tea, pulled a face then held her cup out for a refill, so I assumed I'd passed the tea test.

"I blame your mother," she said with another conversational side swerve.

I bristled. "What for?" I blamed my mother for loads of things but that didn't mean I liked it when others did.

"That Sandra Mitchell, running off with the chirrupist."

I knew, from the many tedious conversations I'd heard in the salon, that 'chirrupist' was Elsie-speak for chiropodist.

"How did you know about that?" Mum had only found out this morning. But Elsie went on as if I hadn't spoken.

"I ask you, talk about selfish. What about my bunions? Do you know how hard it is to get a chirrupist to come all the way out here? According to Olive, who went to school with her older sister, that Sandra always was a flighty piece. Your mother should have kept a better eye on her."

28

"Or Maurice should have." I retorted, refusing to let Mum get the blame for Elsie's neglected bunions.

"Maybe." She shrugged and took another sip of her tea. "Heard you had Lady Duckface in the Salon this morning. After your votes, was she?"

"Well, she's not getting mine," I said, as I remembered the cruel way she'd upset poor little Millie Compton.

"Nor mine. She came round knocking on all the doors in the Crescent last week and I asked her, straight out, what made her think she was good enough to step into Marjorie Hampton's shoes?"

My stomach gave a sickening lurch at her words. The last time I'd seen Marjorie Hampton's shoes they'd been on the ends of her legs which were sticking out of one of Will's dad's freezers where the murdering maniac had planted the poor soul after she'd been killed. It was something that would be imprinted forever on my mind. Even now, almost a year later, I still woke up some nights shaking with the horror of it all.

"So then I said to her, all Jeremy Paxman-like," Elsie was saying. "What was she going to do about the minibus Marjorie used to organise, to take us into Dintscombe to collect our pensions, now that the Post Office has been closed and turned into one of her horrible little holiday cottages? And what do you think she said?"

"I have no idea. Maybe..."

"Only told me that I should have my pension paid directly into my bank account. *Like normal people,* she said. Her very words."

"Well, it would perhaps be safer—" I began, but at that moment, the clock on the mantelpiece chimed.

"Two o'clock," Elsie said. "Off you go. If I don't get my afternoon nap, I fall asleep in front of *Countdown* and it's my favourite programme. So I'll see you tomorrow morning, ten thirty sharp. And wear something more suitable. If Creepy Dave at Number Four sees you in that top that barely covers your decency, he'll have a heart attack. Which would be no bad thing, now I come to think about it."

Chapter Four

You see what my mother had landed me in? Running around after a crotchety old lady and her hooligan dog wasn't the sort of job I'd planned. On the other hand, I reasoned, it was only for a couple of hours a day and would bring in a bit of desperately needed cash, if I was to meet my bank loan repayment this month and maybe have a little left over to go into my scooter fund. And, as I kept telling myself, it was only temporary after all.

Particularly as the only work I had in the diary from *The Ch*ronicle this week was an extraordinary meeting of the parish council, to 'discuss' (that's parish council speak for moan, whinge and generally waffle on about) the outbreak of potholes in the roads around the village with a representative from Somerset Highways Department, on Thursday evening.

I'd covered these 'extraordinary' meetings before – and take it from me, the only extraordinary thing about them is the amount of effort it takes to stay awake for the entire meeting.

I promised Elsie I'd be at her place next morning on the dot of 10.30am and headed back home. When I got there, Tanya's sporty little car was no longer parked in Dad's spot outside the house. With a bit of luck, she'd have said whatever it was she had to say and left.

The house was silent as I let myself in. The salon was closed now the pre-funeral rush was over and there was no sign of Mum.

I still had my piece on the Not-Much-Fun Dog Show to write up. As I went upstairs to my room, where my desk and laptop were, I was already working out how to string it out by including a little bit of unpleasantness between the judges and one of the owners. She'd thought her dog had won the prize for the dog with the waggiest tail, and was not best pleased to discover that her little pug had, in fact, taken first place in the 'dog who looked most like its owner' category.

The subeditors could be pretty picky when it came to the length of a piece and were inclined to chop off the end if it was too long for the available space. But if it stayed in, it could earn me another ten lines, as being freelance meant I got paid linage. The more I wrote, the more I got paid. I figured it was worth the risk.

There was an almost-promise from Mike, the new editor, of 'maybe' a staff job if things worked out and if (and this was the really big if) I could get myself some transport. My job as a local reporter in a rural area was sadly limited when the sole means of travel was my old bike and the number 167 bus that only ran when it felt like it and never on a Sunday or after 6.30pm.

So as well as paying off my bank loan, I was saving every penny I could to buy myself a little scooter or moped to get myself around. At one time, back in the days when I'd had a life, not to mention a proper job, I wouldn't have been seen dead on one. But after a year buried in Not-Much Winchmoor with the pink and mauve bike I'd been given for my thirteenth birthday as my only means of transport, I'd stopped worrying about how uncool scooters looked.

There was a limit to how many lines I could squeeze out of a Fun Dog Show, even allowing for an over-the-top description of the monsoon that had turned the car park into a quagmire. And, of course, Pug Lady.

I was trying to figure out how I could work a remark about soggy doggies into my opening paragraph as I pushed open the door of my bedroom – and froze.

What the—? My bed had disappeared under a mound of suitcases. Various sizes, all in a matching faux leopardskin print. My 'desk' looked more like the dressing table it used to be, as my laptop had been pushed aside to make room for an astonishing array of expensive-looking lotions and potions.

As I stood there trying to work out what had happened, I heard the front door open as Mum came back in. And, from the sound of it, Tanya was still with her. I closed the door of my room and went back downstairs.

"Mum?" I hurried into the kitchen. "What's with the pile of suitcases on my bed?"

"Oh, hello, love. You're back sooner than I expected. Tanya and I have been out to lunch. Have you eaten?"

"No, but…"

"I'm just making a cup of tea. Do you want one?"

I wanted an explanation as to why my bed resembled an airport baggage reclaim area and my desk the cosmetics counter at Boots. But I settled for the cup of tea in the short term.

"What's going on?" I asked, although the expression on Mum's face told me I wasn't going to like the answer to that particular question.

"Your Auntie Tanya—" she began, but Tanya cut across her.

"Really, Cheryl, how many times do I have to say it? Just Tanya, if you don't mind. Aunty Tanya makes me sound like I should be wearing a shawl and pink fluffy slippers."

Mum, who had changed out of her pink fluffy slippers and back into her work shoes, let the barbed remark go, which was more than I'd have done.

"Tanya will be staying here for a night or two," she said.

"A night or two?" I echoed. Judging from the amount of luggage on my bed and the stuff on my desk, it looked as if she was planning on moving in permanently. "But why?"

"It's just while she gets things sorted. She and Uncle Richard are…" Mum looked uncomfortable. She was probably the only person in Much Winchmoor who hated discussing other people's personal problems. "Well, apparently they're having a few... um, a few issues, at the moment…"

"Oh, for goodness sake, Cheryl," Tanya snapped. "Stop pussy-footing around. Katie isn't a six-year-old. She knows the score. The truth is, Katie, your Uncle Richard is, like a lot of men, an arrogant, selfish bastard who's not afraid to use violence to get what he wants."

I stared at her, in astonishment. Uncle Richard? Violent? He was the quietest, most inoffensive man on the planet. He crept about as if apologising for the space he was taking up and prefaced almost every sentence with the word 'sorry'. As for the arrogant and two-timing bit...

"I don't believe it," I said.

Tanya shrugged and examined her long Barbie-pink nails. "Of course you don't, sweetie. You only see the side of him that he presents to the world. The grey, mild mannered chartered accountant who would never say boo to a goose. Least of all raise a hand in anger. But then, let's face it," she turned towards my mother as she went on, "none of us really knows what goes on in someone else's relationship, wouldn't you agree, Cheryl?"

Mum dropped a cup, and was then too busy scrabbling around picking up the pieces to respond.

I answered for her. "I suppose not."

After all, Tanya had a point. Certainly as regards Ratface, I hadn't had a clue what had been going on there. As for my on-off relationship with Will, Elsie had been winding me up when she went on about the new blonde vet – hadn't she? What if there really was something going on? I'd probably be the last to know.

"There's no suppose about it, Katie," Tanya said with a toss of her Dolly Parton mane.

"You're probably right," I conceded. "But Uncle Richard is always such a..." I was going to say *a mouse of a man* but decided against it. I settled for, "He's such a quiet man."

"The quiet ones are the worst, take it from me," she said. "Still waters and all that. I could tell you things about your so-called kind and gentle Uncle Richard that would make your hair curl, which now I think of it might not be a bad thing." She gave my hair a withering look and sighed. "Short and spiky is very last year, you know, sweetie."

Before I could protest, she went on. "And last night was the final straw. He came into the bedroom while I was getting ready for bed and he—"

"I don't think Katie wants to hear all the details," Mum cut in quickly.

She wasn't wrong there. *She and Uncle Richard were the same age as Mum and Dad, for goodness sake!* I shuddered at the thought.

"I'm sure you don't mind, Katie, but I said Tanya could have your bed," Mum said.

Too right I minded.

"But where am I going to sleep? There's so much of your salon stuff in the spare room, there's not enough space for a footstool, least of all a bed."

"We can soon clear some of that out, enough for the little push-under bed from your room. You were always happy enough to sleep on it when you had friends for a sleepover."

But that was because I was eight years old at the time.

It was one of those beds that had fold-down legs so it could slide underneath the other bed when not in use. Then when you wanted it, you pulled out the legs to make a proper-height bed. The only problem was Jules and I had been messing around one day and had snapped one of the legs.

Dad had said it wasn't safe to mend it, and so ever since the bed had only been used at the low level. I'd been happy enough to sleep in it way back when. Not quite so keen at twenty-four.

"But it's on the floor," I protested.

"It's only for a night or two, Katie," Tanya said. "And I couldn't possibly sleep on it. Not with my back. My chiropractor would have a fit if he thought I was even thinking about it. But you don't have to scrunch up in the spare room, sweetie. I'll be quite happy to share with you. It'll be fun, don't you think? We can have some nice girly chats."

"That won't be necessary," Mum said firmly as she placed two cups of tea on the table in front of us.

"Thanks. But no tea for me, Cheryl." Tanya stood up. "You'll have to excuse me. I didn't sleep a wink last night after Richard – well, you know. And I am totally exhausted, both physically and mentally. So if you don't mind, I'm going to go and put my head down for an hour or two."

Which was why I spent the rest of the afternoon in the salon trying not to breathe in too deeply, as the place still reeked from the morning's perm-fest. Meanwhile Mum cooked up a storm in the kitchen. It was something she always did when she was wound up and my heart (and stomach) quaked at the thought of what our evening meal was going to consist of.

I sat on one of the spindly chairs in the Reception area with my laptop balanced on my knees, while I tried to think of fun and original things to say, in as many lines as possible, about the Not-Much-Fun Dog Show.

"Come on, then," Mum said when I'd finally hit 'send' on my Soggy Doggies story and wandered back into the kitchen, which now looked as if Hurricane Harriet had just flounced through. "That's tonight's stew prepared and in the slow cooker. You can give me a hand clearing out the spare room now."

My heart sank as I peered in through the cooker's glass lid. There seemed to be an awful lot of grey, lumpy things floating around in a lurid mustard-coloured sauce. Things were not looking good but I knew better than to say so. Or ask what it was.

"But Tanya said she didn't mind sharing—" I began.

"She might not mind, but I do," Mum said in that *don't-argue-with-me* voice that even the cat obeyed. "I've been meaning to have a clear out in the spare room so it's a good thing really. And it's only for a couple of nights, at the most. Tanya's a real townie. She'll be only too pleased to go back to Uncle Richard after a couple of days in the 'back of beyond,' as she calls it. Just you wait and see."

But, of course, Tanya didn't. It was as if she'd heard what Mum said and was going out of her way to prove her wrong. She had, she announced the next night over dinner, no intention of going back to Uncle Richard, and added that life in the back of beyond 'had its compensations,' whatever that meant.

She certainly couldn't have included Mum's cooking in those 'compensations' as the leftovers (of which there were plenty) from Monday night's lentil and aubergine curry turned up again in Tuesday's aubergine, lentil, and something from a tin with a missing label pie.

Mum's cooking was a bit hit and miss at the best of times but that pie was off the scale of weirdness, even by her not-exactly-*MasterChef* standards. And I was pretty sure she was doing it to starve Tanya into moving on.

Only it didn't work. The original night or two had somehow turned into four, and by Friday she still showed no signs of leaving.

She'd even taken to going for power walks around what she now referred to as 'this charming little village', claiming that the fresh air and exercise were doing wonders for her stress levels.

Good to know someone's stress levels were doing ok. The rest of us were on serious stress overload.

Dad had taken to spending even more time than usual at the Winchmoor Arms, ever since Tanya started smiling winsomely at him and going on about how she'd chosen the wrong brother. Mum had given up on the prune and compote diet completely and was in danger of developing a serious Jaffa Cake habit. Even the cat was sulking because Tanya insisted on sitting in his favourite chair, and had dared to suggest he'd be perfectly happy sleeping on the floor.

The whole family was out of sorts and on edge and I couldn't understand why on earth Mum put up with it. It wasn't as if she and Tanya got on with each other. On the contrary.

But when I'd dared mention it to her, she'd snapped my head off and muttered something about 'families looking out for each other.'

The atmosphere at home became so bad I began to look forward to the two hours I spent at Elsie Flintlock's each morning.

This time last week, I'd have gone up to see Will and have a good old moan to him about it. But I still hadn't heard from him and I was determined that I wasn't going to be the one to back down and call him. Not this time.

So the week dragged on and even Thursday night's extraordinary potholes meeting was slightly less boring than listening to Tanya's endless prattle about the latest celebrity gossip, punctuated by Mum's heavy silences.

But I didn't hold out much hope of any great linage count

from the meeting. There was, as the man from the Highways Department said, precious little money for potholes, either for the parish council or me.

***

Over the week Elsie and I slipped into a routine of sorts. She criticised everything I did and wore, while I cleaned her flat, checked her lottery numbers, walked her manic little dog and did outrageous things to my hair just to wind her up.

I'd meant to get up early on Friday morning and finish writing up my extraordinary potholes piece before going to Crabshaw Crescent, as I'd promised Mike that it would be on his desk first thing that morning.

But I overslept, thanks in part to being kept awake by Tanya talking on her phone, then watching some noisy film on her iPad until late into the night. I promised myself I'd finish the piece as soon as I got back from Elsie's.

It was nearly lunchtime when I brought Prescott back from his walk, my last job of the day. As we turned rather sharply into the Crescent, to avoid Prescott hurling doggie obscenities at the Vicar's cockapoo, Olive hurried out of her bungalow, as if she'd been watching for me.

"Katie, thank goodness I've caught you, dearie."

"What's wrong?"

"It's Jasper, my cat." Her thin face was shrivelled up with worry. "Would you keep an eye on him? I've got to – oh dear. I don't know, I'm sure. I really don't."

As she fretted, a police car drew up outside.

"Look out, Olive," I joked, worried by her extra pale face and hoping to get her to lighten up a bit. "They've come to take you away. Have you not been paying your TV licence?"

"That's why I wanted to see you about Jasper." She darted a glance around to make sure no one else was within earshot. "They've come to take me up our Millie's, and I don't know when I'll be back. Seems she's in a state."

"Jeez, I'm sorry." I wished I hadn't tried to make that silly joke now. "Is it Abe?"

37

"You could say that. The old fool was shouting his mouth off in the pub the other night," Olive whispered as a policewoman walked up the path towards us. "About what he'd do to that Margot Duckface for saying she wouldn't be seen dead drinking his cider."

"But that's just Abe. Everyone knows what he's like when he's trolleyed."

"That's as maybe. But Margot was found dead this morning. Face down in a vat of Abe's HeadBender cider. And they seem to think it was Abe who put her there."

When I'm nervous or shocked, I have this awful habit of saying stupid things. Lucky for me then the policewoman reached us before I could blurt out that, at least this year, nobody could say that Abe's cider lacked body.

Chapter Five

By the time I'd seen Olive safely into the police car and assured her for the twenty-seventh time that Mad Dog Prescott wouldn't get within lip-curling distance of her precious Jasper, Elsie had worked herself into a right frenzy.

She pounced the second I opened the door.

"What's going on?" she demanded, her Brillo pad hair standing up in little spiky tufts where she'd been tearing at it. "Why have the police carted poor old Olive away? Has she forgotten to pay her TV licence again?"

"It's not Olive who's in trouble, it's Abe," I said, as I led Prescott into the kitchen, took his lead and harness off and gave him a drink. "Do you want me to make you a cup of tea while I'm in here?" I called out.

"Of course. I'm parched and it doesn't do for people of my age to get de-hibernated. Just be quick about it. What's that fool Abe done now? And what's it got to do with Olive?"

"Millie's in a bit of a state, apparently. So Olive's gone up there to look after her." I called through to her from the kitchen while I laid out the tea tray to her very specific requirements. Matching bone china cup and saucer ('the one with the violets on, not the chipped one'), with a plate of ginger-nut biscuits on the side.

"Millie's always in a state," she said dismissively. "What's it this time? Has she lost her bus pass again?"

"No." I came back into the living room while I waited for the kettle to boil. "It's something really serious. I'm afraid Margot Duckett-Trimble was found dead this morning."

I felt a little thrill of triumph at being able to tell Elsie something she didn't know. Usually, she had this uncanny knack of knowing everything that was going on. In fact, I often joked that if Elsie Flintlock didn't know about something, then it probably hadn't happened yet.

Only, of course, it had happened. And it was nothing to joke about, I realised with sudden shame. Nor should it be used to score points with Elsie. It was a cruel and horrible murder, not a juicy bit of gossip to be enjoyed over a cup of tea and a plate of ginger nuts.

"Dead?" Elsie's small puckered mouth went slack with surprise. "How? And what's that got to do with Abe Compton?"

"It seems she was found in a vat of Abe's cider," I said as the kettle gave a shrill whistle. "And the police think it was Abe who put her there."

I made the tea, poured it out and took the tray into the sitting room where Elsie was deep in thought.

She hardly looked up as I came back.

"Are you saying the police think she's been murdered?" she said.

"Well, I shouldn't think she put herself in there, would you?" I said, as I moved last week's *Dintscombe Chronicle* and the church magazine to make room for the tray on the overcrowded side table.

I thought of poor little Millie, as short and dumpy as Olive was tall and lanky. The two sisters always put me in mind of a couple of birds. Olive was a stooping, spindly-legged heron while Millie was a plump little wood pigeon, with her bobbing head and soft cooing voice

Only she wouldn't be cooing softly now. Poor, poor little Millie.

"So who did put her there?" Elsie's shrewd blue eyes peered at me over the rim of her cup. "Will you be investigating this one, Miss Marple? Seeing as how you were so successful in finding Marjorie Hampton's murderer?"

A chill ran down my back, in spite of the sauna-like temperature of Elsie's bungalow. Getting involved in another murder was the last thing in the world I wanted.

"That was different," I said quickly. "I knew the police had got the wrong person."

"And you think Abe Compton's the right one?" Elsie shook

her head so vehemently a bit more of her Brillo pad hair unravelled. She brushed it back with an impatient flick of her hand. "Don't be ridiculous."

"Apparently, he was saying some pretty wild things about what he'd do to Margot if she got his cider-making stopped. Which it looked as if she had every intention of doing."

Elsie snorted. "According to Olive, the man's a fool when sober and an even bigger one when drunk. He's barely got the wit to tie his own shoelaces, let alone murder someone."

"It could have been an accident," I said. "Maybe they were having an argument, Margot got a bit too close to the vat, he pushed her in a moment of anger and she toppled over and fell in."

"You can't *topple* over into a vat of cider," Elsie said scornfully. "Olive took me up there one afternoon to have a look round and the top is a good six feet off the ground. With a great big lid that locks down. Take it from me, girlie, she didn't get in there by accident."

"But if it wasn't Abe, then who could it have been?"

"Strikes me there's plenty of folk in the village, aside from Abe Compton, who'd be only too pleased to see the back of her. Myself included."

"Surely you didn't—?"

"With this?" She tapped the plaster cast on her leg. "Of course not. But I can't abide folks who put on airs and graces, pretending they're that much better than the rest of us, when all the time they're no better than they should be. Olive says…"

She broke off and twitched the curtain as a car pulled up outside. The sound sent Prescott into hysterical overdrive. He raced into the hall.

"Surely Olive's not back already?" I had to raise my voice to make myself heard above the sound of Prescott hurling himself at the front door.

Elsie turned away from the window and back to me, her cheeks faintly pink. "Would you believe it?" she murmured. "It's not Olive. It's my grandson, Danny."

I glanced up at the array of photographs of the geeky little boy that covered most of the wall behind me.

The temptation was too much.

"Now, would this be the same Danny, as in, your useless grandson who only lives ten minutes' drive away but can never be bothered to come and see you?" I asked with a grin.

Elsie glared at me so fiercely I thought I'd gone too far. Then she smiled. Not a big, full-on one but a small, wry smile, that softened the hard lines around her mouth and made her bird-bright eyes twinkle.

"Yes, that Danny," she admitted grudgingly. "Now, for goodness sake, let him in, will you? Before Prescott knocks the front door clean off its hinges."

I grabbed Prescott by the collar, herded him into the kitchen, then opened the front door.

Oh wow! I'd been expecting a grown-up version of the geeky schoolboy in the photographs. Danny had grown up all right – and in all the right places. He was seriously gorgeous in a cool Johnny Depp (when he was Jack Sparrow) kind of way.

"Hi," he said and his voice set me off fancying a piece of rich dark chocolate. "I've come to see my grandmother."

He had one of those amazing smiles, kind of slow and lazy. I cursed myself for choosing, today of all days, to wind Elsie up by spraying my hair (which had been toned down from its earlier purple to a rich shade of aubergine) with green and orange streaks. I'd also added a (temporary) tattoo to my left arm that announced I was 'born to be wild' for good measure.

"Come along in, Danny," Elsie sang out. "You're just in time. Katie's made me a cup of tea but she'll soon put the kettle on again for you."

"Actually, my name's Kat…" I began to say, but he was too busy fending off his grandmother's third degree to hear me. I opened the kitchen door and Prescott shot out like a stone from a catapult.

As I waited for the kettle to boil I couldn't help overhearing their conversation. With Elsie's paper-thin walls, it was almost impossible not to – particularly if you stood over by the broom cupboard in the corner and opened the door.

"So you see, Gran, I'm broke," I heard him say. "If you

could just see your way clear to lending me £250, that would be brilliant. I'll pay you back, honest."

The creep. He'd only come to see his gran to touch her for money. I didn't visit mine that often on account of how she was always banging on about what had I done to my hair this time, when was I going to get a proper job and how did I ever think I'd get myself a nice young man if I went around showing everything I've got?

Very much like Elsie, come to think of it. Even so, I wouldn't dream of asking her for money.

I'm referring to Grandma Kingham, by the way, my mum's mum. Dad's mum, Gran Latcham, really got me and would never have given me that sort of grief. She was the one who encouraged me to believe that there was life beyond Much Winchmoor and to apply for uni. It grieved me that she'd died before I graduated.

I still missed her and hated going past what used to be her cottage. It was now one of Margot Duckface's holiday cottages with tasteful Farrow & Ball paint everywhere, a trendy log burner and bare sanded floorboards throughout.

Gran would have hated it. As did I.

"I'm sorry, Danny," Elsie's voice brought me sharply back to the present – and to the broom cupboard. "I don't have that sort of money," she was saying. "I can let you have £20 if that will help?"

"'Fraid not, Gran, but thanks anyway. Don't worry. I'll ask Dad." He sounded remarkably cheerful for someone who'd just been knocked back. "But how do you mean, you've got no money? I thought you'd sold your house in Dintscombe for megabucks? Don't tell me you've been through all that already? If so, you must have really been living the high life these last few years."

"It's none of your business, Daniel," Elsie said tartly. "But I'll tell you anyway. If you must know, I gave the money to your dad."

"What did you do that for? Dad's loaded."

"Because – because he told me…" Even from the depths of the broom cupboard I could hear the tremor in Elsie's voice and wanted to break cover and go and give her a big hug, even though she'd have probably cracked me round the head with one of her crutches for doing so. "He told me he'd put the money in a safe place in case I ended up having to go into a nursing home, where they'd take all my money to pay the fees so the fat cat owners could swan around in their Ferraris. So I did as he asked, and he promised I could have whatever money I wanted whenever I wanted it. Only when I asked him for the money to buy a new fridge the other day, he – he said…"

Danny gave a weary sigh.

"Let me guess. He said there was nothing wrong with the old one."

"He said I wasn't to add to that there globe warning by littering the planet with old fridges."

"Scumbag." Danny echoed my sentiments exactly. "But I don't get it. If you're broke, how did you afford—?" he broke off.

"Go on," Elsie said. "Afford what?"

"Well, I heard you on the phone to Mum the other day about how you'd bought this piece of land."

"Oh that," Elsie laughed. "Yes, I did indeed. It's in a lovely spot, overlooking the village church. You see, when I'm dead and gone…"

I'd heard enough. Poor Elsie. It was bad enough her family didn't visit her from one decade to the next (apart from when they wanted to touch her for money, of course) without them quizzing her on the state of her finances and the contents of her will when they did so.

I took the tea in, glared at Danny as I deliberately slopped it in his (non matching, chipped) saucer and told Elsie I'd see her the same time tomorrow.

"She doesn't seem too friendly," I heard Danny say as I let myself out.

"Boyfriend trouble," Elsie replied, raising her voice to make sure I could hear. "She keeps getting dumped. Mostly likely because she scowls so much and does daft things to her hair. Makes a half-decent cup of tea, though."

44

***

I stood on the doorstep for a while, still smarting from Elsie's parting shot. Not about the hair, of course. That didn't bother me. It was the bit about being dumped. Will hadn't dumped me, had he? It was just that he was busy and had forgotten to call me back. Nothing more.

I wasn't in any hurry to go home, even though I still had my potholes piece to finish. Ok, maybe the use of the word 'finish' was a tad optimistic there, seeing as I'd only got as far as the heading.

"Not much in the pot for Much Winchmoor potholes."

I went next door to make sure Olive's cat was ok then took the long way home, going along the High Street rather than cutting through the back lane that led to our house – and the house guest from hell.

I had no idea why Mum put up with her. But I got such a snippy reply when I suggested that the couple of days Tanya had said she needed to 'get her head straight' was up, and maybe Mum should start dropping hints about her moving on, that I hadn't dare broach it since.

Dad, the coward, voted with his feet and was spending his time either at his allotment or propping up the bar in the pub.

I needed time to clear my head before settling down to work, and Tanya's non-stop chatter was not going to do it for me. The news of Margot's murder had shaken me more than I wanted to let on to Elsie. It had brought back a flood of memories of a horror that had never really gone away.

You watch TV detective shows and murder is just entertainment. A light-hearted puzzle. But the reality is different. Very, very different.

Murder takes your nice, joined-up world and smashes it into a thousand little pieces. It's disorientating and frightening. Cruel and messy.

As for the thought that there could be another murderer loose in our tiny village, that was too horrible to contemplate. Olive must have got things wrong. After all, it wouldn't be the first time. Every time the clocks went back or forward, Olive always managed to be plus or minus two hours out of sync with the rest of the country.

"Too stuck up for your old friends now, I see, Katie Latcham."

I whirled around and saw the girl I'd had my first cigarette with (I was sick, she wasn't); giggled over my first kiss with (I found it gross, she laughed at me when I told her); lusted after Justin Timberlake with (we were as one on that particular question).

"Jules! I was miles away. I didn't see you. And this must be… Oh my goodness, how you've grown," I cooed at the baby, hoping Jules didn't notice that not only could I not remember its name but its gender escaped me as well.

"Not entirely unexpected, seeing as the last time you saw Zeke he was six days old and he's now three months," she said crisply. "Babies tend to grow quite a bit in that time, you know."

"Three months? Has it really been that long? Doesn't time fly? Anyway, how are you?"

"Well, you know," Jules stifled a yawn and pointed at the scarlet-cheeked baby, who was slumped in the buggy like a miniature drunk, a large fleecy hat covering most of his tiny cross face. "Busy. Broke. Bone weary. The usual. What about you?" Her gaze travelled from my (temporary) tattoo up to my aubergine, orange and green hair and rested there. "You're looking pretty cool, Katie," she said in an unflatteringly surprised voice.

I was about to remind her that I preferred to be called Kat but at that moment, in my scruffy T-shirt and dust-covered joggers, I didn't feel much like Kat.

Kat would never have spent an entire morning scrubbing an old lady's bathroom and sorting through the contents of two medicine cabinets.

(Why two? Trust me, you really, really don't want to know.)

"Do you know what's going on?" Jules asked. "Police cars have been up and down the village all morning. And I'm really worried because I've just noticed a whole fleet of them up at Uncle Abe's as I went past the bottom of their road. I've tried

46

phoning Aunty Millie, but got no reply."

Most people in Much Winchmoor are related to each other and the Comptons were no exception. Abe was married to Olive's sister, Millie. And Jules was Olive's granddaughter. So technically Abe was Jules's great-uncle, but take it from me, there was nothing great about Abe Compton, either in stature or intellect.

"According to your gran, Margot Duckett-Trimble was found dead this morning," I told her. I resisted saying Margot Duckface in view of the gravity of the situation. "In a vat of Abe's cider. And the police think he did it."

"Uncle Abe?" Jules' hoot of laughter caused the miniature drunk to stir ominously. "I'm sorry. I didn't mean to laugh. But that's totally ridiculous. Margot's a good six inches taller than him for starters. And way more steady on her feet. He'd be far more likely to tip himself into the vat."

"I know. It's bonkers, isn't it? But he has been sounding off all over the place about what he'd like to do to her, after she persuaded Mary to stop selling his cider in the pub."

"Yeah, but everyone knows Uncle Abe's all talk and not much else." She frowned and checked her watch. "I ought to go up there and check it out but I've got to pick up Jenson from Little Ducklings."

Who is Jenson? I wanted to ask, but didn't dare. At the last count, I'd thought Jules only had two children, but after forgetting this baby's name and gender I wasn't prepared to chance it.

"Little what?"

"Little Ducklings. It's what they call the village playgroup now. Look, I don't suppose you'd do it, would you? Just while I pop up to make sure Aunty Millie's ok?"

Before I left home, I'd kind of got used to Jules landing me in trouble with her mad schemes. And I'd never quite got the knack of saying no to her. But this was something else.

"You don't mean pick up…? Oh no, no. I couldn't – I mean, how old is… is Jason?"

"It's Jenson. And he's three."

"But they won't let him come with me. You know, security

47

and all that," I gabbled. "Besides, I'm no good with children, Jules. I'd probably give the poor little kid nightmares."

Jules gave another hoot of laughter. Once again, the baby stirred, and whimpered.

"Your face!" she crowed. "It was a picture. Talk about panic stricken. Of course I wasn't asking you to collect Jenson. His mother would have a fit. And you're quite right. They wouldn't let you anyway."

I tried not to let my relief show. "So, he's not yours, then?"

"No, thank God. I've got enough with my own two, thank you very much. He's my neighbour's kid. She has Zeke on a Monday when I do my couple of hours up at the Manor. In return, I pick up Jenson from Little Ducklings on a Friday and keep him for a couple of hours so she can do a shift in the pub. Fancy walking with me? We could go up to Uncle Abe's as soon as I've picked up Jenson and see what's going on. Or do you have to be somewhere?"

Like back to Tanya's snarky comments and Mum's tight-lipped responses?

"Sure. So where are these Little Ducklings? Not in the village pond, I imagine?"

"In the village hall." The miniature drunk settled back down again as the buggy began to move. "So, seeing as you're now officially Much Winchmoor's very own Miss Marple, who do you think 'done it'? Because obviously it wasn't Uncle Abe."

I didn't much like being called Miss Marple for the second time that morning. I couldn't knit, for starters. Not to mention the fact that I'm at least fifty years younger than her.

"You're probably right," I conceded. "But the police must think they've got something on him because they've taken him in for questioning. Which is why Millie's lost it."

"What?" She stopped abruptly and the baby was jerked awake and protested so loudly that a pair of rooks spiralled upwards in panic from their perch on the Old Bakehouse chimney. "They've actually arrested him?"

"Helping the police with their enquiries, was how your gran said they put it."

Jules's eyes were wide with shock. "You're kidding."

"Course I'm not. I wouldn't joke about a thing like that."

"But Uncle Abe wouldn't hurt a fly," Jules went on as she jiggled the buggy so hard the baby's hat slipped right over his eyes, making him yell even louder. "Hush now, Zeke. Aunty Millie's always grumbling about how she's the one who has to despatch the chickens, seeing as how the 'girt soft apeth' – her words, not mine – can't bring himself to do it. It can't have been him."

"No, of course it wasn't," I said as we crossed the High Street, then walked along the bumpy path that ran around the village pond because 'Zeke likes to see the ducks,' apparently. Even though Zeke had by now gone back to sleep. Which was just as well as there were no ducks, although a blackbird flew out from one of the overgrown bushes, scolding us as it did so.

"Then who was it?" Jules asked.

"I have no idea. Your gran was in the salon on Monday and was saying that Margot was 'no better than she should be.' What do you think she meant by that?"

Jules laughed. "That's Gran-speak for 'having an affair'. Bet she called her a flighty piece too."

"She did, as it happens. But who was Margot having an affair with?"

"Well, I'm not one to gossip…"

"Blimey, Jules. You've changed."

"I mean, I'm not one to gossip about my employer." She sounded almost as po-faced as Will had done last Saturday when he gave me his 'animal welfare' lecture.

"Ex-employer," I reminded her.

Her face clouded. "God, yes. I hadn't thought of that. That's me out of a job then, I suppose. Are you sure it was murder?"

"How many people do you know who'd commit suicide in a vat of foul-smelling cider?"

She grimaced. "Yeah, you're right."

"Go on then," I prompted.

Her eyes darkened as she looked at me. "You still working for *The Chronicle*?"

"Yes, when I can. Why do you ask?"

"You're not going to write this, are you?"

I stared at her, hurt that she could even ask such a thing. "Of course I'm not. What do you take me for?"

"Ok. But this is just between you and me, right? Promise me you won't let it go any further."

I nodded. "I promise."

"Well, a couple of weeks ago, I had to phone Margot to say I couldn't make it that day because Kylie – that's my eldest, in case you're wondering," she added, her hard stare telling me she hadn't missed the fact that I'd forgotten everything about the new baby.

"Of course, I knew that," I said quickly, while silently repeating *Zeke, Zeke, Kylie, Kylie,* hoping the names would stick in my mind. "Go on."

"Well, Kylie was sick that morning. One of those twenty-four hour things that was going around the school. So I had to phone Margot to say I couldn't make it." We crossed the road and turned into the lane that led down to the village hall. "She sounded pretty annoyed and I felt so bad about letting her down that I asked Gran to have Kylie, left Zeke with my neighbour (Gran refuses to have them both) and went up to the Manor as usual."

"And then?" I prompted as she paused.

"I didn't phone to say I was coming after all, just in case Kylie started playing up, so Margot wasn't expecting me. As I went around the back of the house, there she was, getting up close and personal. And you'll never guess who with?"

"Go on."

Jules' eyes sparkled. She was about to impart a particularly juicy piece of gossip and was determined to make the most of it.

"Gerald Crabshaw."

"You're kidding!" My reaction must have been everything she could have wished for.

"On my life, I'm not. None other than our glorious ex-councillor Crabshaw." She leaned forward to adjust the hat on the now-sleeping Zeke and looked up at me, her eyes wide. "Oh God, Katie. You don't think it was Gruesome Gerald who murdered Margot, do you? A lovers' tiff?"

Chapter Six

Gerald Crabshaw lived with his wife Fiona in a renovated mill on the edge of the village. Unlike most things in Much Winchmoor, Winchmoor Mill was still a working mill that had been patiently and lovingly restored by the Crabshaws.

That is to say, Gerald read some books about restoring old buildings and indulged in a few funny handshakes in order to get various grants to finance it, while Fiona dealt with everything else, from sorting things out with English Heritage to, once the work eventually got under way, making the builders enough cups of tea to float the QE2.

To further fund the restoration, they'd turned every spare room and outbuilding over to bed and breakfast rooms. While Gerald posed about playing the jolly miller, and never passed up an opportunity to drone on to the visitors about how he was single-handedly breathing life into rural communities (the mill was not commercially viable but run as a tourist attraction), Fiona just got on with the cooking, cleaning and generally holding everything together.

She must have cooked enough full English breakfasts to have raised the cholesterol count of the entire nation, while Gruesome Gerald swanned around in his look-at-me Porsche and made out that he was still Much Winchmoor's Big Cheese.

But then, this time last year he was indeed the Big Cheese, even if it was in a very small pond, if you'll excuse the mixed metaphor.

He had been the man with a finger in every pie and a seat on every committee. A Dintscombe District Councillor, he was strongly tipped to be its next chairman. He had been riding high, and no doubt looking forward to the day he was recognised for his services to the community and became Sir Gerald of Winchmoor.

But all that came crashing down when he got tangled up in

a property scam. Thanks to a very clever lawyer, who did the same funny handshake as Gerald, nothing was ever proved against him, but he was still 'invited' to resign his seat on the council.

He'd blamed me for being the cause of his fall from grace ever since.

Certainly, I was the one who'd uncovered the fact that he'd been having an affair with a poor woman who'd subsequently ended up as the murdering maniac's second victim.

And now, Jules was telling me that Gruesome Gerald had once again had an affair with a woman who'd ended up murdered?

As Lady Bracknell might have put it: 'One murdered mistress is unfortunate. But two is downright careless.' Or at least deeply suspicious.

"Gerald was having an affair with Margot? Are you sure?" I asked. I was having trouble getting my head around it. Gerald Crabtree and 'irresistible to women' didn't belong in the same sentence.

He was pompous, portly and puffed up with his own importance. Not to mention slippery, smarmy and downright sleazy.

"I know what I saw," Jules said. "Or, rather, what I heard. They were in the dining room. The windows were wide open and I couldn't help overhearing. 'Here's to our little secret,' I heard Gerald say. 'It's really important my wife doesn't find out,' and then Margot giggled and said that her husband wouldn't be too happy either. Then Gerald gave that sleazy laugh of his. Honest, that guy gives me the creeps."

"Ok, that means he was up to something, I'll buy that," I said. "But not necessarily an affair."

"Yeah, but then a couple of days later I heard her on the phone to him. She was saying how she was tired of pretending and how she just wanted everything out in the open."

"But that doesn't make any sense, does it?" I frowned. "Think about it. John Duckett-Trimble's a good looking guy for his age, in a George Clooney kind of way. And he's obviously seriously rich if he can afford Winchmoor Manor.

Not to mention the way he buys up all the houses in the village. Whereas Gerald Crabshaw…"

I shook my head. I couldn't for the life of me imagine what Margot might have seen in Gerald with his shifty eyes, phoney regimental tie and loud braying laugh.

Jules shrugged. "No accounting for taste, I suppose. Anyway, I went back around to the front door and rang the bell. It took Margot ages to answer and when she did, she looked quite flustered and not at all pleased to see me. And when I went into the dining room, there was no sign of Gerald. He must have sneaked out the back way rather than risk being seen by me. Talk about acting guilty."

"I can see he wouldn't want his wife to know he'd been hobnobbing with Margot, whether or not they were carrying on," I said. "Fiona was in the salon only the other day, moaning to Mum about how the Mill's B&B trade has plummeted since Margot started her holiday lets."

Jules giggled. "Surely you mean her 'luxury self-catering cottages, an intrinsic part of the historic Winchmoor Manor estate,'" she drawled, in perfect imitation of Margot's ultra-plummy accent. "At least that's what it says on the cover of her glossy brochures, which she had printed by the thousand, by the way."

"Whatever she called it, her holiday business hit the Mill hard."

Jules nodded. "So I heard. According to Margot, B&B is 'so last century'. And apparently she and Fiona had a right set-to about it the other day at the Floral Art Society meeting, when Fiona accused her of poaching her customers."

"There you go then. Mystery solved. It was a crime of passion." It was all beginning to fall neatly into place. "Then there's the election, of course. Not only were Margot and Fiona rivals in love and business, but for a seat on the parish council as well."

"Murdered for a seat on the parish council?" Jules' yelp of laughter caused the miniature drunk to stir ominously beneath his fleecy hat again. "I hardly think so, do you?"

"OK. Maybe not. But even so…"

"And while we're on the subject of passion," Jules said with an abrupt change of subject that I didn't see coming. "What's this I hear about you and Will? One minute it's on, next it's off. What's going on with the pair of you?"

You see what I meant about her giving me the third degree every time we met? I should have known I wasn't going to get away with it.

"You might as well tell me," she went on, as we reached the small car park in front of the village hall. "You always do in the end."

She wasn't wrong there. That's my problem. I've never been able to make her (or anyone else in Much Winchmoor, come to that) understand that my love life (or lack of one) was none of her damn business.

I drew a pattern in the gravel path with the toe of my shoe. "Things have cooled between us a bit lately," I muttered. "If you must know, he stood me up on Saturday night."

"Will? Stood you up? I don't believe it. Who's he supposed to have stood you up for?"

"Is that the time?" I avoided looking at her by glancing down my watch. "I really must go."

"Oh no, you don't." She wheeled the buggy round, blocking my escape. "Come on, girl. Spill."

"Not who. *What.*" I glared at her, daring her to laugh. "If you must know he stood me up for a pregnant sheep."

She didn't laugh. Instead, she gave me a look that would caused even Mary Berry's custard to curdle. I flushed and looked away.

"Jeez, you have been away a long time, haven't you?" Her voice was scathing. "The guy's a farmer, for pity's sake. It's bang in the middle of the lambing season. He can't afford to lose any. No sheep equals no money equals no food. Surely he explained?"

I shoved my hands deep into my jacket pockets. "I haven't spoken to him since. He's ignoring my calls and texts."

"If I know Will, it will be more a case of him forgetting to charge his phone for a few days. You know what he's like. A mobile phone's totally wasted on him because he's either left it at home or he's carrying it around with a dead battery. He's a total dinosaur when it comes to technology. So why don't you go up and see him instead of sulking?"

"I'm not sulking," I protested.

"Not much. You're behaving like my Kylie when she doesn't get what she wants." She glared at me and, as she turned away, muttered: "You don't deserve him."

An awkward silence fell, broken only by the high-pitched screams and squeals from the Little Ducklings inside the village hall. What is it about little kids playing that always makes it sound like they're killing each other?

Jules shrugged and said she'd better go.

"Do you want me to look in on your Aunty Millie on my way back?" I asked. "See if there's anything I can do?"

"Like what, exactly?" she flashed, her acid tone telling me she was still mad at me. "Assemble everyone in Uncle Abe's sitting room and unmask who done it?"

"Of course not. But—"

"I'm going up there myself as soon as I've picked Jenson up. Look, I've got to go."

"Of course. Well, it's been great bumping into you like this," I said, trying really hard to make it sound like I meant it. "Why don't we have a girls' night out some time soon and have a really good catch up?"

"Yeah, let's do that. Some time." She sounded about as enthusiastic at the prospect as I was. "Text me. Got to dash. They're about to be let out."

But bumping into my one time best friend hadn't been great at all, I admitted to myself as I watched her approach the group of mums who were clustered around the hall entrance.

I felt as out of place as a terrier at a cat show.

I'd changed. Jules had changed. Even Much Winchmoor had, in some ways at least, changed. And nothing quite fitted together anymore.

Perhaps Will and I didn't fit together any more, either? I'd known him all my life. We'd more or less grown up together and he had been the brother I'd never had.

And when we discovered that there was something more

going on between us, to be honest, neither of us really knew how to handle it. I had feelings for him, certainly. And I knew he had feelings for me.

And things were going along just great until a couple of months ago, when suddenly, out of the blue, he started talking about the future. Our future.

And as he did so something inside me froze. And had stayed frozen ever since.

Because, deep down, I was still working on how to get out of Much Winchmoor. Still chasing that dream job. Still dreaming of that city centre flat and the buzzy city life that I used to have, before it all came tumbling down around my ears.

Whereas Will was as much a part of Much Winchmoor as the village duck pond. His family had owned Pendle Knoll Farm since the days when Judge Jeffreys roamed the Somerset countryside after the Monmouth Rebellion in sixteen hundred and something, looking for rebels to hang, draw and quarter.

Trying to imagine Much Winchmoor without the Mannings was like Marks without Spencer or Ben without Jerry.

As I walked back towards home I stopped by the pond and stood gazing down at the exact spot where Will had fished me out when I'd just turned seven, and had got a bit too adventurous while gathering frogspawn.

Me without Will? The thought made me uneasy and panicky.

I took out my mobile and left yet another message on his dead phone. Only this time, I remembered what Jules had said and tried really hard not to sound like a five-year-old who's just been told she can't have second helpings of chocolate fudge cake.

I left the same cheery message on Will's land line. Neither Will nor his dad were answering, which meant they were out on the farm somewhere, probably leaning on a gate and watching their cows grow. Or, it being the lambing season (as Jules had pointed out) up to their elbows in a sheep's...

I stopped. That particular analogy was a step too far so I turned and headed for home. The potholes were calling.

***

As I passed the road that led up to the Comptons' farm, I saw that the police car was no longer parked outside the house. Were they, at this very moment, asking John Duckett-Trimble to identify his wife's body? I wondered. He'd been called back from a business trip abroad, I'd heard.

Poor guy. When it came to rubbish days, mine was way down the list compared with what he'd be going through right now.

Not to mention Millie and Abe Compton.

Did the fact that the police cars had left the farm mean they'd discovered who had really pushed Margot in to the cider vat? Because, of course, Elsie was right. It couldn't possibly have been Abe.

So was *I* right? Could it have been Fiona Crabshaw in a fit of jealousy? She was a very quietly spoken, seemingly inoffensive woman, the least likely person, you'd think, to commit murder. But then, that's what I, and everyone else, had thought about the murdering maniac this time last year.

I was so deep in thought that, as I walked past the Old Forge cottage, I almost bumped into the For Sale sign that had been fixed to the gate post but now leaned at a drunken angle across the pavement.

As I attempted to push it back to its original position, I jumped back, startled, as the laurel bush just inside the tiny front garden began to move. This was accompanied by a sound that had become all too familiar in the last few days.

The leaves parted and Tanya, complete with her trademark jingling bracelets, stood there.

"What are you doing in there? You're not house hunting, are you?" I added with a laugh. Although the idea of Tanya settling down to life in Much Winchmoor was anything but funny.

"Good Lord, no," she said quickly. "Although as an investment property, this could do very well. I see, from my morning power walks, there are quite a few holiday cottages in this village. Must be a market for it."

"I'm sorry to disappoint you, but the estate agents are a bit late taking the sign down," I said. "This one was sold over a week ago. Houses in Much Winchmoor are snapped up faster than feeding time at a crocodile farm at the moment."

In fact, The Old Forge was the latest of John Duckett-Trimble's acquisitions, but I wondered whether he'd be going ahead with the purchase now.

Tanya extricated herself from the laurel bush. As she did so a police car threaded its way in and out of the parked cars that lined the High Street.

"That's the second police vehicle I've seen this morning," Tanya said. "This place is busier than Bristol city centre on a Saturday night. What's going on?"

"Remember the woman you met on Monday in the salon?" I said. "The one you thought you recognised?"

She gave a small, tinkly laugh. "Silly me. And all the time I was mistaking her for the lady from ITV news. I felt such a fool."

"Her name was Margot Duckett-Trimble. She was found dead this morning. That's what all the police activity is about."

Tanya stumbled as she tripped on an uneven paving stone.

"Dead? This morning?" she echoed when she'd recovered her balance. She looked bewildered. "But she can't be. I was only speaking to her yesterday. What do I …? I – I can't believe it."

She sat down on a nearby garden wall and looked so genuinely upset that I wished I'd been a bit more tactful about the way I'd told her.

"I'm sorry," I said. "I didn't realise you knew her."

"I didn't," she came back, quick as a flash as the colour returned to her face. "As I said, it was just a silly mistake on my part. Was it a car accident? I must say, some of these country lanes around here are death traps. I had a very narrow escape myself on the way here. A tractor wanting all the road and totally oblivious to other road users."

"No. Nothing like that. She was found dead in a barn just up the road. That's probably where that police car had just come from."

"In a barn?" Her face paled again beneath her salon tan. "She didn't – oh my God, you don't mean she committed suicide, do you?"

"Oh no. Nothing like that. She drowned."

"In a barn?"

I nodded. "In a vat of cider."

She hugged her thin arms around her body and rocked slightly. "Oh my God, what a dreadful thing to happen. What a ghastly accident."

"But that's just it. They don't think it was an accident."

Tanya stared at me. "But if it wasn't an accident… and she didn't commit suicide…" Her voice rose an octave. "Do you mean she was murdered?"

"I think the official line, at the moment, is that the police are treating it as a suspicious death."

"But who did it? Have they charged anyone?"

"Not as far as I know." I decided not to tell her about poor Abe being taken in for questioning. The police had obviously made a mistake, so there was no point in adding fuel to that particular rumour.

She shook her head. "It doesn't seem possible. Her poor husband. He must be devastated. Some sort of business man, wasn't he? I seem to remember her saying something along those lines?"

I nodded. "John Duckett-Trimble is, as Margot was always at pains to point out, 'something big' in the city."

"Really? You mean, he's a property developer?"

"I couldn't say. Margot never went into detail. I always had the impression he's a banker or something like that, but I could be wrong. Whatever it is, he has pots of money, which is how he can afford to gazump anyone who tries to buy one of the houses in the village so that Margot can – I mean could – turn them into holiday cottages. He'll end up owning the entire place at the rate he's going. Although I don't suppose he will now. The holiday cottages was Margot's thing, not his."

"So, was he the person who bought The Old Forge?" she said.

I nodded. "Probably."

"Well, I don't suppose he'll want to go ahead with it now, will he?" She tossed her hair back and gave a sudden bright smile. "Every cloud and all that. It leaves me in with a chance of getting the cottage, after all, don't you think?"

I had to hand it to Tanya. She was all heart. Not.

Chapter Seven

Before I could answer her, yet another police car had threaded its way along the High Street. I thought of poor Millie and hoped she was feeling a little better now that her sister was with her.

"Really, this place gets more like *Midsomer Murders* every day," Tanya commented with a giggle. No doubt the prospect of The Old Forge coming back on the market had helped her recover from the shock of Margot's death. "Where's Inspector Barnaby when you need him?"

"Except *Midsomer Murders* is made up," I murmured. "And Margot's murder is real."

Horribly real. Because murder happened to real people. It left families bereft. Their lives changed forever.

Not only that, it left friends and neighbours looking at each other and wondering. *Was it him? Or her?*

Because if it wasn't Abe Compton, in a fit of totally out-of-character uncontrollable rage, then who? I couldn't forget the fact that Marjorie Hampton's killer had turned out to be the last person I, or anyone else, had suspected last year.

Who then, I wondered, as we walked along the High Street with its closed-up, out of season holiday cottages, who in our small, claustrophobic community was the person least likely to have committed the murder? Our elderly vicar? Elsie's neighbour, Creepy Dave? Or even, of course, Abe Compton? Or quiet as a mouse Fiona Crabshaw, who was known to have had a blazing row with Margot and whose husband may or may not have been having an affair with her.

We hadn't got very far when Tanya's phone rang. She looked down at it, swore and stuffed the phone back in her bag.

"Problems?" I asked.

She gave an exasperated sigh. "Richard. He's been phoning me all day. I knew it was only a matter of time before he came crawling to me. He wants us to go to counselling, if you've ever heard anything so pathetic. 'To start a dialogue,' is how he put it. I've told him, the only dialogue I want with him will be through our respective lawyers."

"I take it there's no chance of a reconciliation, then?"

Her eyes hardened. "None at all."

We walked on in silence until we reached the end of the High Street and were just turning into our road when she stopped and looked back. A small smile tugged at the corners of her mouth. She had a look on her face like our cat gets, when he's eyeing up the bird table.

"Do you know, in these last four days I've developed quite a liking for this funny little place, Katie," she said. "And I've just had this really brilliant idea."

"Oh? What's that?"

She gave another of her tinkly laughs. "Oh, I'm not ready to share that with anyone yet. But I'm actually beginning to see why you hang around. Much Winchmoor kind of grows on you, doesn't it?"

You reckon? The only thing about Much Winchmoor that grew on me was the desire to get away from it. Even more so if Tanya was thinking of moving here.

***

"Isn't that your dad's car?" she asked a few minutes later as we reached our house. "And there was your mum trying to make out how he worked all the hours under the sun and that the place would grind to a halt without him. It's all right for some, finishing half way through a Friday."

"He's been working late almost every night this week," I said. "He's probably got an afternoon owing to him."

Our cat Cedric had been sunning himself on the garden wall but stalked off, slowly but purposefully, his tail flicking like a metronome that's lost its oomph as we approached.

We should have named him Slo-Mo because he never did anything at speed, apart from eat, which is why the birds on the bird table were never in any danger from him. Cedric preferred his meals served up to him on a plate. With a side order of salmon flakes or prawn cocktail crisps.

As we reached the back door, my phone rang. My heart leapt, thinking it was Will. I gave Tanya my key, took out my phone and groaned.

Mike.

"Trouble?" Tanya purred, her eyes glinting.

"Of course not," I lied, because of course, it was trouble. With a capital T. "Just work stuff. You go on in. I'll be there in a minute."

Once I was sure she was safely out of earshot, I hit reply.

"Mike, hi," I called, in my chirpiest voice. "I'm glad you called. I was about to call you."

"I'm not in the habit of chasing up my reporters," he said, stonily. "You said I'd have your copy in my inbox first thing this morning. It is now almost two o'clock in the afternoon. So, where is it?"

I swallowed hard. "Yes. Well, the thing is—"

"I don't want to hear excuses," he cut in. "I'm pushed for space this week anyway. So we'll forget it."

Noooooo! Forget the time I'd spent in an overheated school hall, scrunched up on a chair made for a seven-year-old, while the guy from Somerset Highways droned on? He'd taken an hour and forty-three minutes to say, 'Money for potholes? No chance.'

And now Mike was saying my numb bum (not to mention my numb brain) had all been for nothing?

While I was desperately trying to think of a way to make him change his mind, he went on: "This is not good,

Kat. Not good at all. I need my reporters to be one hundred and ten per cent committed to Team Chronicle. If I can't rely on you, we'll have to do a rethink about whether you deserve your seat on the team bus. As I keep saying, there's no I in team, you know."

Did he just say what I thought he'd said, in amongst all that cringe-worthy management speak he was so fond of? He was about to start again, so I broke in before he could say anything that I would regret.

"Look, Mike, I'm really sorry about the potholes," I said quickly. "But the thing is, there's been a murder in the village this morning. I – I thought it would be better if I spent some time getting local reaction. On the spot stuff. That sort of thing."

There was a pause. A very long pause.

"I – I know I can't go around interviewing suspects, or anything like that," I went on. "But I thought it would be good to get a bit of background on the victim, and local people's reaction. You know, 'killer strikes terror in sleepy village,' that sort of thing."

I shrivelled up inside as I said that. I hated it when reporters talked about 'sleepy villages'. It was patronising and cliched. But I was fighting for my job here.

I thought back to the last time there'd been a murder in the village. The staff reporter from *The Chronicle,* an ambitious Irish charmer called Liam, had been on the spot within the hour, interviewing anyone willing to talk to him.

But what had I been doing this morning? Too busy fancying myself as a (young) Miss Marple, filling my head with theories about who might have done it, instead of thinking like the journalist I pretended to be.

But it felt like I was cashing in on John Duckett-Trimble's misery. To be honest, I hadn't even thought about Margot's death being a news story. Until now. Now it had become my hang-on-to-your-job card.

I held my breath, crossed my fingers and waited.

"Ok then," he said finally. "Let's see what you come up with. Only local, peripheral stuff, mind you. I'll liaise with the police. Who's the victim?"

"A woman called Margot Duckett-Trimble. I actually did an interview with her a couple of weeks ago. She is – was – standing for the parish council."

"Oh right. I remember. Two women contesting the seat, wasn't it?"

"Yes."

"So have they charged anyone, do you know? The husband? It's usually the husband."

"Oh no, it can't have been him. He's been away on business all week. Poor guy, what a shocking thing to come home to. I've heard that a local man, Abe Compton, has been helping the police with their enquiries, as they put it. But it couldn't have been him either."

"How do you know?"

"Because I know him. And he's harmless. He couldn't have done it."

"Well, it's not your place to decide who did or didn't do it," he said. "Ok, go ahead. Let's see what you come up with. We might be able to use it. Just a bit of background stuff, nothing too heavy. And no rush. Monday will be fine. I'm warning you now, there may not be space in the end, but it'll be good practice for you."

"Thanks Mike." I remembered to start breathing again. "I'll get on to it."

"Oh. And one more thing, Kat?"

"Yes?" My heart skipped a beat. Had I pulled it out of the bag after all?

"Your coverage of the parish council meeting with Somerset Highways? In my inbox by four o'clock, please. And just the straight account this time. None of this 'aren't I the clever one?' padding, like you did with the dog show. And leave the funny headlines to the subs, ok?"

I was shaky with relief as I ended the call and went indoors. As I did so, I could hear Dad and Tanya in the kitchen, laughing. That's to say, Tanya was doing that girly high-pitched giggle that set my teeth on edge, punctuated by Dad's low rumble.

I could tell from the whine of a hairdryer that Mum was still in the salon so I went straight in there to see if she needed any help before settling down to work.

"Thanks, love, but I've only got Mrs Crabshaw here to finish off, then I'll be free. One advantage of the big rush I had on Monday is that it's made Friday a lot quieter than normal. So your Dad and I are planning on having an afternoon out for a change, which is why he's taken the time off."

"Good idea." I nodded approval then looked in the mirror at Fiona Crabshaw and smiled. She gave me a small, tight smile back that didn't quite reach her strange green-gold eyes, fringed with sandy eyelashes. The colour always reminded me of that lemon and lime marmalade Gran Latcham used to be so fond of.

Everything about Fiona Crabshaw (apart from those strange eyes) was beige. She wore mid-calf length skirts, with long, droopy cardigans in varying muted shades of browns and creams. Looking at her was like looking at one of those old, sepia photographs. Her hair was the colour of curtains that have been left in the sun too long (no highlights or lowlights for her, in spite of Mum's best efforts to persuade her otherwise) and she always wore it coiled in a neat bun at the nape of her long, bony neck.

I wondered why Mum bothered to blow dry that fine shoulder length hair into some sort of style when Fiona always wound it into the same neat bun (she never trusted Mum to do it) as soon as Mum finished.

Fiona always looked fragile, as if 'a puff of wind 'ud roll her over,' as Olive often said. But that day, she looked even more fragile than usual and her pale beige face was etched deep with weariness. I reckoned sitting in the chair while Mum did her hair was probably the longest time she'd sat still in ages.

"How was Elsie today?" Mum raised her voice above the noise of the drier as she carried on blow-drying Fiona's hair.

"Fine," I said. "Getting more mobile by the day. In fact,

she had a visitor this morning. Her grandson."

"That would be Danny," Mum said, putting the finishing touches to Fiona's hair. "Such a clever boy. He went to Cambridge, you know. King's College, so I believe. Would you like some hairspray on that?"

"Thank you. But I won't." Fiona's soft voice was apologetic, as if she expected her refusal to offend.

"She's that proud of him," Mum went on, picking up a hand mirror and angling it so Fiona could see the back. "He's such a lovely boy, taking the time to visit his grandmother like that."

Hmmm. 'Lovely boy' wasn't exactly the phrase I would have used to describe him.

"Do you know, Katie," Mum went on. "Your Grandma was only saying to me the other day how long it is since she and Grandad saw you. She said the last time you visited—"

"Have you heard the news?" I asked, cutting her off. Once she got started on my shortcomings, we could all be there for the rest of the afternoon.

I hadn't been going to say anything about Margot until Mum was on her own, but speaking to Mike had changed everything. Getting the reaction to Margot's death from a rival would be as good a place as any to start my report. I meant rival in the parish council election, of course. Not for the attentions of Gruesome Gerald. I still couldn't quite buy that one.

"You know I don't approve of gossip, Katie," Mum said.

"But this isn't gossip. This is fact. Margot Duckett-Trimble was found dead this morning. In one of the vats in Abe Compton's cider barn."

Both Mum and Fiona gave a horrified gasp. What little colour there had been in Fiona's pale face drained away, so that her eyes stood out, in sharp glittering relief, against ashen cheeks.

If she hadn't been sitting down, she would have fallen. Instead, she swayed slightly and gripped the arms of the chair so hard, she looked as if she was in the front seat of a roller coaster ride. And hating every minute of it.

"But that's terrible," Mum said as she turned towards me. Her eyes, too, were wide and startled. "Just terrible."

Then she looked back at Fiona.

"Are you all right, Mrs Crabshaw?" she asked. "Would you like some water?"

"No. No thank you. I'm fine. It was just... just such a shock, that's all." She looked across at me as she struggled to regain control. "How – how did she...? I mean, what happened?"

"They think she was murdered." I said.

"Murdered!" Fiona gasped. "Oh no. That's not possible."

"Of course it's not," Mum said. "It must have been some horrible accident. Oh, the poor woman. She was such a lovely lady."

Only my mother would describe Margot Duckett-Trimble as a 'lovely lady,' but it didn't seem appropriate to contradict her.

"They've taken Abe Compton in for questioning," I said. "That's how I knew about it, because I was there when a policewoman came to take Olive up to be with Millie, who is, it seems, in a bit of a state."

"Well, yes, of course. She would be. Poor little Millie," Mum said. "It's a mistake, obviously. I mean, Abe, for goodness sake. What on earth are the police thinking of?"

"The police are very good at making mistakes," Fiona said, her voice stronger and clearer now. "If you recall, it took them ages to admit they'd made a mistake over Gerald. And by the time they did, the damage to his reputation had been done."

The general consensus of opinion around the village was that Gruesome Gerald had got off lightly last year. But Fiona still looked very pale and neither Mum nor I were about to contradict her.

"Anyway, I'm sure the police will soon realise their mistake and arrest the real murderer," Mum said. "If, indeed, it was murder. Katie has a tendency to dramatize things, Mrs Crabshaw. She always has done. You wouldn't believe the stories she used to come out with when she was little."

"I do not..." I protested, but she went on as if I hadn't spoken.

"Besides," this was accompanied by one of her 'don't you dare say another word' looks. "As you so rightly say, the police have been known to make mistakes before."

I cleared my throat. It was now or never. "I'm doing a piece for *The Chronicle,* Mrs. Crabshaw. You know, just general background stuff about Margot. And I wondered if you'd like to comment?"

"Me?" She gave a startled gasp. "But why on earth would I?"

"Well, there won't have to be a parish council election now. You'll be elected unopposed. I thought perhaps you'd like to pay tribute to your rival, something like that?"

Fiona's head shot up so quickly, she almost knocked Mum's comb out of her hand.

"I hardly think it's appropriate for me to comment, given the circumstances," she said coldly as she pushed the chair back and stood up. "Thank you, Cheryl. That's lovely."

Mum passed her a handful of pins. "But don't you want to put your hair up?"

Fiona took the pins, stuffed them into her pocket and handed Mum her credit card. "I'll do it later, thank you, Cheryl. I'm in a bit of a hurry today. If you'd just make out my bill, please?"

"Really, Katie," Mum hissed as she passed me on her way to get the ancient card machine that looked as if it should belong in a museum. (None of that modern contactless payment nonsense in Much Winchmoor, thank you very much). "Have you nothing better to do than stand around here gossiping? Go and see if your father wants any lunch. Otherwise he'll just munch his way through half a dozen packets of crisps then tell me he's had his five a day because they were cheese and onion. There's a very nice salad in the fridge."

"Dad doesn't do salad," I pointed out.

She shrugged. "It's in the round Pyrex dish. A new recipe."

My heart sank. Believe me, 'new recipe' was not something you wanted to hear in our house.

"What is it?" I asked.

"It's actually tofu and sesame seeds with soba noodles. But don't tell him. He'll eat it if he's hungry."

I crossed Fiona Crabshaw off my list of possible interviewees and headed for the kitchen. But not before I'd seen the little flicker in those lime marmalade eyes, when I mentioned that her seat on the parish council must now be a done deal.

It was only the briefest of flickers. Was it hope? Or maybe even triumph? And it was only there for a nanosecond before she ticked me off for my 'inappropriate' comment.

Of course I didn't seriously think she could have murdered Margot. But she was surely going to be one of the people who stood to benefit from her death. If only for an uncontested seat on the parish council. And then there was the damage that Margot's holiday cottages had been doing to Fiona's B&B business.

Who else, I wondered, stood to gain from Margot's death? I couldn't believe it was her husband, as Mike had suggested. Unless, of course, he'd found out that she'd been carrying on with Gruesome Gerald? But, in any case, he'd been out of the country on business since Tuesday.

I was puzzling over this as I went in to the kitchen, to see if I could persuade Dad that tofu and sesame seeds with soba noodles was really just a poshed-up version of mac and cheese.

I pushed open the kitchen door but stopped dead in the doorway, unable to believe my eyes.

Tanya and Dad were over by the sink, tangled around each other like tights in a washing machine.

Chapter Eight

"Dad? What the…?"

As he whirled round I almost laughed out loud at the expression on his face. It reminded me of one of Will's ewes when Tam, the sheep dog, had it cornered.

Desperation bordering on sheer, blind panic.

"Ah, Katie, thank goodness you're here, sweetie," Tanya cooed as she stepped away from Dad. As she did so, he sort of crumpled back against the kitchen sink and pushed his hand through his non-existent hair. It's always a sign my dad's under stress when he forgets he lost his hair twenty years ago.

"This is so silly," Tanya giggled. "I've got my hair caught in the zip at the back of my top. Your dad was trying to free it for me. But you know how useless some men can be when it comes to doing things with their hands. All fingers and thumbs he was. The way he was yanking at it, he was in serious danger of tearing my top clean off. Isn't that right, Terry?"

"Well, um, no. Not – um, not exactly," Dad mumbled, as he reached once again for his long-departed hair.

"Do you think you can be a love and free me, Katie?" Tanya went on. "It's actually quite painful. I don't know how it happened."

Her hair was, indeed, trapped in the zip at the back of her close-fitting jersey top. I was very tempted to give it a good, hard yank.

"It's well stuck," I said. "Shall I get a pair of scissors? Or ask Mum to do it?"

"Oh no, no need to bother her. Look, just see if you can ease the zipper down, there's a good girl. Ouch! Not that hard. You'll pull my hair out by the roots."

Talking of roots, up close I could see hers needed doing quite badly, but I didn't think she'd appreciate me pointing that out. A few less-than-gentle tugs and I'd worked it free.

While I was intent on doing this, Dad murmured something I couldn't catch. The next thing, I heard the click of the back door.

"There," I told her. "That's got it."

"Thanks." She ran her hand along the back of her top then fluffed out her hair, like a chicken having a dust bath. "There you go, no harm done."

No harm done? That wasn't what Mum would say when she came in. Because while Tanya and I were fiddling around with her hair, the click I'd heard was the sound of my father escaping, faster than Cedric used to whenever Gran Latcham brought her dog round. The arrival of the dog was the only thing that ever got that cat out of crawler gear, as he leapt for the safety of the shed roof where he'd stay, mouthing cat curses until Gran and the dog left.

Dad, however, was not heading for the shed. He was, without doubt, on his way to the pub. And that was the problem. Because once he'd had a couple of pints at lunchtime, particularly before he'd had anything to eat, that would be him finished for the rest of the day. He'd come home, relaxed and at peace with the world, sit down in his chair and fall into a such a deep sleep, his snores could be heard from one end of the village to the other. And nothing or no one would be able to wake him.

And that was the end of Mum's afternoon out.

...

"Where's your dad?" Mum asked, the minute she came into the kitchen. "Was that the back door I heard just now?"

If I was quick, I reckoned I could nip along to the pub and drag Dad out before he reached for his second pint. I was about to mutter something about not being sure where he was, but Tanya beat me to it.

"He said something about wanting a lunchtime pint. I'm thinking about joining him. What about you, Cheryl? Shall we go now you've finished in the salon?"

"I have better things to do," Mum said crisply as she crossed to the fridge and took out the round Pyrex dish containing what only she would ever describe as a 'very nice salad.'

She slapped it down in the middle of the table. It smelt like wet dogs. It looked like something even Prescott (whose idea of a tasty snack was rabbit poo) would turn his pointy little nose up at.

"And while you were out, Tanya," she went on, "Richard rang. In fact, he's been phoning all morning. I said you'd call him back when you got in."

"Thanks for nothing," Tanya muttered.

Mum picked up a serving spoon and began ladling dollops of the 'salad' into three bowls. "You can't avoid him forever, you know. If you take my advice, you'll sit down and talk to him. I know it's none of my business, but I always find nothing's so bad that it can't be talked through, quietly and calmly."

"You're absolutely right, Cheryl," Tanya flashed, two vivid spots of colour high on her cheekbones. "It is, as you say, none of your bloody business. Perhaps you should sort out your own marriage problems before you start commenting on mine."

For a second, the sudden stunned silence was broken only by the ticking of the kitchen clock. I held my breath. Then Mum let the spoon clatter to the table. Her head shot up and she and Tanya faced each other across the 'nice salad', like two boxers waiting for the bell.

Mum was the first to look away.

"I'm sorry, I didn't mean to offend you." She stared down at the 'nice salad' as if committing every detail of its ghastly grey gloopiness to memory. "I was upset. I'd been looking forward to going out this afternoon. But now Terry's taken himself off to the pub, he'll be fit for nothing except sleeping in his chair when he gets back."

What was the matter with her? She wasn't usually so meek and mild, particularly on the occasions when Dad went AWOL. It was like she was scared of upsetting Tanya. Which was weird. I mean, they'd never exactly been best buddies, any more than Dad and Uncle Terry were, even though they were brothers. In fact, Mum always used to say Tanya was a sight too 'up herself'. Why, then, wasn't she just telling her to pack her things and go?

Tanya flicked her hair back and gave a soft, low laugh. "Tell you what, why don't you go and join him in the pub and I'll stay here? You know I don't like playing gooseberry. Whether it's here in your village pub or in that bar in Bournemouth, remember?"

She turned to me, her eyes narrowed, her smile as false as her sparkly purple fingernails.

"Did your mum ever tell you, Katie, about the amazing weekend she and I had in Bournemouth a while ago? I kid you not, you wouldn't have recognised her. She…"

"That's enough!" Mum snapped. "You can stop that right now."

I felt like applauding her. She looked furious. In fact, I don't think I'd never seen her so angry, not even on the day when I backed her precious little pink car into a five bar gate. For one glorious moment, I wondered if Tanya was going to end up wearing the gloopy grey noodles.

But Tanya just laughed. "Well, well, I wondered what it would take to make the worm turn."

"I've had it with your hints and innuendoes." Mum snatched up the spoon, gripped it like an offensive weapon and advanced towards Tanya. "This stops right now."

But Tanya stood her ground.

"You reckon?" she sneered. "I've only just begun. And here's something for you to think about. I'm opening a salon of my own right here in this precious village of yours and when I do, it'll wipe you clean off the map, Cheryl. I'm going to bring this place screaming and kicking into the twenty-first century."

"Don't be ridiculous," Mum said. "You don't have the financial backing, for a start. Not without Richard. Your divorce settlement won't be that good, from what I hear."

"I don't need Richard. I'm going to see someone who, I reckon, will be a more than willing partner, once I explain my plan. In the meantime, I'm off to join Terry. I could do with a drink."

"Tanya, I'm warning you," Mum called out as Tanya headed for the door. "If you say anything to him, I swear I'll kill you."

Tanya laughed and slammed the back door behind her. As she did so, a small quavery voice called out, "Hello? Is that you, Cheryl? Oh dear, I hope I'm not interrupting but have you forgotten my 2.15pm appointment? Or have I got the wrong week again?"

There was a startled silence. Mum didn't move but stared at the elderly lady in the shabby grey coat who stood framed in the doorway that led from the kitchen into the salon.

"Um, it's er – it's Mrs Yarcombe, isn't it?" I said, when it looked as if my mother was going to stay rooted to the spot for the foreseeable future. Doris Yarcombe lived over the road from us. A retired school teacher, she'd become increasingly frail following her husband's death a few years earlier.

"That's right, dear," she gave me a sweet twinkly smile. "I'm sorry to intrude but there was no one in the salon. I called out but couldn't make anyone hear. Then I heard voices." Her smile was replaced by an anxious frown. "I hope you don't mind."

Mum's appointment book was on the kitchen table. I picked it up and turned to today. The afternoon, as Mum had said earlier, was completely clear after Fiona Crabshaw.

"Did you say you had an appointment?" I said. "Only I'm afraid there's nothing in the book. Not for this week, at any rate." I flipped forward to next week. "It's next Friday. At 2.15pm."

Her small, wrinkled hand fluttered across her mouth like a moth looking for somewhere to land. "Oh dear, I am so sorry. There I go, getting things muddled again. Last week it was the dentist and now this. You won't tell my son, will you? He worries about me, you know. Says I'm not safe to live on my own. And sometimes, dear, I think he might be right."

"Of course I won't tell him." I smiled at her, trying to reassure her. "As for getting dates muddled and forgetting things, I do it all the time. Don't I, Mum?"

Doris Yarcombe glanced across at Mum, who gave no indication of having heard me.

"I'm so sorry to have troubled you, Cheryl," she said. "I'll see you next week."

She turned to go but as she did so, the movement seemed to snap Mum out of her trance.

"What? Oh no, no. Mrs Yarcombe." She rubbed her hand across the back of her neck. "Please don't go. I'm sorry. I've just had a bit of a – well, it's all been…"

"I'll see you next week, Cheryl," the old lady said gently. "I can see you're not quite yourself, my dear."

"Oh no. It's all right. I'm fine, I promise you. I've just got the start of a headache, that's all. Nothing a cup of tea and a couple of paracetamols won't cure. And seeing as you're here now, I might as well fit you in. It's not like I've anything planned for the afternoon."

I preferred it earlier when she was angry. Now, she sounded defeated and sad.

"But Mum," I protested. "I thought you and Dad were going to—"

"Go on through to the salon, Mrs Yarcombe. Katie here will get you gowned up."

She gave me another of her looks. Other people's mothers communicated with words. Some even used texts and messages. Mine used a variety of looks. It was getting to be her communication method of choice.

I took Doris Yarcombe into the salon, assured her that she really, really was no trouble and stayed chatting to her until Mum was ready.

Then I settled at the kitchen table to jot down some

notes for my piece about Margot. I thought I'd start by Googling her for some background stuff. But the only things I could find were her website and the Facebook page for her holiday cottages. The Winchmoor Manor Estate, as she called it, making it sound as if the Duckett-Trimble family had owned the Manor and most of the village from the year dot.

But, in fact, they'd only moved into the Manor a couple of years ago. They'd bought it at auction, after the previous owner, an old man who was virtually a recluse, had died. He'd left the house to a distant cousin in Australia who, very wisely, had stated that he had no desire to move from the beautiful city of Melbourne to a dreary little English village in the middle of nowhere, and had promptly put the place up for auction.

It was the same with Margot's Facebook page. It was all about the cottages and nothing else. No personal stuff, just loads of happy family snaps from satisfied customers and pictures of chic cottage interiors that looked as if they belonged in smart, urban apartments, not Much Winchmoor High Street.

"Had a totally wonderful time, living the simple life in the Old Bakehouse," cooed one couple, under pictures showing iPads, a wide screen TV and a bottle of Moet, artfully arranged with the label showing. Another commented on a picture of two boys, who had lifted their heads from their phones just long enough to scowl at the camera: "Tarquin and Josh loved Bluebell Cottage and so enjoyed their taste of real country life."

I really, really hoped Tarquin and Josh were here the week Will opened up his silage pits for the first time of the year. The all-pervading stench of fermented grass that enveloped the entire village at this time would have given them a 'taste of country life' that would remain burned in their psyche forever.

I gave up on Margot and tried Googling John D-T to see if I could work in a bit about his background, but turned up blank. But that's the problem with Internet searches, isn't it? It's fine about coming up with answers – as long as you ask the right questions. And I was obviously not asking the right questions.

I was getting nowhere with my background stuff. Google had let me down. But I knew someone who was Much Winchmoor's answer to Wikipedia.

I didn't dare disturb Elsie now. It was her time for her pre-*Countdown* nap. So I put it on my to-do list for tomorrow and went back to my potholes.

I worked steadily, if boringly (it's difficult to do otherwise when you're writing about potholes, particularly when Mike had warned me against any padding to liven things up) until I heard Doris Yarcombe leave.

"He's not back yet, then?" Mum said as she came back into the kitchen.

"What? Oh, you mean Dad?" I tried to sound all casual, like I hadn't been itching for him to come back before she finished with Doris Yarcombe, so that I could have a go at him about being an idiot.

I did, at one point, think about slipping out and having a quiet word with him in the pub, but Mum has the hearing of a bat and she'd have heard me go. Besides, the story that I'd been sent down the pub to get him to come home would have gone around the village faster than our so-called high-speed broadband (which is anything but). She'd have thanked me for that! Not.

"I'm not sure where he is," I went on. "I've been that busy I've hardly looked up. He may have gone up to the allotment…"

"Don't bother trying to cover for him," she said wearily. "We both know where he is – and with whom."

"Look, Mum." I took a deep breath, in the full knowledge that what I was about to say was extremely risky, but I chanced it anyway. "You shouldn't let Tanya wind you up like that. And you know what she's like. She'll flirt with anything that's got a pulse, if it's male."

"Except your dad's not likely to have a pulse when I catch up with him," she growled.

"Well, if it's any consolation, I think Dad escaped to the pub to get away from her. There was nothing more to it than that."

"Nothing more to what than what?" she demanded, all trace of weariness gone.

Whoops! Didn't think that one through.

"I could hear the two of them in here giggling away like a couple of school kids," she went on. "So what exactly was going on? People don't say 'there's nothing more to it than that' for no reason."

"Nothing was going on, honestly." I couldn't make things any worse so pushed on. "Look, I probably shouldn't be saying this, but why do you put up with Tanya? She's had everyone at each other's throats ever since she got here. Why don't you just tell her to push off?"

Mum stared at me for what seemed like an hour. Then she took a deep breath and leaned forward as if she was about to confide in me. At the same time, we heard the click of the front gate.

"You're absolutely right, Katie," she said quietly as she straightened up. "You shouldn't be saying it."

I decided I didn't want to be around when Dad came in so I picked up my laptop and escaped to my on-the-floor bed, in the store cupboard that used to be our spare room. I balanced my laptop on a carton of shampoo bottles and went back to my potholes.

I took my phone out and saw, to my annoyance, that it was completely dead. I'd meant to charge it when I got back from Elsie's but in all the excitement had forgotten to do so.

I plugged it in and after a few minutes it came back to life with a ping to say I had a voice mail. To my surprise, it was from Will.

He doesn't normally leave messages and I wondered what was urgent enough to make him change the habit of a lifetime.

"It's Will here," he said, like I wouldn't recognise his

voice. "Katie – oh no, sorry, I mean Kat. I keep forgetting that's what I'm supposed to call you." He gave a self-conscious laugh. "Anyway, Kat," he went on, laying heavy emphasis on the name. "I'm sorry I haven't been in touch."

My heart gave a worried leap. Why was he being so polite? And why call me Kat? Even if it was in an almost snarky kind of way. He always called me Katie, never Kat, because he knew it wound me up.

I hated it when Will acted out of character. It worried me.

I swallowed hard and tried not to think about pretty blonde vets. Whatever the reason for this ultra-polite call, it had to be bad news. Was I about to get the 'it's not you, it's me' brush off again? First Ratface, now Will?

At least Will was telling me (almost) to my face, and not leaving me to find out the hard way, like Ratface had.

"I've been crazy busy this week and I'm really sorry about last Saturday night," Will's message went on. "Lambing's all but done now so I've fixed up a real treat for you for tomorrow night to make up for it. It's going to be a surprise but you'll love it. Wear something smart and don't eat too much lunch. That's all I'm going to say. I'll pick you up about seven tomorrow night, ok... er, Kat."

I started breathing again. Now I knew I wasn't about to be dumped, I played the message again and listened more carefully this time. Wear something smart? Don't eat too much lunch? On the face of it, it sounded exciting.

But knowing Will as well as I did, I figured the reality would probably turn out to be a pork pie and a pint at the rugby club, with a packet of wine gums that had probably been sitting around in the glove compartment of his Land Rover since last Christmas for dessert.

Even so, it beat staying in with my parents for a second consecutive Saturday night, especially if Tanya was still going to be around.

Chapter Nine

I stayed upstairs for the rest of the afternoon, not even coming out when I heard Tanya clip-clop up the stairs and start banging around in my room.

After a while, the banging stopped and there was a knock on my door.

"Can you be a love and help me down with these, sweetie?" she asked. She pointed at the faux leopardskin suitcases piled on my bed.

My desk now looked like the cosmetics counter at Boots at the end of the first day of the January sales. Most of the lotions and potions had gone, leaving only a few used cleansing wipes, an almost-empty bottle of bubblegum pink nail polish and a can of very fancy hair spray.

"You're leaving?" I tried, for the sake of politeness, not to sound too pleased at the prospect.

She nodded. "Now, I've left you some silver highlighter that I think would work really well for you. Don't overdo it, though. As I always say, less is more."

Obviously the advice didn't extend to her own collection of jingly bracelets or the mascara that was so thickly applied, it looked like a couple of black hairy caterpillars had settled on her eyelids and were squaring up to each other every time she blinked.

Still, it was a nice gesture on her part so I thanked her.

She shrugged. "Don't thank me. I was going to bin it. It's a tad over the top for my taste. But I thought it might tone your hair colour down and make you look a bit less like a Halloween party reject."

I was so made up at the thought of getting rid of her, I let the insult pass. Besides, the silver highlighter sounded intriguing. And it was a very pricey brand, way out of my budget.

"Are you going back to Uncle Richard?" I asked.

"Good Lord, no." Her eyes widened in horror at the prospect. "I wasn't joking when I said my future plans are, for the moment at least, here in Much Winchmoor. Richard features nowhere in those plans, except, of course, in reference to my divorce settlement. And if he thinks he's going to weasel out of paying me what's rightly mine, he's got another think coming."

"So, if you're not going back to him, where are you going?"

"I'm moving in to the Winchmoor Arms. It's just until I've got something that's in the pipeline finalised. It's only a matter of time but until then I've just had a long chat with Mary, the landlady, and she's agreed to let me have one of her rooms at a very fair rent. In return for which, I shall be availing her of the complete range of my skills – hair styling, makeup, manicures. The full salon treatment. I might even include a facial. Goodness knows," she pulled a face, "Mary could do with one. I don't think the woman has ever heard of cleanse, tone, moisturise."

"She's very busy," I murmured. "Runs the place single-handed."

"A woman should always find time to look her best, no matter how busy," she said. "And while I'm dispensing free hair and beauty advice, Katie, here's some for you. Forget the spikes. They're so last year. Your hair would look much better teased into little feathery fronds around your face. I could do it for you, if you like? No need to wait for my salon to open. Come to my room at the pub. Only don't tell your mother."

"Thanks, but I couldn't do that. As for Mary, she's one of Mum's best customers." As soon as the words left my mouth, I knew I shouldn't have said them, as a gleam of triumph flickered in her eyes. "Aunty Tanya, you can't. Families don't do that to each other."

"I think you'll find that your mother and I are no relation whatsoever," she said crisply as she picked up her Stella McCartney bag and shrugged it on to her shoulder. "We merely happened to have married two brothers. And now I'm about to divorce one of them that severs the relationship completely, wouldn't you say? Now, be a dear and help me downstairs with these cases. I would ask your father but he seems to have disappeared."

"No, it's fine. I'll do it," I said quickly before she could change her mind about leaving.

***

I'd hoped Tanya's departure would ease the tension between Mum and Dad but, if anything, it got worse. By the next morning, the long heavy silences had got longer and heavier and the only way they communicated was through me.

I looked back on the previous Saturday with nostalgia. Watching the *Eurovision Song Contest* with them had been as exciting as a wet Wednesday in Weston-Super-Mare but at least they'd been talking to each other then, if only to argue about who deserved *null points*.

I found myself actually looking forward to going to Elsie's, even though she'd assured me that Saturday was the day Millicent Lydiard always turned out the airing cupboard. But half an hour before I was due there she phoned.

"Don't come this morning," she announced. "I shan't be here."

"Oh, right." I was disappointed (a) because I needed the cash and (b) because I'd been hoping to get a bit more background information on Margot from her. "Are you going anywhere nice?"

There was a pause. Elsie believed information gathering was strictly a one way process and I thought for a moment she was going to tell me to mind my own business.

"I'm off to my son's for lunch," she said eventually.

"That's nice. What about Prescott? Would you like me to walk him?"

"No, he's coming with me," she said with a wicked chuckle. "It annoys the hell out of my daughter-in-law. She hates him and spends the whole time running around after him, brushing dog hairs off anything he's been anywhere near. Oh yes, and don't bother coming in tomorrow either. I don't pay double time for Sunday working."

I spent the rest of the day up in my room checking out the job market, both in *The Chronicle* and online. Nothing. I checked out my work schedule for next week. Again nothing. I went back to my notebook to see what, apart from the piece on Margot, I could submit for the coming week. Another big fat zero.

If I couldn't get together enough background for my piece on Margot, the only thing I could hope for in the paper this week was my report of the potholes meeting, a sure contender for most boring piece of journalism of the year award, following Mike's snippy comments about padding. It was just as well I'd cycled to the school hall where the meeting had been held. If I'd driven there, the linage money wouldn't have covered the cost of the petrol.

I really needed to work on him to persuade him to give me more assignments. I was that hard up, if my bike got a puncture, I'd have to increase my overstretched overdraft to buy a puncture repair kit.

I turned from the depressing state of my finances to my next big problem. One that had been bugging me for some time.

What on earth was I going to wear tonight?

Will's advice to wear something 'smart' was not as helpful as it sounded. Usually, his idea of dressing 'smart' was to swap his muddy wellies for a pair of trainers. I'd tried several times to ask him where we were going, and to be a bit more specific when it came to his definition of 'smart,' but, as always, he was out of communication range.

In the end, I settled on a skirt I'd bought in the January sales and hadn't had a chance to wear yet. It was short, black and clingy and looked really cool with my spiky-heeled boots. I matched it with a pink, sparkly top and long, tasselled earrings that brushed my shoulders when I moved my head.

I'd taken Tanya's advice, too, and washed the purple and orange out of my hair, added a few streaks of her posh silver highlighter and finger-dried it into a light, choppy style that framed my face. I checked it out in the mirror, ready to ditch it and go back to my usual spiky style, but what do you know? Tanya was right. It looked really cool.

Much as it pained me to admit it, she knew her stuff when it came to modern, sassy hairstyles. I'd have been worried for Mum's business if I thought her customers were in fact looking for anything remotely modern, least of all sassy. Most of them were still firmly locked into the regular monthly perm, interspersed with shampoo and sets and the occasional Blue Hyacinth rinse.

Usually when I'm going out it takes me less than ten minutes to get ready. But that night, it took for ever. Partly because it was so nice to have my bedroom back that I was actually glad to spend a little more time in it. But also because it was better than being downstairs and battling the permafrost whenever my parents happened to be in the same room.

As I took one last look at myself in the mirror, I was pretty pleased with the overall effect. Even more pleased by Will's reaction when I opened the door to him that evening.

"Wow, Katie... Kat!" The look in his eyes sent my pulse – and my confidence – soaring, and I forgave him for making my name sound like a chocolate bar. "You look..."

"Yes?" I prompted when his voice faded away. He dragged his hand through his hair as he searched for the word.

Gorgeous? Hot? Sexy?

"You look... um, you look good."

It would have to do. Will didn't do long, flowery speeches. It was one of the things I liked about him, but also one of the things that annoyed the hell out of me about him at the same time.

OK, maybe I didn't want the long, flowery speeches (Ratface had been good at them and look where that got me), but a short, not-quite-so-flowery one would have done very nicely.

But, for now, 'um, you look good,' would have to do.

Besides, he um, looked good himself, especially the way his hair stood up in little tufts where he'd raked his hand through it, giving him that tousled, bed-head look that sent my thoughts spiralling.

And his eyes had those little white fans in each corner because of all the time he spent outdoors, squinting against the sunlight. He was also wearing chinos and a crisp blue shirt that matched his eyes. Did he do that deliberately, I wondered?

But whatever, the overall effect was a far cry from his usual faded jeans and T-shirt.

"So, is this smart enough for the rugby club?" I asked. "Or do you want me to go back and change into a full-length ball gown?"

"Who said anything about the rugby club?"

"OK, then," I said, as I opened the passenger door of his battered old Land Rover and, out of habit born of painful experience, brushed my hand across the seat before trusting my brand-new skirt to it. Short, black and covered in straw and other agricultural unmentionables was *so* not a good look. "So where are we going?"

"There's this restaurant in Dintscombe," he said. "It comes very well recommended, so I thought we'd give it a try."

"It's not the Friendly Fryer, is it?" I had grim memories of the last greasy burger I'd had from there five years ago. My digestive system still hadn't recovered.

"No, that's long gone. It's a kebab shop now."

I glanced across at him. "Oh my God, Will, I haven't got myself all togged up like this to go to a kebab shop, have I? I think on balance I prefer the rugby club."

He sighed. "What do you take me for? I'm not going to tell you where we're going now. You'll to have to wait until we get there."

He parked the Land Rover in the main car park in Dintscombe and we set off along the High Street. I was, as usual, almost running to keep up with him until someone called his name and he stopped so abruptly I cannoned into him.

"Hi, Will. How's the ewe today?"

"Oh, hi, Anna. She's fine now, thanks. And the twins are thriving. You did a great job, thanks. Oh, yes—" he went on as I nudged him in the back, a tad harder than I perhaps should have done. "This is Katie. Katie, this is Anna. She's…"

"The new vet." I forced a smile. I could have said 'the pretty young blonde vet,' as indeed she was all of those things, and then some. But I didn't.

"Hi, Anna. And my name's Kat, by the way. Not Katie." I added, as I glared at Will.

"Hi Kat, great to meet you. How did you know I was a vet, by the way?" She gave a soft, low laugh. "Don't tell me I've still got mud on my shoes, or something worse?"

"Nothing like that. I just happen to work for a witch who knows everything that goes on in Much Winchmoor and the surrounding areas before it happens."

She gave a cute little puzzled frown and wrinkled her tiny, tip-tilted nose. She was, as Elsie had said, pretty. But it was more than just pretty. I could have handled that. She was small, dainty and feminine and, far from having muddy shoes, they were elegant and stylish and made my spiky boots look like snowshoes.

And, try as I might – and believe me, I tried really, really hard – I couldn't envisage her with her hand up a sheep's bottom.

'Gentlemen prefer blondes,' Elsie had said and, from the look in Will's eyes, I could see where she was coming from. Ok, so my hair was no longer the colour of a pickled beetroot, but neither was it soft and smooth, like spun silk. I felt clumpy and awkward standing next to Anna and my clothes, which I'd thought were fun and exciting when I picked them out, now seemed silly and over the top.

"Well, I mustn't keep you," she breathed. "You two look as if you're off somewhere. Anywhere nice?"

"Yeah, I hope so," Will said. "We're going to try out Michael's, seeing as it came so highly recommended."

She gave a small, tinkly and oh-so-feminine laugh. How did she do that? If I tried it, it would come out as somewhere between a hiccup and a sneeze. I caught a glimpse of the two of us mirrored in a shop window and realised I looked like a cart horse standing next to a thoroughbred. I moved as far away from her as I could, and got my heel wedged in a crack in the pavement as I did so.

87

"I'm so glad you took my advice, Will," she was saying while I focussed on freeing my heel without toppling over and making myself look a complete loser. "I promise you, you won't be disappointed. I was thrilled to find such fine dining in a place like Dintscombe. Wasn't expecting that at all. Do try the lobster thermidor if it's on, won't you? It's the best I've tasted outside of Nathan Outlaw's. Anyway, I'd better not keep you. The *maitre d'* can get very sniffy if you're late. Don't forget, you owe me that drink. Another time, eh? Great to meet you, Kat. Bye."

Will and I walked on in silence. That is to say, he walked, I hobbled as my heel now felt decidedly wonky.

I'd been looking forward to a quiet, stress-free evening with Will, pouring out my worries about Mum, Dad and Tanya over a pint or two, so that he could tell me I was fretting over nothing.

Now it looked as if it was dinner for two, with starched tablecloths, an even starchier *maitre d'* and so many knives and forks I wouldn't know where to start.

Suddenly, the rugby club, and maybe even the kebab shop, seemed very appealing.

***

Michael's Restaurant was situated in Dintscombe's only hotel. It was one of the town's oldest buildings and legend had it that the notorious Judge Jeffreys had stayed there during his search for rebels.

Local wags claimed that the place – and that included the bed linen – hadn't changed since then. Indeed, the hotel reception was as drab as ever, with its dark panelled walls hung with faded prints of Cheddar Gorge and Glastonbury Tor that had obviously come from the same closing down sale as the ones in the Winchmoor Arms.

But, according to the advertising feature they'd run in *The Chronicle* a few weeks ago (and, no, I hadn't had the chance to write it, more's the pity), the room that used to be a rather soulless hotel dining room, with two long rows of tables set out like a school canteen, had had a makeover.

Before we could find out for ourselves, the starchy *maitre d'*, who was even starchier than I'd expected, glided across to us. He looked us up and down as if trying to find a reason to refuse us entry.

"You have a reservation?" He peered down his long, hooked nose at us and made me wish I hadn't washed off the temporary tattoo. Just to see if his eyebrows would reach what used to be his hairline.

"Will Manning, table for two, 7.30pm," Will said.

"Would Sir like an aperitif in the bar while you peruse the menus?" he asked, never once casting a glance in my direction.

"Madam would like…" I began, but Will beat me to it.

"Two gins and tonics, please," he said, as the *maitre d'* pointed his long bony nose skywards, like a trail hound who'd just caught the scent, and invited us to follow him.

"The barman will be with you shortly," he announced, before he and his nose left us to it and he slithered off to 'welcome' more guests.

The made-over dining room was broken up by huge, floor-standing pots of foliage. A corner had been partitioned off by yet more foliage to create a small bar, in exactly the same way Mum had used pots of artificial geraniums to mark out her reception area.

The bar's spindly chrome chairs were no more comfortable than Mum's, although they didn't wobble. Instead of dog eared copies of *Hello!* each chrome and smoked glass table held a large dark blue leather-bound book embossed with silver which, it turned out, was the menu. It was the size of a telephone directory and looked more like a royal proclamation than a bill of fare.

The other thing the bar had in common with Mum's reception area was that the tables were packed so tightly together it was almost impossible not to include the people on the next table in your conversation, whether you wanted to or not. Elsie Flintlock would have loved it.

As Will went up to the bar I glanced across and smiled at

the woman at the next table. She wore a long beige dress, a string of pearls around her neck and her pale golden hair was neatly coiled in a bun at the base of her neck.

"Good evening, Mrs Crabshaw," I said.

With the air of a startled fawn, Fiona Crabshaw looked up from the menu she'd been studying so intently. She gave me a puzzled stare, as if trying to place where she'd seen me before.

"It's Kat," I said. "Cheryl's daughter. From the salon. Much Winchmoor."

"Yes, of course. Forgive me. I was miles away." Her soft voice had a frosty edge that told me she'd known exactly who I was but still hadn't forgiven me for my inappropriate comment about the parish council election.

She gave a flicker of a smile that did not reach those lime marmalade eyes and went back to her menu.

I don't know why I did what I did next. I've thought about it a lot since. And I can only say, in my defence, that I was feeling rattled. By the starchy *maitre d'* and his even starchier restaurant. By the fact that, as we'd made our way to the 'bar,' I'd had a quick glance at the dining room and my worst fears were confirmed.

It was, indeed, all starched tablecloths, sparkling glassware and so much cutlery it looked the homeware department of Harrods.

This came hard on the heels of my encounter with tiny, dainty gentlemen-(even-farmers)-prefer-blondes Anna. Will's muttered, "You look, um, good," was erased from my memory bank by the look in his eyes when he saw her. And I couldn't get Elsie's dig about pretty young vets out of my mind.

So, I wasn't really thinking straight when I looked across at Fiona Crabshaw as she pored over her menu. In a bid to distract myself from pretty young vets, I did what I always do when under stress. I said the first thing that came into my head.

"Did you know the police now think Margot was killed some time on Tuesday night?" Elsie had delivered that particular nugget of information yesterday morning with all the relish of a conjuror producing a bunch of paper flowers out of a rabbit's ear.

Fiona's pale face went several shades paler.

"No. No, I didn't," she said and went back to her menu. It was, as I said, a very long menu.

"Apparently, they've let Abe Compton go because he had an alibi for Tuesday night," I went on. "So that means they're questioning everyone as to their whereabouts then."

"Oh, really?" she said faintly, "That's good news about Abe Compton. His wife must be very relieved."

"She is, of course. But the thing is," I went on, "If it wasn't Abe, then who was it?"

She shook her head. "I can't imagine. But I think these things are best left to the police, don't you?"

"Of course. They'll probably do a house-to-house of the entire village now, asking everyone where they were at the time."

"Probably."

"So, tell me then, Mrs Crabshaw, where were you on Tuesday night? I hope you and your husband have got your alibis sorted."

She stared at me, her eyes wide with horror. Then she looked across at her husband, who was leaning against the bar, talking to Will and the barman.

"Gerald. Please!" she said in what was for her a very loud voice.

"What is it?" he asked. There was a hint of impatience in his voice until he turned, saw me and glared. "What the hell are you doing here?"

I lifted my chin. Gerald Crabshaw and I had crossed swords many times before and I was not going to be intimidated by his bullying tone.

"Having dinner. The same as you, I imagine," I said with quiet dignity.

"Gerald." Fiona darted an anxious look at him, her voice low. "She's just told me the police have let Abe Compton go. And that they're going around the village asking everyone where they were when Margot was killed. Gerald, she asked me if you and I had an alibi for that night."

91

Gruesome Gerald's face went the colour of the rare venison loin that was, according to page twenty-three of the menu, chef Michael's signature dish. He stalked across the tiny bar and halted in front of me. He was breathing so hard, I quite expected to see steam coming out of his nostrils.

"How dare you upset my wife like that?" he hissed.

Behind him, Will asked, "Katie? What's going on?"

I closed the menu, replaced it on the tiny chrome and glass table and stood up.

"I've decided I don't want to eat here after all, Will. Shall we go?"

Chapter Ten

I stalked out without waiting for Will, and was half way down the High Street before he caught up with me.

"What the hell was all that about?" He held my arm and pulled me around to face him. "What's got into you tonight?"

"I'm sorry," I said. "But I wish you'd said where we were going. I really don't like that sort of place, Will. I've had a hell of a couple of days and just wanted to go somewhere quiet and relaxed where we could have a chat. Not sit there fussing over which knife and fork went with what and having to get my French dictionary out to translate the menu. Nor do I like the idea of you having to mortgage the farm to pay the bill. Did you see the prices?"

He grimaced. "The G and Ts were so expensive, I actually asked the barman if he'd made a mistake. I'm sorry, though. I thought you'd like somewhere a bit more sophisticated than the rugby club."

"Well, yes, I would. But let's face it, almost every pub in town passes that criterion. That place was so up itself. As for that *maitre d'*…"

He laughed and we began to walk on, his hand still on my arm. "He was a bit much, wasn't he?"

"He was a lot much."

"But what did you do to upset Gerald Crabshaw? One minute he's talking to me about the rugby international, the next he's snorting like a riled-up bull."

"You know Gerald," I said vaguely. "He's only got to look at me and his blood pressure goes off the scale."

"Come on, then," he said as we were walking past the Red Lion. "Will this do for you, Madam?"

"Yes please," I said. We settled for a table in the corner by the fireplace where a real log fire hissed and crackled in the

93

grate. As Will went up for the drinks, I leaned back in the comfortable old chair, stretched my legs towards the fire and watched showers of sparks spiral up into the darkness of the wide chimney. As I did so, the tight knot of tension in my neck and shoulders slowly began to unravel.

"So, come on, spill," Will said as he came back with a couple of drinks and a menu that was just one page long. And in English.

"How do you mean?"

"You're wound up like a coiled spring. What's wrong?"

It felt so good to be able to tell him about the atmosphere at home.

"But things should improve now that Tanya's moved out, surely?" he said when I'd finally talked myself to a standstill.

"You'd think so, wouldn't you? But if anything it's worse. She's talking about setting up in business against Mum."

"Where?"

"In Much Winchmoor, she reckons. Says she's already got her finances in place."

"Much Winchmoor?" Will laughed. "That's not going to work, is it?"

"It's not just that." I told him how the only way Mum and Dad were talking was through me.

"It's doing my head in, Will," I sighed as we both tucked into Doreen's Saturday special with relish. You could keep chef Michael's lobster thermidor. Doreen's steak and mushroom pie, with its crisp, buttery pastry and rich, dark gravy was the food of the gods. Especially after Mum's tofu and sesame soba noodles.

"There's one way out of that," he said, as he pinched a chip off my plate and used it to mop up the last of his gravy.

"Oh? What's that?"

"Well, you could move in with me." He held my gaze for a second then looked down at my plate. "Are you going to finish the rest of those chips?"

I shook my head and stared at him, unsure what he meant or how to answer him.

The only thing I was sure of was that, if ever I did move in with Will, or anyone, it would be because we loved each other and were ready to move our relationship on to another level.

It wouldn't be as a matter of convenience. Or because I wanted to get away from my warring parents.

"Well? What do you think?" Will was still happily munching his way through my chips, which was just as well because if I'd tried to eat them now, they'd have tasted like sawdust, even though a few minutes earlier they'd been heavenly.

Did I get that wrong? Had Will just asked me to move in with him? Or was he simply offering me a place to doss down, like any mate would?

"Have you and your dad let the washing up pile up again, then?" I joked. "Besides, someone had better stay at home and play referee between my parents. Otherwise there's going to be another murder in the village."

Will stared at me. It was as if a shutter had just come down behind his eyes.

***

Although it was great to be back in my own bed, and my own room, sleep didn't come easily that night after Will had dropped me off. There was just a casual peck on the cheek and a 'see you,' before he hurried off to count his sheep. Or whatever farmers do to get to sleep.

Was it my fault he'd gone all cool on me? He'd been as relieved as I was to leave the starchy restaurant (especially when he realised he'd have to sell a tractor or two to pay the bill) and things were fine until he suggested I move in with him and his dad.

But it wasn't a serious attempt on his part to take our relationship – if that's what we did have going – to the next level, was it? After all, earlier on in the evening, I'd been wondering if he fancied the pretty blonde vet.

I assumed he was just being a mate and that he felt sorry for me, caught in the crossfire of marital meltdown. When we were kids I often stayed over at his house, sleeping in the little attic bedroom with its tiny windows and sloping ceilings. That was what he meant, wasn't it?

So it was ok to answer him with a laugh, surely? It wasn't as if it was a serious question.

Once I'd reached that conclusion, sleep came a bit easier and eventually I drifted off, waking up too late for my usual pre-breakfast run.

"How did it go last night?" Mum asked as I wandered into the kitchen, still groggy from my restless night.

"Good, thanks." I gave information to my mother strictly on a need-to-know basis. Although I couldn't help wondering what she'd say if I went on: "Will asked me to move in with him and I laughed at him. Oh yes, and I upset Gerald and Fiona Crabshaw by asking them if they had an alibi for the night Margot was killed. But, apart from that, it was great."

Mum was standing at the cooker, Dad was at the table, pretending to be interested in reading the report of last month's Women's Institute meeting in the parish magazine.

I'd hoped that an evening on their own last night, without the excitement of Eurovision, would have given them a chance to clear the air a bit.

"I'm making scrambled eggs, if you want some?" she went on.

"Yes, please," Dad and I chorused in unison.

She cracked another couple of eggs into the pan. But when she'd cooked them, she served them up on two plates. One for me. One for her.

Obviously no clearing of the air last night, then. Mind you, Dad wasn't missing anything. Only my mum could scramble a few eggs and turn them into something you could use to fill the cracks in the living room ceiling.

I took a deep breath. "Mum? Dad? Don't you think this has gone on long enough?"

But before either of them could answer – or, judging from their mulish expressions, refuse to answer – there was a sharp rap on the back door.

Uncle Richard stood there, worry lines scoring deep furrows in his narrow face.

"I've come to see Tanya," he announced, rocking back on his heels slightly as he stuffed his hands in the pockets of his immaculate grey flannel trousers and jingled his loose change.

Mum and Dad stared at each other, each waiting for the other to say something. I reckon they'd have still been there now if I hadn't stepped in and broken the tense silence.

"She's not here, Uncle Richard," I said.

He stopped jingling and swore in a very un-Uncle Richard like way. He took his hands out of his pockets and clasped them together so hard his knuckles cracked. For one crazy moment, I could almost see those long, bony fingers closing around Tanya's neck. I shuddered and pushed the thought aside.

"You'd better come in," I said. "Would you like some tea?"

He shook his head without glancing in my direction. His attention was one hundred per cent focussed on Mum.

"She's with him, isn't she? I should have known." His usually soft voice was brittle, edgy. "Come on, you might as well tell me the truth. She told me she was coming to stay with you for a bit and when I spoke to you on the phone, you confirmed that. So have you been covering for her again, Cheryl?"

Mum flushed. "Of course I haven't. She was here when you phoned the other day. But since then, we – well, if you must know, we had a bit of a disagreement." She shot Dad a look that would have boiled oil. "And she left."

"Do you know where? If she's gone back to him— "

"No. I don't. She just came back yesterday afternoon, grabbed her suitcases and drove off without a word. Not even a 'thank you for putting me up.'"

"That sounds like my wife," Richard muttered.

"And who's this 'him' you're talking about?" Mum went on. "Tanya didn't say anything about there being another man. She said she'd left you because—"

She stopped, looked down at her scrambled eggs, then pushed the plate away with a sigh.

Dad cleared his throat, more than willing to take over where Mum had left off.

"She said she'd left you because you threatened her with violence." He looked accusingly at his brother. "How could you do that?"

"Me?" Richard's voice rose to a reedy squeak. "She said I was the one who threatened her? And you believed her?"

Dad and his brother stared at each other across the kitchen table. I'd never thought they looked a bit alike. Uncle Richard was tall and thin, with a faint stoop and neat, swept-back hair. Dad was short, with a beer belly that spilled out over the top of his trousers like a badly-set *panna cotta,* a round face and a shiny bald head that glowed like a bright red beacon when he'd been on Abe Compton's cider.

But, at that moment, both men had identical expressions on their faces as they squared up to each other, like a pair of bantam cockerels scrapping over a little bantam hen.

"I had no reason to think otherwise," Dad said stiffly. "The poor woman was beside herself. She said at one time she was in fear of her life."

Mum and Richard both let out snorts of indignation and began to speak. But Richard got there first.

"Not that it's any of your damn business, Terence…"

Dad grunted. He hated being called Terence but I guessed Uncle Richard knew that.

"If there was any violence threatened to my wife that night," he went on. "It was from the woman who'd just discovered Tanya had been having an affair with her husband."

"I should have known," Mum huffed, but Uncle Richard ignored the interruption.

"It seems Tanya's so-called personal trainer had been getting a damn sight too personal, if you see what I mean." he went on, "Until his wife found out. She came to the house threatening to tear Tanya's hair out by the roots if she ever went near him again. So yes, there was indeed violence threatened that night. But I can assure you, the threats came from the wronged wife. Not from me. I wanted to sit down quietly and calmly and talk about it. But Tanya refused to do so and stormed off to her room. We have separate rooms, you see," he gave a slightly embarrassed shrug. "She says I snore.

Anyway, when I came down in the morning, I found she'd gone."

"She never told us that," Mum said. "I'm sorry, Richard. When she talked about violence, we thought... well, to be honest, we didn't know what to think."

I did. I knew Uncle Richard wouldn't have the nerve to threaten Tanya with violence. But I wasn't going to say that in front of him.

"It's ok," he gave a wry smile. "Tanya can spin a very good yarn. So, where is she?"

Mum shook her head. "Honestly, I don't know. And that's the truth. Maybe Terry knows."

She glared at Dad.

"Terry?" Richard asked.

Once again, the two squared up to each other. Dad blinked first. "I don't know," he said quietly, "And that's the truth."

I looked across at him and frowned. Why was he lying? He must have been in the pub when Tanya came in and fixed everything up with Mary. So why was he trying to pretend he didn't know where she was? He could, at least, make a pretty good guess.

I'd had enough. The whole thing was doing my head in.

"I told Elsie I'd walk Prescott again this morning," I said, picking up my bag and heading for the door.

"Surely she doesn't expect you to work on a Sunday, does she?" Mum said. "That's exploitation, that is."

"No, she doesn't expect it. But the dog doesn't know it's Sunday, does he?" I said. "He needs his walk."

And I need to get away from this toxic atmosphere, I could have added, but didn't. I didn't know why my dad was lying about not knowing where Tanya was. But I didn't fancy hanging about to play referee between the two brothers.

Gran Latcham used to say the pair of them fought like tigers when they were little boys. And the way they were looking at each other, it didn't appear either of them had grown up any in the interim.

***

I stood outside the Winchmoor Arms. It wasn't quite noon and the front door, with its flaking green paint and tarnished brass door knob, wasn't open yet.

I went around the back to see if the door to the public bar was shut too. As I crossed the car park, I was almost knocked over by the arrival of a great big bear of a man on a very small scooter. He was crouched low over the narrow handlebars, his huge rugby player's shoulders hunched, his knees almost touching his chin.

"Hi Shane," I smiled as he parked the scooter, straightened up and removed his helmet. "You haven't grown into that thing yet?"

Shane Freeman shook out his mop of thick, dark curls and scratched his head. "Don't knock it," he said. "It gets me from home to here and is a damn sight better than that old push bike you pedal around on. Cheap as chips to run, too, which was the main reason for getting it."

Shane lost his job as a lorry driver last year. He now worked in the pub at weekends and had a job as a night filler in the supermarket at Dintscombe during the week. Neither job paid particularly well, hence his need for cheap as chips transport.

"We're not really open yet, sweetheart," he said. "But if you're that desperate, and seeing as it's you…"

"I haven't come here for a drink, Shane," I said as I followed him into the bar.

"No? Well, that's a shame because would you believe it, we're clean out of designer handbags at the moment. Not to mention fancy cupcakes. We do a fine line in ladies' lingerie, though, if you fancy a private viewing?"

Shane and I had gone to school together. Like Will, he'd been in the year above me. Even back then he'd fancied himself as a comedian. Pity no one else did.

I gave him a brief smile. "I'm looking for my aunt, Tanya. Skinny blonde with big hair and lots of bracelets. She said she was staying here. Do you know if she's around?"

He looked around the empty bar. "Can't see her anywhere."

"But she is staying here, isn't she? She told me yesterday she'd taken a room."

He grinned. His teeth needed a good scale and polish and it was not a pretty sight.

"How would I know? I've only just got here. Besides, I don't do room service," he added with a leer that made me take a step backwards.

"Is Mary around?" I reckoned I'd get more sense from her.

"She'll be up to her elbows in parsnips and carrots at the moment, getting ready for Sunday lunch service." he said. "She always gets very wound up around this time and won't thank you for disturbing her. Nor thank me for giving out confidential information about her guests."

I was losing patience. "For goodness sake, Shane. I only want to know if my aunt is in. I'm not asking for the details of her bank account."

He grinned. "All right. All right. Keep your hair on. I'm only teasing you. 'Struth! You always were a feisty one, Katie Latcham. I'm surprised Will puts up with you."

He saw he'd gone too far, and held out his hands. "Sorry. Sorry. Look, I'll risk getting my head bitten off and go and ask Mary. Stay there."

He disappeared into the kitchen. I looked around the bar. It was a depressing sight. It hadn't changed since the previous landlord's day, more's the pity. The faded prints of Cheddar Gorge (out of the same job lot as the ones in the hotel last night); the forlorn spider plant in the window; even the same dust-laden fir cones in the never-to-be-lit fireplace.

Shane reappeared a couple of minutes later.

"So what did she say?" I asked.

"She says, did I think she has nothing better to do than keep track of everyone's comings and goings? And why was I hanging around like a spare part, getting in her way, when we have a party of ten booked in for 12.15pm?"

"But did she say anything about Tanya?"

"She said she thought your aunt went out, about ten minutes ago. And no, before you ask, she didn't say where she was going. But she can't have gone far because that fancy car of hers is still in the car park."

"Thank you – I think."

"Shall I give her a message when she comes back?" he asked. "All part of the Winchmoor Arms customer care package. In fact, I could give you a ring when she gets back, if you give me your number?"

Give Shane Freeman my number? In his dreams.

"Just tell her I was looking for her, and I'll catch up later," I said.

Then I hurried out, preferring the company of a bad tempered, snappy little dog with an attitude problem to hanging around in that dreary, draughty bar with the smell of over-boiled cabbage drifting out from the kitchen.

Chapter Eleven

Elsie had given me a key to her bungalow a couple of days before. For a few brief moments I'd felt a warm glow, touched by her trust in me, until she spoilt it by adding: "It's only while I'm in plaster, mind you. And I don't want you wandering in and out of here like you own the place. So this is just to save me the trouble of getting myself to the door to let you in. Be sure to knock and call out, though. I don't want you creeping up on me and giving me a heart attack."

So as instructed, I knocked and called out: "It's me, Mrs Flintlock."

"Katie? What are you doing here?" *The Chronicle*, spread across her bony knees, was open at her favourite section, the obituary pages. She always studied each entry with such fierce concentration, she'd have got an A star if they ever brought out a GCSE in the subject. "I said not to come today. You're not getting double time or anything like that."

"I'm not expecting any pay at all. But it's a lovely day and I thought I'd come and take Prescott for a walk. Would you like a cup of tea while I'm here? There's something I'd like a quick chat about, if that's ok?"

She looked across at me, with those bird-bright eyes that missed nothing.

"It's not a lovely day at all," she sniffed. "Looks like it's going to pour down any moment."

I opened my mouth to ask her about Margot, but before I could do so she went on, "Happen things are better at home now the trollop's taken herself off to the pub, instead of making your mother's life a misery?"

"How did you know that?" I asked before I could stop myself.

"It's my ankle that's broken. There's nothing wrong with

my hearing. Or my eyes. Besides, Creepy Dave was in the pub yesterday lunchtime and he told me how your dad came in, followed a few minutes later by your aunt, who took herself off to the far corner of the bar where no one could hear and had a long chat with Mary. After a bit she left, but came back a little later with enough suitcases to stock a shop."

See what I mean about Much Winchmoor? I kid you not, if someone sneezed at one end of the village, someone at the other end would hear it and speculate as to what they'd been doing to catch a cold, where, and with whom.

I shrugged and went in the kitchen to make the tea (Elsie didn't hold with coffee. Said it gave her 'paltry-pations'). I was hoping by the time the tea was made she'd have finished with the goings-on of my parents, and would be ready to answer my questions about Margot.

No chance.

"And what about that lanky streak of nothing?" She peered at me over the rim of her favourite bone china teacup (with matching saucer).

"Who do you mean?"

"The trollop's husband. Richard, isn't that his name?"

"Yes. But…"

"Olive says she saw him pull up outside your place this morning in his flash car. Said he had a face like thunder."

"He's there now." No point in denying it.

"No wonder you got yourself out the way. Those two boys have never got on. Your gran used to fret over them, right up to the day she died, God rest her soul. She always said there'd be trouble between them, sooner or later."

I knew I shouldn't encourage her. But couldn't help myself. "How do you mean?"

She took a long, slow slurp of tea before answering.

"Of course I wasn't living in the village at the time. But your gran told me all about it. How it was your mum who first started going out with Richard. Engaged, they were."

"What?" *Mum and Uncle Richard?* This was news to me.

Elsie nodded. "They'd set the date of the wedding, booked the reception and everything. It was all going smoothly until

Cheryl made the mistake of introducing Richard to the trollop —"

"Do you mean Tanya?"

She sniffed. "Your mum's so-called best friend. At least, she was at the time. She batted her eyelids at him and next thing anyone knew, the pair of them had run off together. Cancelled the wedding and everything."

I started at her, shocked. I'd had no idea. Poor Mum, no wonder she'd been so understanding when Ratface did almost the same thing to me. Although, in my case, there was no broken engagement and cancelled wedding, just a great big hole in my finances. And a shed-load of dented pride.

I made a promise to myself at that time that I would never ever let a man do that to me again.

"But how did Mum end up with Dad?" I really shouldn't be gossiping about my parents to Much Winchmoor's gossipmonger-in-chief. But I was dying to know.

Elsie knew when she'd reeled in her audience, and was milking it for all she was worth. She picked up a ginger biscuit (which, as per instructions, I'd set out on a matching bone china plate) and dunked it before continuing.

"According to your gran, Terry had been sweet on Cheryl since the moment Richard first brought her home. And after Richard jilted her, I dare say young Terry made a very good shoulder for her to cry on. If you ask me, your mother got the best of the bargain. Your dad's a good honest man."

"Are you saying Uncle Richard isn't?"

"Of course I'm not." She put her cup down and shot me an indignant look. "How could I? I don't even know the man."

I thought about pointing out how that didn't usually stop her speculating. But decided against it.

"A man who runs off with another woman, leaving his fiancée to cancel the wedding, is hardly good husband material, wouldn't you agree?" she went on.

I was still trying to take it in. It explained why Dad and Uncle Richard were always so edgy with each other. I'd thought it was nothing more than sibling rivalry that they'd never grown out of. It also explained why Mum and Tanya didn't get on.

Why, then, had Mum agreed to her coming to stay with us this week? And why did she go on that girlie weekend to Bournemouth with her a year or so ago, that Tanya kept harping on about? It didn't make any sense.

"Well?" Elsie suddenly demanded. "Are you going to stay there staring out of the window all day? What were you going to ask me?"

I was still trying to get my head around my parents' merry-go-round relationship. Or should that be pass the parcel?

"You said you wanted to talk to me about something," Elsie prompted. "I hope it wasn't anything to do with Danny. Because, last I heard, he was spoken for. Actually, he said he might look in later."

I felt my cheeks burn. "No, of course it wasn't about him. It was actually about Margot. The editor at *The Chronicle* wants me to do a background feature on her."

"Does he indeed?" She looked at me sharply. "That's a far cry from last week's dog show."

"Yes, well, that's local journalism for you, isn't it?' I said quickly before she could winkle out the truth that Mike hadn't actually asked. I had offered. "Never the same story. The trouble is, I can't find anything about Margot before she came to the village. Where she came from, why they decided to settle in Much Winchmoor, that sort of thing. And obviously, I can't ask her husband. Not at a time like this. So I thought of you."

There was a small silence. I glanced at her sharply. Silence was not Elsie's usual response.

"I don't really know where to start," I went on. "She's not on any of the usual social media sites, apart from Facebook. And that's only about her holiday cottages."

Elsie snorted. "Let's hope those cottages will go back on the market now, so that local people who really need them can buy them."

You reckon? I'd never had Elsie down for one of life's optimists. But I let it pass.

"So, you don't know much more about the Duckett-

Trimbles than I do," I said.

Her head shot up as if I'd just challenged her to an arm wrestling contest.

"I didn't say that. They bought the Manor at auction after old Mr Jenkins died. He lived there like a recluse after his wife passed away. It was the new-monials that did for her. Not surprising, the place was that cold and damp. But they were a very strange couple. She used to cycle around the place on one of those old three-wheeler bikes with a basket on the front handlebars. Used to carry a small dog in it. She came from Wiltshire," she added as if that explained the old lady's eccentric behaviour.

I didn't want her to go off on a tangent, so steered her gently back. "And the Duckett-Trimbles? Do you know where they came from?"

"No. I don't. Lady Duckface wanted to know everybody's business but was very close when it came to her own. Now," she said briskly as she picked up *The Chronicle* and smoothed it across her knee. "Are you going to leave me to read my paper in peace and walk my poor little dog?"

Her poor little dog was snoring loudly in his basket by the radiator. But I needed to have a think and a brisk walk always helped.

So, even Elsie didn't know anything about the Duckett-Trimbles before they moved to Much Winchmoor. Very strange.

"Come on, Prescott," I called. "Walkies."

There was no response until I collected his lead and harness from the kitchen. At the sound of which he leapt into the air then hurled himself at the front door.

***

Prescott and I cut through the churchyard. As I threaded my way through the graves I recognised the tall thin figure leaning over the wall, looking at the small triangular wedge of land that was between the churchyard and the road. I nipped behind one of the yew trees before he spotted me.

It was Danny. And he had this great big grin on his way-too-handsome face.

So this was indeed Elsie's plot of land. It was just about big enough for a small house, I supposed, although the way they squeezed things in nowadays, it would probably end up with a row of five 'executive town houses', suitable only for families of 'executive' mice who had no need or inclination to swing a cat.

It would be a shame to see the plot developed, though. It was fringed with hazel and blackthorn bushes and studded with apple and pear trees, their blossom a picture every spring, their fruits scrumped by every kid in the village come the autumn. In fact, the first buds were just beginning to show on some of the trees and the thought that they might never turn into apples made anger well up inside me.

While I was watching Danny, Prescott had busied himself burrowing in the nearby compost heap in the corner of the churchyard. He'd dug himself in so deeply that only his back legs and stubby little tail was visible. I gave a sharp tug on his lead, stepped out from behind the yew tree and walked towards Danny.

The tag on Prescott's collar jingled like a bicycle bell as he shook off the last of the leaf mould, grass clippings and goodness know what else he'd been digging in. Judging by the smell, I preferred not to know.

Danny looked up at the sound. "It's Katie, isn't it?"

I was going to say something snippy about how property developers were ripping the hearts out of small villages. But instead, I nodded curtly and returned his smile with a hostile glare. And went to walk on.

"Look, don't rush off," he said. "I'm glad I've seen you. The thing is, I'm a bit worried about Gran. Is she really as hard up as she makes out?"

"Worse," I snapped, furious with him for touching the poor old soul for cash and then pretending to be worried about her. "She's hardly got enough to eat at times and has to sit with her coat on most days because she can't afford to turn the heating on. It's terrible when you get old and nobody cares about you, isn't it?"

At least that wiped the smile off his way-too-handsome face, I thought, as I stomped away.

Of course it wasn't true. Elsie had more than enough to eat which explained why her waistbands wouldn't do up, even though she always blamed it on her clothes 'shrinking in the wash.' And her bungalow was like a sauna most days. But I wanted to make Danny feel bad.

And by the shocked look on his face I'd succeeded.

***

Walking through the village with Prescott was, as always, a nightmare. He barked at everything, from the discarded crisp packet that scudded along the pavement in front of us to the For Sale sign that, in spite of my efforts to right it yesterday, now lolled against the wall of the Old Forge. He also insisted on stopping to sniff at every bush, gate and lamp post.

I decided to take him up Pendle Hill, in the hope that the wind (which was always a full-on gale up there, no matter what it was doing anywhere else) might blow away the smell of the churchyard compost heap which still clung to him. Also, once up there I could let him off his lead and get in a half-decent walk.

The route to Pendle Hill took me past the entrance to Winchmoor Manor. The wrought iron gates, usually tightly closed, were open. As I stood there, waiting for the dog to leave his 'Prescott was here!' messages all over the elegant stone pillars, I caught sight of a flash of bubblegum pink in the bushes just inside the gate.

Was that Tanya? But before I could check it out, I heard the crunch of tyres on gravel and John Duckett-Trimble's long, sleek car came down the drive.

At first I thought the car was being driven by his chauffeur, a surly guy with a face that looked like it would crack if he broke out a smile. But as it got closer I could see it was John himself at the wheel and my heart went out to him. He was almost unrecognisable.

He was away on business a lot and didn't mix much in village life, apart from an occasional pint in the pub. But when he was out and about he was always polite and friendly, with a smile and a wave for everyone, and was usually dressed like an advert for an upmarket Savile Row tailor. Smart, well cut suit, snowy white shirt with crisp cuffs and collar, expensive silk tie. The archetypal successful businessman.

But that day, he looked dreadful. He was wearing an old sweatshirt that was as grey as his face, while his usually trim hair made him look, as Olive would say, like he'd been 'dragged through a hay-rick upside down.'

He also looked like a man who hadn't slept for a fortnight. He was probably jet-lagged after being called back from his business trip in such terrible circumstances.

I yanked Prescott away from the stone pillars and stood aside as the car whispered past, engine purring liked a contented cat. I felt like I'd been caught peering through his letterbox, but he didn't even appear to have seen me as he turned right on the road out of the village.

What must it be like, to lose someone you love in such dreadful circumstances? To live with the knowledge that out there somewhere was a person who hated your wife so much they could do such a dreadful thing to her.

But who? Who would that be? There was no doubt Margot had managed to upset almost everyone in the village at some time or another. Margot was to tact what Darcey Bussell was to mud wrestling.

But you didn't kill someone just because they'd told you your frontage was letting down the look of the entire High Street (Mary in the pub) or that the WI was stuck in the past and needed a good shake-up (and maybe a nude calendar). Or even that the Young Wives Group should be renamed, as none of its members would see sixty-five again (the entire membership of the Grumble and Gossip Group). Even our elderly vicar didn't escape (boring sermons and too many hymns).

I thought of Fiona Crabshaw's reaction last night to my innocent remark about the police asking people where they were at the time of the murder. It wasn't true, of course. According to Elsie, poor old Abe Compton was still suspect number one. And I'd only said that to Fiona to rattle her. Because, at the time, I was rattled myself. I'd let the encounter with the pretty blonde vet and then the starchy *maitre d'* get under my skin.

I'd regretted the words the moment they left my mouth. But the memory of her extreme reaction (and that of Gruesome Gerald) got me wondering if I hadn't, after all, struck a nerve.

"Katie?"

I looked up to see Tanya extricating herself from yet another bush. What was it with her and bushes, I wondered? First, the laurels outside The Old Forge and now the rhododendrons here at the entrance to the Manor.

As she clip-clopped her way towards me, bracelets jangling, Prescott growled. She looked down at him as if I had a rat on the other end of the lead.

"What sort of a dog is that? He seems a particularly unpleasant little creature."

I thought so too. But there was no way I was letting her know that. I suddenly felt quite protective towards my bad-tempered little canine friend whose bite was, as I knew to my cost, most definitely worse than his bark.

"His name's Prescott," I said, raising my voice slightly to cover his low, rumbling growl. "I'm walking him while his owner's recovering from a broken ankle."

She tutted and looked at me with mock pity.

"You poor darling. The things you have to do to earn a few pennies around here. Never mind, when I open my salon I could well have an opening for you, if you're interested."

I stared at her in astonishment. "Of course I'm not. For starters, I'm a qualified journalist." Well, she didn't need to know that the 'qualified' bit wasn't totally true. "And you're planning to set up in opposition to my mother. I couldn't do that to her, even if I wanted to. Which I do not."

She shrugged. "Suit yourself, sweetie. I'm sure there are plenty of people who'll be only too happy to work in a trendy, upmarket salon that caters for younger people, with not a perm or a shampoo and set in sight. Talking of which…" she peered at my hair. "I was right, wasn't I? That style suits you so much better."

I thought of Will's 'um – very nice' last night. And felt a little glow – until I went on to remember the way he'd looked at Anna.

"I don't understand why you're doing this to Mum." I scowled at her. "What did she ever do to you?"

If what Elsie said was true, it was more a case of what Tanya, and Richard, had done to Mum.

She gave that tinkly laugh that always set my teeth on edge – and set Prescott off on another of his long, low grumbles.

"Whatever gave you that idea? This is purely business, sweetie. Nothing to do with your mother."

"You're still going ahead with your idea for opening a hair salon here, then?"

"Not just a hair salon." Her eyes shone, her bracelets jangling as she waved her arms expansively. "It's going to be the ultimate one-stop pamper-shop. Spa, perfumery, tanning salon, nail bar – a complete beauty package, all under one roof. Maybe even a juice bar. So, yes, you'd better believe it's going ahead. And there's not a damn thing your mother can do about it. She might as well sell up now."

Chapter Twelve

I'd have been worried for Mum, if the whole thing wasn't so ridiculous. The Old Forge was one of the larger higgledy-piggledy cottages at the far end of the High Street. But even so it was hardly big enough for the sort of set-up Tanya was talking about.

It probably wasn't true, anyway. Chances were, she was just telling me all this in the hope I'd tell Mum.

"I wouldn't have thought there was enough room in The Old Forge for all that," I said. "Unless, of course, you're planning to turn the old stone shed that used to be the outside privy into a space for a hot tub?"

She gave a slow, catlike smile. "Who said anything about it being in the Old Forge?"

"You did. At least that was what you were talking about yesterday."

"Yes, I was, wasn't I?" Another catlike smile, only this time it was more of a smirk. "What is it they say? Twenty-four hours is a long time in politics? It is in business as well, sweetie." She looked like a kid who has a secret that's just bursting to be shared. "It's all very hush-hush at the moment but I've just set up a meeting which, if it goes my way – and I've got a very strong feeling it will – will put Much Winchmoor well and truly on the map. Watch this space, as they say."

I wasn't sure that Much Winchmoor wanted, or indeed, deserved, to be put on the map. Unless it was one of those 'places best avoided' ones.

Before I could say so, she went on. "But whatever happens, I'm this close to finalising a deal on The Old Forge." She closed her thumb and forefinger in a circle "That, at least, is all going perfectly to plan."

I flashed her a suspicious frown. "You haven't been up to see John Duckett-Trimble, have you?"

"Of course I haven't." She looked indignant. "It's all being done through his agent."

"So what were you doing hiding in the bushes?"

"Being nosy, the same as you. I saw the gates were open and thought I'd have a wander up the drive and see if I could take a peep at the Manor. Just out of curiosity."

"And did you?"

She shook her head. "I didn't get very far when I heard his car coming, so got myself behind a bush, in case he thought I was trespassing."

"Which you were."

"Well, yes. I suppose. And if he'd stopped and said something, I was going to..." she broke off and bit her lip. "The thing is, I know something. Something about Margot, and I'm not quite sure what to do about it."

I felt a stirring of excitement. "Hey, that's great. You might be able to help me then. I'm doing a background piece on her for the paper and—"

"Oh no, no." She backed away, hands outstretched as if to fend me off. "It's nothing like that. And certainly not for publication. So don't you dare write a word."

"How can I? You haven't told me anything."

"And I don't intend to." She gave her Dolly Parton mane an extra-large toss, as if to emphasise the point. "Not that there's anything to know," she added.

"So, is what you know relevant to her murder?" I asked.

She shrugged. "Probably not."

"You should go to the police," I said forcefully. "Just in case."

She shook her head. "No. At least not until I've checked something out. But, whatever, it's nothing to do with her death. And certainly nothing the police would be interested in."

"You should let them be the judge of that."

She shook her head. "I can't stand here chatting all day. Mary's promised me one of her famous Sunday lunches. I'm

114

told they are legendary."

I smothered a grin. Mary's overdone roast beef, soggy boiled cabbage and dishwater gravy was indeed legendary. But like all things, there are good legends. And bad legends.

Mary's Sunday roasts definitely fell in the latter category.

I thought about telling Tanya this. But then I thought about what she and Richard had put my mother through – and were still continuing to do. So I decided against it.

It wasn't until Prescott and I were half way up Pendle Hill that I remembered I hadn't told Tanya that Richard was in the village, looking for her. And could, even now, be 'enjoying' Mary's legendary roast beef himself.

The pair of them thoroughly deserved it.

***

The top of Pendle Hill is the highest point for miles around. Part of it is pastureland, the rest steeply sloping woodland. Will and I used to play in the wood when we were kids, building dens and making rope swings in the trees. There was one particular place where a tall beech tree grew over what was almost a sheer drop, where the land fell steeply away. We used to call it the Cliff of Death, and dare each other to swing out over it. It scared the living daylights out of me, to be honest. But there was no way I'd ever let Will know that.

There were no cattle in the field that day so as I set off across it, I let Prescott off his lead. He took off like a bullet and was soon buried deep in the far hedge, where, I hoped, the undergrowth would rub off at least some of the churchyard compost heap smell. Or replace it with something less noxious.

I zipped up my coat as the chilly wind flattened my hair and stung my cheeks. As I walked on, towards my favourite viewpoint, the knot of tension across my shoulders, that seemed to have been there forever, finally began to loosen. Hands thrust deep in my pockets, I stood and looked at the view that always took my breath away. In the distance, the Somerset levels stretched as far as the eye could see, with the unmistakable Glastonbury Tor sticking up like a pimple in the distance.

From up here, you could see the pattern made by the willow-fringed rhines (rhymes with beans and is the local name for the deep, ruler-straight drainage ditches that keep the low-lying fields from flooding – at least some of the time). They divided the fields into neat, patchwork squares. The narrow road across the moors followed the lines of the rhines, with sharp right-angled bends that have caught out many unwary motorists hoping for a quick short cut.

I loved it up here. Will had taught me to recognise the different birds and my attention was caught by a keening cry above me. I looked up and saw a pair of buzzards, their huge wings outstretched as they drew lazy circles in the big open sky. They wheeled around each other, as graceful as a pair of skaters performing an intricate, elegant ice dance.

As I watched, they flew towards the village. I looked down on Much Winchmoor, and my feeling of peace and all's right with the world vanished abruptly. The tension knot across my shoulders returned, tighter than ever.

Somewhere down there, a voice inside my head said, *is a murderer.*

I shuddered, hugged my coat closer and wished I'd worn something warmer. I turned away from the village and looked across to where Pendle Hill Farm nestled into the side of the hill. A curl of smoke rose from the farmhouse's old stone chimney before it was snatched away by the wind.

"Come on, Prescott. Let's go," I called. Suddenly cold, the idea of toasting my toes in front of that fire, enjoying a cup of coffee with Will and his dad (even though Will's coffee always tasted like something you could paint a fence with) was very appealing.

I called Prescott again. But he ignored me. Nothing new there. I finally managed to hunt him down, half-way into a rabbit hole. I grabbed him by the harness, clipped his lead on and we headed back to the farm.

As we got closer, I could see a car that I didn't recognise parked in the yard. It was a silver estate. Closer still and I could make out the sign in the back window. Dintscombe Vets.

What was wrong? Whatever it was had to be pretty serious for Will or his Dad to have to call a vet out on a Sunday.

As I watched the farmhouse door opened. I heard a familiar laugh and saw Will and Anna come out and cross the yard towards the car. Anna still managed to look chic and neat even when wearing jeans that looked as if they had been poured on, trendy Hunter wellies, the cost of which would have bought me a small car, and a quilted gilet that wouldn't have looked out of place at a polo match. She was laughing up at something Will had said. Neither of them looked as if there was any sort of animal-related crisis going on.

Suddenly, the idea of a cup of coffee and a cosy fire didn't seem such a good one after all. Prescott was happily investigating the gate post but I dragged him away before he drew attention to our presence by barking.

I was aware of my wild, windswept hair, my ratty old waterproof coat and my saggy tracksuit bottoms. It seemed like everywhere I turned these days I came across Dintscombe's pretty new blonde vet, with her designer clothes and annoyingly well-behaved hair.

I headed back to Elsie's and hoped that Danny wasn't there. I thought of the problems between Dad and Uncle Richard, then money-grabbing Danny and 'um, you look nice' Will, who was certainly looking at Anna in a way he never looked at me.

Was it any wonder that I decided, then and there, that men were more trouble than they were worth?

***

As I'd hoped, Danny wasn't at Elsie's when Prescott and I got back. But Olive was. She and Elsie were in the sitting room, empty tea cups by their side.

"How's Millie?" I asked.

"She's bearing up, thank you, my dear," Olive said, with her usual sweet smile. "A lot better now that her fool of a husband is back home, that's for sure."

"They've decided he didn't do it, then?"

"Of course he didn't do it," Elsie snorted. "Don't know what took them so long to realise that."

Olive stood up. "If you don't mind, Elsie, I'll be off now. I baked a fruit cake this morning and promised I'd take some up to Millie. Abe loves a bit of my fruitcake, he does."

"Thanks again for lunch," Elsie said. "That's one more I owe you when I can get up and about more."

"Bless you, dearie, that's what neighbours are for," Olive said. "Friends and neighbours should be there for one another, you know."

I thought for a moment she was going to start singing the theme tune to an Australian soap.

"Very kind of you," Elsie said gruffly then turned to me. "Olive brought me lunch, you see."

"Well, everybody loves a roast on a Sunday, don't they?" Olive said. "I'm cooking for myself. No trouble to dish up some extra for you. And it's company for me."

"So it was just the two of you for lunch, was it?" I asked, trying to sound casual. I didn't want to come out and say I'd seen Danny. Just in case he'd only come to the village to check out his grandmother's plot of land and hadn't bothered to come in and see her.

"No," Elsie said. "George Clooney popped in. And that nice Hugh Grant. We had quite a party, Olive, didn't we?"

"Did we?" Olive looked confused. She didn't do sarcasm. Or get it when someone else did. "Oh no, dear, it was just the two of us."

That answered that question then. And Danny went even further up the league table of men I didn't like. So he had, indeed, come to the village just to check out the plot of land. He'd been within a two-minute walk of his grandmother's house and hadn't bothered to call in on her.

What a lowlife. Suddenly, he was right up there, competing with Ratface for top spot.

***

I left Elsie's the same time as Olive.

"Do you have any idea where Margot and her husband lived before they came to Much Winchmoor?" I asked her as we walked down Elsie's path together.

She paused outside her front gate. "No, dear. I'm afraid I don't. She may well have said, but I'm afraid my memory isn't what it was. My daughter's always telling me my memory's like a…" she frowned. "A colander? Or something like that. Is it important?"

"I'm doing this piece for *The Chronicle*," I explained. "Just a bit of general background stuff about Margot."

"For *The Chronicle*, eh?" She couldn't have looked more impressed if I'd said *The Sunday Times*. "You always were a clever girl. I said you'd go far."

Go far? Yeah, right. I'd gone as far as Bristol, only to come back with my tail between my legs when the money ran out. Oh yes, I'd gone far, right enough. All the way there and back again. But it was sweet of Olive to say so.

"Thanks," I said. "But the problem is, I'm not doing very well. No one in the village seems to know anything about Margot's background."

She pushed open her gate. "Our Julie might be able to help you. After all, she worked for them for… oh, I don't know. Several months, I'm pretty sure. Have you asked her?"

I thought about the last time Jules and I met – and how we'd parted. I was probably the last person she'd want to see. She'd made that pretty clear.

"She's busy," I mumbled. "I don't want to bother her."

"Don't be silly. It's not a bother. And she was only saying to me the other day how she misses you."

I imagine that was before our little falling out outside the village hall the other day.

"Why don't you call in and see her?" Olive went on. "I happen to know her Eddie is off working today. He's managed to get himself some casual work over Glastonbury way. Or was it Gloucester? Somewhere beginning with a G anyway. And, as you know, they need all the money they can get now they've got another little mouth to feed. So she'll be on her own with the kiddies and glad of the company, I'm sure."

I wished I shared Olive's optimism on that score. But she was quite right. Jules could well be able to fill in some of the gaps for me.

Jules and Eddy lived in the cluster of new houses over the other side of the village. It was yet another of those executive-style family home developments, which is property developer speak for 'let's see if we can beat our own record for the greatest number of houses squeezed into the smallest possible piece of land.'

I thought about texting her first. But it took me so long to work out what to say that I decided, in the end, it would be quicker to walk over there and just wing it. I'd know by the look on her face if I was welcome or not.

"Katie!" She squealed with delight the second she opened the door. "OMG, I was just texting you. You look frozen. Come on in. Kylie's just finishing her lunch. Have you eaten?"

Kylie was slurping her way through spaghetti hoops with a fried egg on top. My favourite comfort meal ever, after chocolate Hobnobs. But what I needed to say couldn't be said with a mouthful of spaghetti hoops.

"Sit down." Jules pulled out a chair, moved a pair of fairy wings on to the draining board and gestured to me to sit. "Tea? Coffee? Vodka?"

I shook my head and took a deep breath.

"I'm sorry…" We both said the words at the same time.

"No, let me," Jules said. "I need to say this before we go any further. Katie—"

"Kat." I couldn't help myself.

She sighed. "Sorry, Kat. I'm sorry about the other day. I was way out of order."

"No. I'm sorry. What you said was right. I was acting like a…" I looked across at Kylie, who beamed at me, with her orange spaghetti moustache and beard, and changed what I'd been going to say to: "Like a complete idiot."

"Even so," Jules said, when I'd been hoping she'd contradict me. "I was wrong to say what I did. I was tired and cranky, haven't had a decent night's sleep for months. But that's no excuse. What goes on between you and Will is none of my business."

I thought of Little Miss Perfect Anna and considered telling Jules that, as things stood between me and Will, what he got up to and with whom was none of my business either.

"Forget it," I said. "Anyway, I didn't come here to talk about Will. But Margot."

She frowned and glanced towards Kylie. I got the message.

"Nothing like that," I said quickly. "I'm just trying to put together a background piece on her. For *The Chronicle*. Trouble is, no one, not even Elsie Flintlock, seems to know anything about her before she came here. Your gran thought that maybe you might."

I thought back to the way she'd gone all starchy on me when I'd asked her about Margot before, and hurried on. "Look, it's ok. I know you don't want to talk about your employers. I get that. I don't want to quote you or use your name. I just wondered if she ever told you where she lived before they came to Much Winchmoor, to give me something to work from?"

Jules shook her head. "Afraid not. She wasn't much for talking, except telling me I hadn't dusted the Dresden china to her high standard, things like that." She looked across at her daughter. "Have you finished, Kylie? Good girl, come here and let me wipe your face. Then you can go and watch Peppa Pig. Don't have it on too loud though, sweet pea. We don't want to wake your brother, do we?"

She wiped the little girl's face and I tried not to look too longingly at the leftover spaghetti hoops on her plate, as I realised that I hadn't even had time for breakfast that morning, let alone lunch.

"Sure you won't have that cup of tea?" she asked. She always did have an uncanny knack of reading my mind. "I've got a packet of chocolate Hobnobs with your name on."

I laughed. "You remembered my weakness for them, then?"

She gave me a long straight look. "I remember all your weaknesses, girl!"

Then we both burst into gales of laughter and, as we did so, the years fell away. And with them, the awkwardness between us. I took the tea – and two chocolate Hobnobs – and felt much, much better. There are few things in life that don't feel better after a chocolate biscuit or two. Mum seemed to have stopped buying them since Tanya had finished off the packet on her first day with us, and I'd been getting serious withdrawal symptoms.

"Sorry I can't be any more help," Jules went on through a mouthful of biscuit crumbs. "She didn't seem to have any friends, unless you count Gruesome Gerald. I never saw anyone else visit. But I used to hear her on the phone to her husband sometimes, when he was away. Always full of plans." She sighed. "Such a pity, isn't it?"

"What sort of plans, did she say?"

Jules shook her head. "It was usually about her holiday lets. She was quite single-minded when it came to them. Probably had ideas for buying up even more. At the rate they were snapping up village properties, the only ones left not part of the Winchmoor Estate, as she insisted on calling it, would be these houses and the old folks' bungalows."

"Did you know my aunt Tanya is hoping to buy The Old Forge?"

"The blonde stick insect?" She pulled a face. "Why? I wouldn't have thought Much Winchmoor was her scene. Unless she's buying it as a holiday let."

I shrugged. "Who knows?" I thought about telling her what Elsie had told me about Mum and Uncle Richard. But decided against it. "Well, thanks for the tea and biscuits. They were a life saver. And I promise I won't write anything that will make life awkward for you."

"Don't worry about it. They're not my employers any more. Mr D-T phoned me this morning to say he's leaving the village. Selling the house, the cottages, everything. So there goes my job. Give him his due, he's given me a very generous pay off. But even so…"

"Did he say where he was going?"

"Hardly. We're not exactly on those sort of terms."

"But what about the funeral?"

"I asked him about that. Said I wanted to know, so I could pay my respects. He said the police haven't released the body yet."

I shivered as if the cold March wind that had been blowing so hard up on Pendle Hill had suddenly made its way into Jules' tiny, overheated kitchen. But before I could say think of anything suitable to say, a loud wail came from upstairs. Jules sighed and stood up.

"That's my five minutes over and done with," she said with weary resignation. "I'll just go and get him. Sounds like he needs a nappy change. I don't suppose you'd mind?"

The swoosh of panic I felt in the pit of my stomach must have shown. Jules gave a sudden hoot of laughter.

"Your face! Talk about panic. Don't worry, I'm only teasing. Unless, of course…" she added, raising her voice to make herself heard above the noise that would soon be bringing the ceiling down. "Unless you insist on doing it."

"I'll pass, if you don't mind." I tried not to look too eager as I made my way to the door. "I've got loads to do this afternoon."

Chapter Thirteen

The village was deserted as I walked back along the High Street. Most of the cottages had been turned into holiday homes and it was still too early in the year for visitors to start arriving. As for the few that weren't holiday lets, there was no sign of life in them either. The days when villagers stood out on the street chatting away to their neighbours were long gone.

Now, if they were at home, they'd be more likely to be chatting to their 'friends' on the other side of the world, via social media.

And, while the cluster of bungalows where Elsie lived might not be as chocolate-box pretty as the ones on the High Street, I reflected, at least Crabshaw Crescent showed signs of real life and didn't resemble an abandoned film set.

Always assuming, of course, that real life was how you'd describe the sound of Elsie yelling at Prescott, the sight of Olive's smalls waving about on her washing line or the smell of Creepy Dave frying onions again.

As I walked on, a car drove by and the driver tooted at me. It was Stuart Davies, the chairman of Much Winchmoor parish council. He'd always been very good to me, welcomed me to the council meetings and made a point of ensuring I had all the information I needed. He'd be a good person to talk to for my piece on Margot and I made a mental note to call him when I got back home.

As I walked past the pub, Big Shane Freeman was ambling across the car park to his scooter.

"Katie." His booming voice echoed down the quiet street. "Thought you'd like to know your aunt's come back. She's in the bar now, if you want to see her. Looks like she's settled in for the afternoon. I've left her putting the world to rights with Mary."

"Thanks, but I've already seen her."

He beckoned me towards him. "You should have been here half an hour ago," he went on, lowering his voice by only a fraction. "She and her old man put on quite a floor show. Least I assumed he was her husband. Only a married couple could go at each other the way they did. More hammer and tongs than a B&Q stock take."

He paused to allow me time to laugh at his witticism. I forced a smile.

"At one point I thought I was going to have to throw them both out," he went on. "Disturbing the peace, and on a Sunday, too."

I groaned. "Is Uncle Richard still in there? Or my dad?"

Shane shook his head. "Haven't seen your dad since yesterday lunchtime. But you've just missed the other guy. He stormed off about ten minutes ago, face like thunder. Your aunt just sat there, looking like the cat who'd got the cream, then calmly ordered a double gin and tonic. Knocked it back in one, she did."

'Well, let's hope she'll spend the rest of the afternoon sleeping it off," I said and added silently, "She's caused more than enough damage for one day."

Only she didn't sleep it off because the next moment, the pub door opened and Tanya came out, phone clapped to her ear, killer heels tapping an urgent rhythm as she crossed the car park. She was nodding and listening and gave no indication that she'd seen either Shane or me.

But whoever she was talking to, it couldn't have been Uncle Richard because she wasn't angry. Instead she looked as happy and excited as a teenager on a first date.

Could it be she was going to meet the man she'd been having an affair with? It certainly looked like it from the way she was laughing and tossing her hair as she ended the call.

The next thing, she got in her car and drove off. For a moment I had a horrible feeling she was heading for our house, but to my relief, she turned at the end of the High Street and roared off down the road that led out of the village.

"You on your way home, then?" Shane asked.

"Yeah." Although Jules' biscuits had filled a small hole in my stomach, I needed something else to eat.

"I'm going fishing this afternoon on Cheddar reservoir," Shane said. "You're welcome to come along. If you promise not to talk too much and scare the fish off. And, of course, you'll have to ride pillion and hang on to my fishing gear."

"Ride pillion?" I looked down at Shane's scooter which seemed to get smaller the closer he got to it. "There isn't room for you on that thing, least of all a pillion passenger."

He grinned and spread his arms wide. "Then you'll have to snuggle up extra close, won't you?"

And, do you know, for one crazy minute I was almost tempted. Not the snuggling up, of course. God forbid. Nor the fishing, which I find about as exciting as watching paint dry. And, while Shane was ok in small doses, he was the only person in the entire universe who thought his one-liners were funny.

But that's what a dreary Sunday afternoon in Much Winchmoor can do for you. Especially when your home has suddenly turned into a battleground.

I missed Will more than I'd have thought possible, and really wished we could turn the clock back to the days when we were still good mates. Before things got all awkward and weird between us.

And before there were any pretty blonde vets on the scene.

I could have told Will what Elsie had said about Mum and Uncle Richard, and he'd have told me it was in the past and none of my business. I could also have told him about Tanya's crazy plans and he'd have told me I was worrying over nothing. Then told me it was none of my business. And that I'd been spending too much time with Elsie Flintlock.

But I wouldn't have told him how I was struggling with what I thought was my big chance to impress my new editor, with my perceptive yet sensitive piece on Margot D-T. He'd have probably said that was none of my business either.

I could always rely on Will to put things into perspective – and to tell me to mind my own business.

I gave Shane a wry smile, thanked him for the offer and set

off to spend the rest of the afternoon wrangling my laptop, trying to find something to write about Margot that wouldn't sound as if I had just made it all up.

Thank goodness for Stuart Davies. He, at least, should be good for a quote.

***

As I reached our garden gate I saw what looked like a rhubarb tree staggering down the road towards me. I peered through the foliage and saw Dad, obviously on his way back from the allotment.

"Blimey, Dad, are you going for rhubarb world domination by buying up the entire crop?" I asked.

He attempted a smile that didn't quite make it. "It's all that rain and the bit of sunshine we had last week," he said. "It's brought it all on like crazy."

I groaned at the thought of all the tongue-shrivelling rhubarb crumbles we had to look forward to. Mum didn't believe in adding sugar.

Dad must have had the same thought because he went on, "Mary in the pub gave me this recipe for rhubarb vodka. I thought I'd give that a try before your mother gets her hands on it. Otherwise it will be a freezer full of crumbles again. I don't think I can face any more of that rhubarb and elderflower she made last year. As for the rhubarb and ginseng —"

"Dad," I put my hand on his arm. "Before you go in, don't you think this nonsense between you and mum has gone on long enough?"

He sighed, pushed away his non-existent hair with his free hand then turned towards me, his face puckered with worry. "You're right, pet. Of course you are. I've been up the allotment, hoeing the onion patch and that always clears my head. And I can see why your mother was a bit upset yesterday. It must have looked a bit suspicious. But it was all totally innocent, I promise you. I've never so much as looked at another woman since I met your mother. And never will. I

127

knew she was the girl for me the first time I saw her."

Even though she was engaged to your brother at the time? I wanted to ask. But didn't. Instead, I gave his arm a reassuring squeeze.

"Of course there was nothing to it. I was there, remember? And I tried to tell Mum that. But she'll be ok now she's calmed down. She was just a bit disappointed because she'd been looking forward to an afternoon out, just the two of you."

He sighed. "I know. And I feel bad about that. It's just… I don't know. I just can't seem to do anything right at the moment. It's like everything I do or say gets on her nerves. I don't know what it is with her."

I had an uncomfortable thought. "You don't think it's because of me, being back home. Getting in the way and all that, do you?"

"Of course not. Your mother loves having you back home."

I noticed he didn't say that he loved having me home. He was obviously still hankering after his snooker table.

"You wouldn't believe how much she worried about you when you were in Bristol," he went on. "She'd like nothing more than to see you and Will, happily settled and living—"

"Whoa, hang on there," I cut in quickly. "Will and me – it's not like that."

He gave a wry smile. "Maybe not. But you know your mother. The first time you went out with him, she wouldn't stop going on about how happy Will's mum, God rest her soul, would have been to have seen the two of you together. I think from the day you were born, Sally and your mum were planning the wedding for you and Will. I dare say she's already bought her hat."

"Then she'd better return it and get her money back," I said quickly. "Because Will and I…" I broke off and kicked at a loose stone on the path with the toe of my shoe.

"Go on, pet," he said, but I shook my head.

"Come on, Dad. Let's go and unload that rhubarb before you drop the lot." I gave him a quick hug and opened the back door for him.

He went in ahead of me. I almost bumped into him as he

stopped abruptly and swore. Rhubarb cascaded to the floor, landing in an untidy heap at his feet.

I eased past him and the rhubarb to see what had happened.

Talk about kitchen sink dramas! This was getting seriously weird.

It was almost an action replay of yesterday afternoon. Only instead of Dad and Tanya in a clinch up against our kitchen sink, it was Mum and Uncle Richard.

They broke apart at the sound of the rhubarb avalanche and turned to stare at us, eyes wide, faces white and strained.

"Terry, Katie." Mum was the first to find her voice, although it came out as a strangled whisper. "I was just – Richard was just—"

"Richard was just going," Dad said in a voice I'd never heard before. Not even the day of my twelfth birthday when I was showing off my new bike to Jules, lost control, and ended up crashing through his precious sweet peas just three days before the village Flower and Produce Show.

Then he'd been scarlet with rage. But now, he was all ice cold, quiet fury. He didn't look like my dad at all. Instead, he looked like a stranger who was really, really struggling to control himself.

"Oh, for heaven's sake, Terry," Mum snapped. "Stop being so ridiculous."

It was an unwise choice of words. His tenuous hold on his self control slipped.

"Oh, ridiculous, am I?" he snapped back as he stepped over the rhubarb and advanced towards them, fists clenched, eyes sparking with fury. "That's all I am to you both, isn't it? A figure of fun. To be laughed and sneered at. Well, I can tell you, I've had enough of it. Get out, Richard."

"Terence – sorry, sorry." Uncle Richard said quickly as Dad rounded on him. "I mean, Terry. Look, I—"

"Get. Out."

"But—"

"You heard me. Get out of my house. Now."

Richard shrugged, looked across to Mum and said quietly: "Will you be all right?"

She nodded.

"Ok then, I'll go. Thanks for listening, Cheryl. I appreciate it."

Then he left by the back door with as much dignity as was possible for someone who'd had to wade through a forest of rhubarb to reach it.

***

There was a long silence, broken only by the sound of Uncle Richard's car driving off.

My parents were still facing each other across the kitchen table. Mum with her back to the sink, Dad gripping a kitchen chair so tightly, his knuckles were white.

Both were breathing heavily as if they'd just run a marathon. Neither spoke.

I'd never seen them like this before. They'd had their spats in the past, of course they had. Mum would rant and rave and Dad would go all quiet and mutter. And then, a couple of hours later, they'd get over it. And everything would go back to normal.

But this was something else.

They were looking at each other like two angry strangers. And I didn't know what to do.

I wished Gran Latcham was still alive. I still missed her terribly, but never more so than at that moment. She'd been a feisty, birdlike little woman, who barely came up to my shoulder, let alone Dad's or Uncle Richard's. Yet her sharply spoken, "Boys! Behave yourselves!" would have the pair of them trembling like naughty kids who'd been caught raiding the sweet jar. What would she say if she could have seen her 'boys' just a moment ago, I wondered, squaring up to each other like a pair of bare knuckle fighters?

"Mum. Dad," I said but neither of them took any notice of me.

"It was always him, wasn't it?" Dad said bitterly. "I was only ever the consolation prize. And now it looks as if he's a free man again – that's what he came here to tell you, wasn't it? That Tanya is absolutely set on a divorce."

"No, it wasn't that. If you must know, he came to warn me – to tell me that Tanya said she was going to—" she broke off, looking across the room as if she'd only just noticed me.

I cleared my throat. "Look, um, you two, well, you obviously need to talk. I – I'll just pop up and get my laptop then I'll head off. Give you some space."

"There's no need," they both said at the same time. At least they could agree on something.

"You're going nowhere," Mum said suddenly. "I am."

She picked up her car keys from the hook by the door, grabbed her coat and left.

"Where's she going?" I asked Dad.

He shrugged and shook his head.

"Don't you think you should go after her?"

Again, he shook his head.

"She looked pretty upset, Dad. She shouldn't be driving when she's in that state," I fretted. "Shall we go after her? I'll come with you."

"No need," he said. "She's probably gone to see your Grandma, who'll tell her what a waste of space I am and how she married the wrong brother. It's what she's always thought."

"Of course she doesn't," I lied, because, in fact, that was exactly what Grandma Kingham thought – and said. Whenever she got the chance. And if she didn't use those exact words, it was what she implied.

Before Elsie told me about Mum being engaged to Richard, I'd always thought it was just because she didn't like Dad. She was a terrible snob and looked down on his job as a stone mason. She thought he should be doing a 'proper' job, like his accountant brother who went to work in a collar and tie, rather than dusty old overalls.

"And if she hasn't gone to her mother's, then she's with Richard," Dad said. He let go of the kitchen chair, pulled it out and sat down heavily. His shoulders sagged as all the fight went out of him. He looked sad and defeated.

"Don't be…" I was about to say *ridiculous* but stopped

131

myself as I remembered how he'd reacted when Mum had used that very word. "Of course she hasn't. For goodness sake, there's nothing between Mum and Uncle Richard. What we saw when we came in just now was as innocent as what I saw when I walked in on you and Tanya yesterday."

"You reckon?" He didn't look convinced.

"Look, call her. Not yet, obviously, because she'll still be driving and won't pick up anyway."

"There's no point," he said. "She won't answer."

"Of course she will."

"I don't think so." He pointed across to the dresser, where Mum's phone lay on top of her well-thumbed copy of *Recipes to Cleanse Your Body from the Inside Out*.

"Do you want a cup of tea?" I asked him. "Or something to eat? I think there's probably some of yesterday's mac and cheese in the fridge."

He pulled a face. "No thanks, love. I'm not hungry. I think I'll just…" He looked down at his watch.

"The pub's shut," I said quickly. "Shane was leaving as I went past just now. And you know Mary doesn't stay open too long on a Sunday afternoon."

"I wasn't planning on going to the pub," he said. "At least not for a drink."

"Dad!" I scowled at him. "You weren't thinking of going to see Tanya, were you? How's that going to help anything?"

His chair scraped across the tiled floor as he stood up. "I just want to know what's going on, love. You heard what your mother said. Something about Tanya saying she was going to… going to what? That bloody woman has been dropping hints ever since she got here that she has something she's dying to tell. And I intend finding out what it is. Once and for all."

"But there's no point. Tanya's not there. She drove off while I was talking to Shane."

His shoulders sagged again and he looked like a little lost boy. "In that case, I might as well go back to the allotment. There's plenty more onions needing hoeing."

I gave him a hug and let him go. He obviously had more

thinking to do. I picked up the abandoned rhubarb, piled it on the draining board and opened the fridge.

Yesterday's tofu and sesame soba noodles looked even less appealing that they had then. I closed the fridge door and opened the freezer instead.

Today was turning out to be one of those days when only a huge tub of double chocolate chip ice cream was going to hit the spot.

Chapter Fourteen

The ice cream helped. It helped a lot.

I loved my parents and didn't want them to split up. But on the other hand, if they were making each other miserable, that wasn't good for either of them. Dad had been right about one thing. Mum had been getting more and more edgy recently. But it had started way before Tanya's arrival.

I still worried that I was part of the problem. After all, our house wasn't that big, particularly as a good proportion of the downstairs was taken up by the salon. So, we were rather jam-packed in, which was fine when we were all getting along. Not so good when we weren't. Like now.

I thought about Will's suggestion last night that I should move in with him and his dad and, for a moment, I was tempted. Until I remembered Anna and the way she and Will had been laughing together in the yard. And the way he'd looked at her when we'd bumped into her in Dintscombe.

If Will really was interested in her, I didn't think I could bear seeing their romance blossom.

When we were growing up and were still good mates, I always used to take a keen interest in his love life and, to a lesser extent, he in mine. I'd pester him for details of each new romance and would often give him a nudge as to which girls fancied him and whether they were worth bothering with.

Now, of course, it was the last thing I wanted to hear about.

Not for the first time since it happened, I wished we'd never had that first kiss. Or any of the other ones. Not that I hadn't thoroughly enjoyed them at the time. Will was a fantastic kisser. And even now my knees turned to water just thinking about how warm and soft his lips were, how the corners of his eyes crinkled when he smiled, how he made me feel safe and warm in his arms.

But that first kiss had changed everything, and not

necessarily for the better. Because now, we were not exactly a couple, despite what the Grumble and Gossip Group thought. We had the odd date, like last night, but it was all getting a bit awkward, like we didn't know how to behave towards each other any more. We certainly weren't the easy-going friends we used to be, and I missed that like crazy.

Right now, I needed a friend. But there was as much chance of finding one of those in Much Winchmoor that Sunday as there would be of finding the 167 bus. Maybe I should have gone fishing with Shane after all.

The house was unnaturally silent. There was no excited chatter from Sunday afternoon football on the TV in the sitting room. No humming from the driers in the salon or the buzz of chatter and gossip. No clattering of pots and pans as Mum whipped up one of her concoctions.

It was almost as quiet outside. Much Winchmoor on a Sunday afternoon isn't so much sleepy as comatose. I could hear some of Will's ewes up on Pendle Hill, calling for their lambs to stay close. And somewhere in the distance came the wail of a siren whilst, nearer home, there was the drone of a tractor.

I opened my laptop and settled down to work. I checked through the precious few notes I had on Margot and found the press release she'd given me when she'd first put herself forward for election to the parish council.

"I don't give interviews to members of the press," she'd announced as she'd peered down her long beaky nose at me. "But I think you'll find everything you need in here."

It was all about her plans about improving the village, cleaning up the environment, sorting out the recycling collection muddle and various other schemes for saving the planet single handed. But nothing personal and, when I'd asked her for some background stuff, she'd refused. Said it was the future that mattered, not the past, and that was the trouble with places like Much Winchmoor. People kept harping back to the past instead of concerning themselves about the future.

There was also a load of bumf about her self-styled

'Winchmoor Estate' and her holiday cottages, none of which I could use.

I'd managed to get just twenty-seven usable lines out of it. Most of the available column space had been taken up with Margot's photograph, more's the pity. They say a picture's worth a thousand words, but not to someone like me who gets paid linage. I'd settle for the words any day.

I looked up Stuart Davies' contact details. I could usually count on him for a quote, and this time was no exception.

"Yes, of course. I'd be happy to contribute to an article about Mrs Duckett-Trimble," he said. "Such a tragedy. I didn't know her very well, but I feel that, if she'd got elected, she'd have made a very valuable contribution to the parish council. She had such drive and energy. It was a pity that both ladies couldn't have been elected. I did say to them that vacancies arose quite often. In fact, it's unusual to have a seat contested. People aren't usually queuing up to serve on the council."

"What will happen now?" I asked. "Will Fiona Crabshaw be elected without there having to be an election?"

"No. The poll will be abandoned and the Returning Officer will order a new election to fill the vacancy, which will have to take place within thirty-five days of the date fixed for the first election."

"And will Fiona have to go through the nomination process all over again?"

"No. At which time, of course, if no other candidate comes forward, she'll be returned unopposed." He sighed. "I don't suppose she'd have wanted to win that way, though."

I thought of the way her eyes had lit up when I'd said that she'd now get her seat. She'd smothered it quickly, but not before I'd seen that little gleam of excitement in those unusual lime marmalade eyes.

"Of course, there's always a chance another candidate will come forward," he went on. "But I think that's highly unlikely."

I thanked him for his time and settled down to finish off my article, trying hard to puff it up to more than twenty-seven lines this time. But it was difficult to stay focussed as I kept listening out for either Mum or Dad.

It was beginning to get dark when Dad came home. Mum didn't come back at all.

"Should we call Grandma?" I asked for what was probably the fifth time, later that evening. "Just to see if she's there."

Dad shook his head. "I'd rather not know."

"But something might have happened to her. She may have had an accident."

Dad gave an impatient sigh. "Of course she hasn't. You're worrying over nothing. I can tell you now, love, she'll be either at her mother's or she'll be with my brother. Either way, I really, really don't want to know, as I've already said. Now, I'm off to bed. And I'd advise you to do the same. It'll all sort itself out in the morning, you'll see."

He stood up and was about to go up to bed when, from somewhere in the house, a phone rang.

"Is that yours?" Dad asked.

But it wasn't my phone ringing. I certainly didn't have a ringtone that belted out Michael Bublé. But I knew someone who did.

Mum. I hurried into the kitchen and picked up her phone.

"Mum?" I said, which was pretty silly, seeing as it was her phone.

There was no answer. I looked at Caller ID and saw a number I didn't recognise.

"Who is this, please?" I asked.

"Katie? Is that you?" The voice on the other end sounded puzzled. But it was a voice I recognised.

"Uncle Richard?"

"Sorry. I thought I was phoning your mother. I must have got the wrong number."

"No. You didn't. This is her phone."

"Oh right. Is she there?"

Relief surged through me. I knew Dad had got it wrong. Of course she wasn't with him. She must have gone to Grandma's after all.

"No, she's not at the moment. Can I give her a message?"

The pause went on for so long I thought he'd ended the call.

"Uncle Richard? Are you still there?"

"Sorry, Katie. The signal keeps going. And no, there's no message. I might…"

But I never found out what he might, or might not, do because there were three beeps and a 'call failed' message appeared. I tried to call him back but it kept going to voice mail, so in the end I gave up.

"Who was that?" Dad asked as I went back into the sitting room.

"Uncle Richard. He was calling Mum. So, you see, she can't be with him. Otherwise he wouldn't be calling her, would he? She must be at Grandma's. Shall I call her? Just to be sure?"

Dad's eyes hardened. "Don't bother. What was Richard phoning for? Did he say?"

"No. But it was a very bad line. It sounded as if he was in his car. Or something like that."

"No doubt he was calling to fix a time and place for them to meet up," he said. "Now, I really am off to bed. I've got work in the morning. And please, promise me you won't phone your Grandma. I don't want your mother to think I'm chasing after her. I have my pride, you know."

I promised, reluctantly. I knew from long experience there was no point trying to get my dad to change his mind once he'd made it up. So I finished off the last of the double chocolate chip ice cream, then headed off to bed myself.

***

I woke early next morning. I could hear Dad moving around downstairs, getting ready for work. He wasn't doing very well because, when I went down to the kitchen, he was sitting at the table, staring down at a piece of burnt toast on the plate in front of him. He looked like he – and the toast – had been sitting there for some time.

"Do you want some more toast?" I asked.

"No thanks. I'm not hungry."

"Shall I make you up some sandwiches, or something for

138

your lunch box?" I asked. "There's still some of that mac and cheese."

"No there isn't," Dad said. "It's in the bin. Best place for it. And I'll grab myself something for lunch at work."

"Dad? I don't suppose…?"

He shook his head. "She didn't come back, if that's what you were going to ask."

"Well, at least it's Monday so I don't have to worry about the salon. But I'm telling you now, Dad, I'm phoning Grandma, whether you want me to or not."

"She won't thank you for phoning at this time of the morning."

"I don't mean now. I mean later."

He shrugged. "You must do what you like. I'm going to—"

He never got to finish his sentence. There was a sharp rap at the door. We both looked at each other.

Who the hell would be calling at this time of the morning?

Unless, I thought with a flicker of hope, it was Mum. Maybe she'd forgotten her key as well as her phone. But then I remembered that her house keys would have been with her car keys.

Not Mum then.

There came another rap, a little sharper this time. Whoever it was, they weren't going away.

"I'll go," I said, when it looked as if Dad had been turned to the very stone he spent his working hours chiselling away at.

"Ben!" I opened the door and gave a huge sigh of relief, as I recognised one of my old school friends standing there. "It's a bit early. But come on in. Do you want a coffee? I'm just making some."

Ben Watkins shook his head. "No thanks. I'm afraid this isn't a social call, Katie," he said.

"Kat," I said automatically.

"Sorry, Kat. Like I said, this isn't a social call. I'm on duty."

"Really?" I took in his fancy leather coat, his chinos, his smart linen shirt. "You don't look much like you're on duty to me."

"I'm CID now."

"Oh, wow! That's brilliant," I forced a smile. "You'll end up Chief Constable at this rate. Are you sure you won't have that coffee? I make a really good one, you know."

I was babbling. I knew I was, but I couldn't stop myself, as all my previous anxiety about Mum came rushing back, brought on by the sombre expression on Ben's face.

"Katie – Kat. I'm afraid there's been an incident. On Long Moor Drove. A car was found in the rhine and..." He looked across the road, where Doris Yarcombe was casting curious glances in our direction as she took forever to put something in her bin. "Look, I think it would be better if I came in."

I staggered back as if he'd punched me. But I held firmly to the door. In fact, I really, really wanted to close it in his face.

"Incident? You mean – an accident?" I clung to the door as if it was a life raft and I'd just jumped off the Titanic. "When? When did it happen?"

Because, of course, it couldn't be Mum. He was going to tell us the accident happened yesterday morning, when she was still here. And then that would be fine. And I could start breathing again.

"We're pretty sure it happened about four o'clock yesterday afternoon," he said, and I remembered the siren I'd heard as I was settling down to work.

"Is she...?" My mouth had gone dry. My tongue stuck to the roof of my mouth. I couldn't believe what I'd been about to ask. And I sure as hell didn't want to hear the answer.

"Dad!" I called as I hurried back into the kitchen. Ben followed.

Dad was sitting at the kitchen table, still staring at the same piece of toast. But judging from the expression on his face, he'd heard everything Ben had said.

Ben cleared his throat. "I'm afraid there's been an incident, Mr Latcham. Out on Long Moor Drove. A car was found in the rhine."

"Is she...?" I tried again.

Ben nodded. "Yes. I'm very sorry. I'm afraid she was dead long before the paramedics arrived on the scene. There was nothing they could do for her."

Chapter Fifteen

There was a stunned silence. At least I think there was. There was certainly a stunned silence inside my head as my brain struggled to take in what Ben was saying.

Accident… Car in rhine… Dead…

But it was like a cold, grey fog had swirled into our kitchen and flooded my brain. Dense. Dark. Disorientating.

No. No. Noooooo. It was a mistake.

I don't exactly remember but I think I looked at Dad. And I think he looked at me. Maybe we said something. Or maybe not. Maybe we just stood and stared at Ben while he took his notebook from the pocket of his cool leather jacket and clicked his pen.

"I'm sorry to be the bearer of bad news," he said when it became obvious that both Dad and I had been robbed of the power of speech. "Is your wife here?"

Dad looked blankly at him. "My… wife?"

I, too, was staring at him, while my heart crashed and banged in my chest like a canary having a panic attack.

"You mean, the woman in the car? It's not…? She didn't…?" I was having trouble getting my tongue to work, let alone my brain. "Who – who was it?"

"We don't want her name released yet because we haven't traced her next of kin. But we believe it to be a Mrs Tanya Latcham. Although that has yet to be confirmed officially."

I sat down with a thump. Dad looked like someone had just cut him off at the knees.

"Aunty Tanya? Dead?" I was still trying to get my head around the fact that it had been Tanya and not my mum in that car in the rhine. Trying, also, to suppress the urge to punch the air and shout alleluia. Not alleluia that Tanya was dead, of course. But that my mother – my infuriating, bossy, worst

141

cook in the world mother – was alive. And I vowed that, from this day on, I would eat and pretend to enjoy every single thing she dished up.

"She is related to you, then?" Ben asked. "I thought she might be, which is why I'm here. Yours is a fairly unusual surname."

"Yes, she's my aunt," I said as it was beginning to look as if Dad would never speak again. "Married to Dad's brother, Richard. She'd – she'd been staying with us for a few days."

"And do you know where Richard Latcham is?" Ben asked. "Only he's not at the family home in Bristol. Neighbours say they haven't seen him since yesterday morning."

"He came down here yesterday morning. Oh, poor Uncle Richard," I said as the reality of the tragedy began to sink in, now the first surge of relief that it wasn't Mum had passed. "I don't know where he is, but he phoned last night."

I figured Ben didn't need to know that Richard had actually called to speak to Mum and went on: "It sounded like he was calling from his car. But he didn't say where he was or where he was going."

Ben didn't comment as he wrote in his notebook.

"He's going to be devastated," I added. "What happened, do you know? That road across Long Moor can be treacherous, especially if you don't know it."

I didn't want to add that Tanya had been drinking in the pub, which may well have contributed to the accident. The police would find that out soon enough, no doubt.

Ben hesitated. "Look, maybe I shouldn't be saying this. But we have reason to believe that Mrs Latcham's death was not an accident."

"What?" Dad jerked back to life as if someone had kicked him hard.

"What do you mean?" I said. "If it wasn't an accident, then…?"

"We are treating her death as suspicious."

"Suspicious? Do you mean she was murdered?" I gasped "But how?"

"I can't disclose that at the moment," Ben said. "I'm afraid

I am having to question anyone who was in contact with her in the last twenty-four hours. When did you last see her?"

"Oh, right. I see," I said. "Well, she stayed here for a few days, then moved into the pub on Friday. Mary will be able to show you her room and all that."

He wrote something in his notebook then looked at Dad. "And your wife, Mr Latcham? Do you think I could speak to her?"

Dad and I exchanged worried glances.

"She's…" I began.

"The thing is…" Dad cut in. "She's popped out. Early."

One of Ben's eyebrows lifted. "Really? Popped out where, exactly?"

"Do you know, I'm not absolutely sure," Dad answered. "She does a few home visits, you know. Every now and again. People who can't get in to the salon. Why don't you call back later, when she'll be back?"

"I'll do that. The thing is, I have to ask you all this question. Just so we can get a picture of who was where and when. So, Mr Latcham? Where were you at four o'clock yesterday afternoon?"

"Four o'clock, you say?" His glance darted around the room as if searching for an escape hatch. "Was that the time of the… of the… um… the accident?"

"So where were you?" Ben stood there, notebook open, pen poised.

"I was at my allotment. Over by the old railway embankment. Well, you'll know where I mean, being a local lad."

"I do. And did anyone see you?"

Dad's hand went up to smooth his non-existent hair. "I'm not sure. It was Sunday afternoon and there was football on the telly. I was the only person up there."

Ben turned to me. "And you, Katie?"

"Kat." The response was automatic. I was still trying to figure out what the hell Dad was thinking about by lying to the police about Mum's whereabouts. "I was here, working. I write for *The Chronicle* and was doing a piece about Margot

143

and I..." I broke off as something occurred to me. "Margot! That makes two murders in the village within a few days. First Margot, and now Tanya. You don't think the two are connected, do you?"

"It's not my place to speculate," Ben said. "And were you home alone?"

"Yes," I said quickly, before Dad could jump in with another lie. "Mum had gone out. I'm not sure where. You'll have to ask her."

"I will," he said. "So, when was the last time you saw your aunt?"

"That would be yesterday afternoon. Just a little before three o'clock. I was passing the pub when she came out, got into her car and drove off."

"Did you talk to her?"

"No. I don't even think she saw me. She was too busy chattering away on her phone."

"She had a phone?"

"Of course. Who doesn't these days? Why do you ask?"

He didn't answer but gave me a look that implied that he was the one who got to ask the questions, not me. Then he snapped his notebook shut, put away his pen and turned to go.

"I'll be back later to speak to your wife, Mr Latcham. In the meantime, if either of you think of anything else, or if Mr Richard Latcham gets in touch, I'd be grateful if you'd call me at this number."

He took out a card and laid it on the table. Dad stared at it as if he feared it was about to spontaneously combust.

The card might not. But I was in danger of doing so. I saw Ben to the door then came back and rounded on Dad.

"What the hell did you do that for?" I demanded furiously.

"Do what?" His look of studied innocence didn't fool me for a nanosecond.

"You know what. Why did you lie to Ben about where Mum was? You'll be in all sorts of trouble if he finds out the truth. Lying to the police at any time is serious, but during a murder enquiry it's absolutely..."

I stopped before I called him something I'd regret.

144

"I didn't want to make things worse for her," he muttered. He picked up Ben's card and pretended to read it.

"Worse for her?" For a moment I stared at him, bewildered. Then I got it. "For pity's sake, Dad, you don't think Mum had anything to do with it?"

"No, of course I don't. But that doesn't mean the police won't. Not after that row they had."

"How did you know about that? You weren't here at the time."

"I know, but Tanya told me. Said she'd never seen your mum so wound up. Didn't know she had it in her. She said she'd actually threatened her and told her to get out while she still could. Tanya said she was afraid your mum was going to do something terrible to her if she stayed."

I glared at him. "And you believed her? Mum said nothing of the sort. You know what Aunty Tanya's like…" I paused, a sinking feeling in the pit of my stomach as I corrected myself. "What she was like. You know how she loved to exaggerate. Yes, Mum was pretty mad with her, but at no time did she threaten her with violence. And I'm shocked that you could think that."

"Well, I didn't really. But you've got to admit, your mother hasn't exactly been herself lately."

"True," I admitted. "But anyway, we should call Grandma right away, see if Mum's there, and tell her to come back pronto."

Dad nodded. "You'd better do it, though. If your grandmother hears me on the line she'll put the phone down."

I called Grandma's number. It rang for so long I began to think she was out. Eventually, though, she answered. As always, she sounded cross, as if she'd been interrupted doing something incredibly important, like completing the Daily Telegraph crossword or counting the silver teaspoons after her cleaning lady had been.

"Kathryn." She was the only person on the planet who called me Kathryn. Even though I was christened Katie, Grandma had wanted me to be called Kathryn after a great-aunt. But although Mum had stood firm (Katie had been Dad's choice) Grandma Kingham always insisted on calling me Kathryn. "To what do I owe the pleasure of this singularly unusual occurrence?"

"I just wondered if Mum was with you?"

"And that's it? No *how are you this morning, Grandma? And is your arthritis better today*?"

"Sorry." I controlled my impatience with difficulty. "How are you this morning, Grandma? And is your arthritis better this morning?"

"The answers to which are: mustn't complain; no, and no she is not."

"Mum's not with you? Are you sure?"

She tutted. Grandma Kingham's tuts were legendary. One tut from her and Grandpa Kingham would shrivel like a leaking balloon. Or stand smartly to attention, depending on the nature of the tut and the amount of trouble he was in at the time.

"It's really important," I went on. "Please, let me speak to her."

The little pause on the other end of the line told me what I needed to know. Mum was there.

"This isn't a trick to get her to speak to your father, is it?" Grandma said. "Because I can tell you this for nothing – she doesn't want to speak to him."

"No. I promise it's not. I really, really need to talk to her."

"What about?" Grandma asked.

"I – I've just had some bad news. Mum will want to know."

That was the clincher. The only thing Grandma liked better than a bit of bad news was a lot of bad news. There was the sound of a chair being pushed back, some low muttering and, a few minutes later, Mum came on the phone.

"Katie?" She sounded worried. "What's wrong?"

Just the sound of her voice made me weak with relief. And it brought back the memory of the overwhelming fear I'd felt when Ben had first told us of the body in the rhine and we'd thought it was Mum. My throat tightened and my eyelids prickled.

"Aunty Tanya's dead," I blurted out. The exchange with

Grandma had wiped all the carefully worded phrases I'd planned on using clean out of my head. "The police think she's been murdered."

There was a long silence.

"Mum? Hello? Are you still there?"

"I'm still here," she said faintly. "When did this happen? And where? Does Richard know?"

"It happened on Long Moor Drove. Her car was found in the rhine yesterday afternoon. And as far as I know, Uncle Richard doesn't know yet, as he's not at home and the police haven't been able to trace him. Do you know where he is?"

"Me?" She sounded surprised. "No, of course I don't. Why would you think that?"

"Because he called you last night. You left your phone on the dresser in the kitchen, did you know that?"

"I thought I must have. You say he called? Did he say what he wanted?"

"No. Just that he wanted to talk to you. And that he'd call later. Are you coming home?"

There was a pause. "I'm not sure."

"Please, Mum." I broke in before she could say anything. "I really think you should. Because the police want to talk to you."

"The police?" There was an edge to her voice I couldn't quite identify. "Why on earth would they want to talk to me?"

"They want to talk to anyone who saw Tanya yesterday."

"But I didn't see her yesterday. I haven't seen her since she moved out on Friday."

"Anyway, Dad told them that you were out, doing a bit of mobile hairdressing this morning."

"Why would he do that?"

"I suppose he didn't want anyone to know that he didn't know where his wife was." I didn't want to tell her that Dad had thought, however briefly, that she might have something to do with Tanya's death. Things were weird enough between them at the moment, without adding that little gem into the mix.

"So, are you coming home?" I prompted.

She didn't answer.

"Mum?" I tried another tack. "I'll just give the police Grandma's address then, shall I? I bet that'll please her when the Blues and Twos rock up to her door."

"Well, I suppose…"

"Please, Mum? It's – it's really creepy here right now. First Margot, now Tanya. It makes you think there's a serial killer on the loose."

She sighed. "Really, Katie. You and your vivid imagination. Look, I'll be home in time for lunch. I take it your father's gone to work?"

"He's getting ready now," I said. "Do you want to speak to him?"

"No. Not at the moment. Tell him – tell him I'll talk to him this evening." I heard her take a long, shaky breath. "I think it's about time your father and I had a proper chat."

Chapter Sixteen

Dad was pacing the kitchen like a caged bear all the time I was speaking to Mum. He pounced the second the call ended.

"Well?" he growled, his face creased with anxiety. "Is she coming?"

I nodded. "She'll be home by lunchtime. And she says that she wants to have what she called a 'proper chat' with you this evening. That's Mum-speak for don't take yourself off to the pub on your way home from work."

"It hadn't crossed my mind," he said, which was clearly a lie, seeing as he stopped in at the Winchmoor Arms every evening for what he called a 'quick one'. He took his work coat from the hook on the back of the door, shrugged himself into it. "Did she say what this 'proper chat' was about?"

"Afraid not. She sounded pretty serious, though. Are you off to work now?"

He stood there, jingling his car keys. "Better had. We've got an urgent job to finish this week. Need to crack on while the weather holds."

"And I can't let Elsie down," I said. "So it's carry on as usual, eh?"

He attempted a smile. "Something like that, love."

He drove off and I got ready to go and see Elsie. I was, as always, there on the dot of 10.30am. Any later and she probably wouldn't have let me in.

I'd been wondering how much to tell her about Tanya's murder. But I needn't have worried. I should have realised she'd know more about it than I did. And she couldn't wait to pass it on.

"Hit over the head, so I heard," Elsie said. "With a blunt instrument."

"How do you know that?"

"Never you mind." She gave a furtive, sideways glance, as if she suspected the room might have been bugged. She'd obviously been watching those old reruns of *Tinker, Tailor, Soldier, Spy* again. "I have my sources."

"But what I don't understand is what Tanya was doing out on Long Moor in the first place," I said, as, under her eagle-eyed supervision, I flicked a feather duster with extreme care over the framed pictures of Devious Danny. "It's not as if the road goes anywhere, except in a great big loop that ends up eventually in Glastonbury. And even so, there are easier ways of getting to Glastonbury from here than across the moor. And it's not like there's anything along there. So what was she doing?"

"Nothing out there except that falling-down old barn half way along," Elsie said. "It belonged at one time to some man who used to grow cannabis there, until the police raided it. Apart from that, it's nothing but farmland."

"She must have taken the wrong turning. Then, when she got out on the moor, found there was nowhere to turn around. Or maybe that was the way her satnav sent her."

Elsie snorted. "I don't hold with all these sack-nab things, or whatever they call them."

"Satnav. It stands for satellite navigation."

"Whatever. It's all spy in the sky stuff and shouldn't be allowed. Folks should take the trouble to learn to read maps, like they used to in my day."

A sudden thought occurred to me. "I saw Tanya in the pub car park yesterday afternoon. She didn't see me because she was talking on her phone. Tossing her hair back and chattering away like she does…" I broke off as I remembered to use the past tense. "I mean, like she did, when she was excited. I thought at the time she looked like someone fixing up a date. I reckon she went to Long Moor to meet someone. After all, it would be a perfect meeting place, wouldn't it? A scarcely-used road, with no one around apart from a few sheep and cattle."

Elsie looked unimpressed with my theory. "Doesn't sound very likely to me. Particularly for a townie like her. She'd be more likely to opt for one of those trendy coffee bars that are everywhere these days. Talking of which, where's that other cup of tea I asked for about half an hour ago? Folks could die of thirst waiting for you to stop gossiping. Doesn't do for us oldies to get de-hibernated. And you've dusted that particular picture of Danny at least four times now. But I've already told you, he's spoken for. So there's no point mooning over him."

What? Me, mooning over him? No way. But there was no point telling her that. I'd just be wasting my breath.

I went into the kitchen to make her a second cup of tea, and was still so rattled she could think I was remotely interested in her money-grabbing grandson that I wasn't paying enough attention to what I was doing. Which was how I came to open the fridge without thinking.

Now, there was a knack to opening Elsie's fridge. As you pulled the door back, you had to put one hand out to keep the plastic rack that holds the milk and other things in place in the door.

Only that particular time, I forgot. Before I could stop it, the plastic rack flopped down, tipping the milk, a carton of orange juice and a partly-used tin of baked beans on to the floor.

Luckily, the milk carton stayed intact. But that was as far as my luck went because the orange juice and baked beans did not. They pooled across the floor in a sticky orangey beany mess. It was touch and go as to whether I reached it before Prescott.

Prescott won. He hoovered up the beans without taking a breath. Although he passed on the orange juice.

I then had to wash the kitchen floor for the second time that day and promised Elsie I'd bring some superglue with me tomorrow to see if I could fix the broken rack.

***

Because of having to re-wash the kitchen floor, there wasn't enough time for the dog's preferred walk up to Pendle Hill and back. Usually I walked him away from the village as quickly as possible, as his habit of barking at everything that moved (and lots of things that didn't) was embarrassing and

151

annoying.

But that morning I only had time for a quick circuit of the village. Though it wasn't that quick, given that Prescott insisted on stopping at every lamppost. But at least I managed to steer him away from the churchyard compost heap this time.

As we passed the pub, I noticed the door to the public bar was open. I tied Prescott to a fence post, told him I wouldn't be long and went inside.

Mary was putting some mixers in the chiller cabinet behind the bar. She straightened up as she saw me, and sighed.

"What can I get you?" she asked wearily.

You know how some publicans smile and greet you warmly when you go in to their pub? That wasn't Mary's style. No friendly, 'How are you today? Good to see you.' Mary didn't do warm and friendly.

In fairness, she'd never asked for this job. She'd been a barmaid for more years than she could remember and had been happy enough doing that, if a bit on the snippy side with the customers when the mood took her, which was most of the time. She'd retired about five years ago and had been acting as relief landlady for the brewery, covering holidays and so on when called upon. Which, given her unfriendly disposition, wasn't that often.

"I haven't come for a drink," I told her. "I suppose you've heard about what happened to my aunt, Tanya?"

Mary's round face darkened. "Poor soul. And to think, this time yesterday she was sitting where you are, chatting away to me like she didn't have a care in the world."

"That's what I wanted to ask you about," I said. "I saw her when she was leaving and she was on her phone to someone. I don't suppose you happen to know who it was?"

She scowled at me. "Of course not. I don't listen in to my customers' telephone calls. And I'll thank you not to go around inferring that I do, young lady."

"Oh no, no, I didn't mean that," I said in a desperate attempt to smooth her ruffled feathers. "It's just that, well, sometimes people shout when they're talking on their phones, don't they? And you can't help hearing what they say."

"Well, I don't," she said firmly, as she closed the chiller and turned her attention to the glass washer. "And what's it got to do with you, anyway? You're not going to put this into that scandal rag you write for, are you?"

The Chronicle? A scandal rag? If I tell you that last week's lead story was about the theft of a load of washing from a launderette in Dintscombe, you'll understand the sort of paper *The Chronicle* is. And the biggest scandal we've had in Much Winchmoor in recent years (apart from the odd murder or two, obviously) was when the captain of the Winchmoor Arms skittles team was accused by a team from the pub in the next village of ball tampering.

"That's not fair to call it a scandal rag," I murmured, feeling the need to defend the paper. "*The Chronicle* gives very good local coverage."

"Tell my sister that," she sniffed. "She's got this pug and was not well pleased to see herself featured last week in your report on the Dog Show."

"Oh." I felt my cheeks getting hotter. "I'm sorry about that."

Suddenly she smiled which, for Mary, was a very unusual occurrence.

"Don't be," she said abruptly. "My sister gets right on my nerves. As for that silly dog of hers... Your write-up gave me the best laugh I've had in a long time. So I'll answer your question, although this is strictly off the record, you understand."

"Of course. I'm not doing this for the paper. Tanya was my aunt. I – we are all anxious to know what happened to her."

Mary took a couple of glasses from the washer and hung them on the rack above her head.

"She did have a phone call while I was in the bar. And she seemed very pleased and excited about it. Ended up saying that she'd call whoever it was back. Then she asked me where Long Moor Drove was and how to get there. I told her that it was – pardon my French – the arse end of the universe and that she didn't want to go there. 'Ah now, but that's where you're wrong, Mary,' she said, looking very pleased with

153

herself. 'I want to go there very much indeed. And as far as I'm concerned, it could well be the end of the rainbow.'"

"So I was right," I breathed. "She was going there to meet someone. But who? Did you hear her mention any names?"

"If I had, I'd have told you," Mary said, back to her normal snippy self. "And is that your damn dog making all that noise out there?"

"Oh, right. Sorry, that's Elsie's dog, Prescott. I tied him to your fence, knowing you don't like dogs in the pub."

"I don't like dogs anywhere," she growled. "And if that dog has damaged my fence, there'll be the devil to pay."

"Ok. I'll sort him out. Don't you worry. And thank you, Mary."

She grunted. "I didn't tell that nosy young policeman what I've just told you. Like I said, I don't gossip about my customers, even to the police. But I liked your aunt, for all her airs and graces. She treated me like a human being, you know, not just someone who works behind the bar."

"Perhaps you should tell the police what you've just told me," I said.

"Indeed I will not," she said. "Any more than I'll tell them that Tanya told me why she wanted a room in the pub."

"Oh?" I began to feel uneasy. "What did she say?"

"Some nonsense about how your mother had threatened her with violence. But, of course, I didn't believe that for a moment. So I'll not be passing that on either."

I thanked her, let her get back to hanging up the glasses, and went to sort out Prescott.

But he stopped barking before I reached him. And when I got to the car park, I could see why.

He was lying on his back in the middle of the car park, paws in the air, a blissful expression that I'd never seen before on his pointy little face. He was having his tummy tickled. By Will.

"Will? What are you doing here?" I asked.

Prescott leapt up at the sound of my voice and tried to pretend that he hadn't been behaving like a great big softy, and that he really was a big, fierce dog with attitude.

"Calming your dog down, for a start," Will said. "Another couple of minutes and he'd have dragged the fence from one end of the High Street to the next. So, what's this?" He pointed to the pub door. "A bit early in the day for you, isn't it?"

"Don't be daft, I haven't been for a drink. I was just seeing Mary about something." My heart sank. "Oh, Will, you haven't heard about Tanya, have you?"

"Yes, I have," his face clouded. "That's why I'm here. I went to your house but there was no one there. Then I realised you'd probably be walking this little monster here. Jeez, Kat. I'm really sorry about your aunt."

He pulled me into his arms. I made no attempt to resist, but sank into him. It was like coming home after you've been away and you're cold, tired and hungry. And then you're home and all you want is to be there. Just standing there, safe and warm. Back where you belong.

But safe and warm wasn't enough for long. I raised my head and looked up at his dear, familiar face. Saw his eyes darken. Felt his breath quicken. Heard him give a little half-sigh, half-groan as he bent his head.

The touch of his lips on mine was as soft and gentle as the brush of a butterfly's wing. Something inside me melted. My hand snaked around the back of his neck, pressing him closer. Wanting him. Needing him. Closer. Closer.

"Oh God, Will, " I groaned as I remembered where we were and tried to pull away. "We shouldn't—"

But I got no further. "You talk too much," he growled as he kissed me again.

So I stopped talking. Stopped caring about where we were or who might see us. Stopped thinking about anything except the joy of being in his arms.

No thoughts of murders or of Mum and Dad having a 'proper talk' which would probably involve the word 'divorce'. Above all, there were no worries about pretty young blonde vets. Just me and Will. And his dear familiar scent.

And, of course, Prescott, whose lead was looped around Will's wrist.

Which was why it was suddenly yanked away from me as

Prescott spotted the huge tabby with a chewed ear who lived in the pub. The cat's favourite sport was sitting by the sign that said 'no dogs allowed,' then sending smug looks at any passing dogs as he stalked, tail erect, into the pub. Or, and this is probably what had set Prescott off in the first place, prowling up and down the pub fence, as he was doing now, particularly if there was a dog tied to it.

By the time Will had regained control of his wrist and the dog, the moment had passed. And sanity had returned.

"I'm sorry," I said. "The dog's a maniac, and I haven't had time to give him his proper walk today so he's got a bit of surplus energy."

"So I see," Will said. "I heard you up on Pendle Hill yesterday. Why didn't you come in?"

I felt my face burn. "You heard me?" I said playing for time.

"I heard you calling the dog. Quite a lot. Not very obedient, is he?"

"I – um, well, as I went down the lane, I saw the vet's car in your yard and assumed you had some sort of emergency going on. I knew you and your dad would probably be busy."

"One of the young heifers managed to get herself entangled in some barbed wire and needed stitching."

"Is she ok now?"

"She's fine. I can't say Dad was, though, having to call the vet out on a Sunday. He's still whingeing about it now."

"I'll bet." And then because my head was all over the place, thanks to Prescott's intervention, I said the first thing that came into my mind. "I bet you didn't whinge, though. Seeing as the vet was the lovely Anna. "

Will's eyebrows shot up. "What?" He looked at me and grinned. "Are you jealous?"

"Of course not. Should I be?"

He shook his head. "Nah, she's way out of my league. "

And I'm not, I suppose? I stared at him, wondering if he even realised what he'd just said. So, what was I? Third Division South? Certainly not Premier League, that was for sure.

156

"I'd better get this dog back before Elsie accuses me of dog-napping and calls the police," I said, taking Prescott's lead from him and preparing to walk away.

"I'll come with you, if you like. There's something I want to talk to you about. It's about—" he began but at that moment, my phone rang. It was Mike.

"Sorry," I said to Will. "It's Mike from *The Chronicle*. I've just sent him some background stuff, nothing about the actual murder, of course. But I do need to take this."

He stepped away. His eyes, which moments earlier had been soft and warm, were now as hard and cold as flint. "Is that all this is to you? The chance to make a name for yourself? I suppose you see yourself as *The Chronicle*'s new crime reporter now, do you? The one with the inside story?"

"Of course not," I snapped. "I wouldn't do that. And I wasn't talking about—"

"It wouldn't be the first time, though, would it?" He cut across my protests, not giving me chance to explain that I'd been talking about writing about Margot, not Tanya. "Kat Latcham, intrepid crime reporter."

The way he said my name was not to please me, but to wind me up.

"Just go away and leave me alone," I hissed. I turned my back on him and answered the call.

"Hi Mike," I said, sounding a lot more upbeat and chatty than I felt. "Good to hear from you."

"I got your piece about Margot," he said. "And I just wanted to say well done. It was good. I hope I can use it, although I'll probably work it in with something else now. But don't worry, you'll get the by-line. And, of course, the linage."

"Something else? What, exactly?"

"I hear there's been another murder in your village. What's going on? Is it something they've put in the water down your way that brings out the murderous tendencies in everyone?"

I watched Will walk away. One part of me wanted to call him back. The other part wanted to whack him around the head with a baseball bat. First the dig about Anna being out of his league. That had rankled. But then to think that I would use

Tanya's murder as a way of furthering my career. How could he?

But, said this annoying little voice inside my head that had a habit of popping up at the most inconvenient times, *isn't that exactly what you were doing with Margot's murder? What's the difference?*

Damn it. I wish I hadn't thought of that. Now I was going to have to apologise to him. Or I would have, if he hadn't been so po-faced and pompous.

I promised myself I'd call him later, and forced myself to focus on Mike.

"The thing is, Kat," he was saying. "I've spoken to the police but they say they're not releasing the identity of the body found in the rhine just outside your village. Only that they're treating the death as suspicious. I don't suppose you could ask around, could you? Using your local knowledge?"

"I'm sorry, Mike, I can't do that. The victim was my aunt. It wouldn't be... appropriate."

I couldn't help wishing that Will had hung around long enough to hear me say that. But, even if he had, he'd probably have said he'd shamed me into doing it. So, on balance, I was glad he'd stormed off when he did.

"Oh right. I'm sorry to hear that. Well, can you send me through some details about her? You know what we need. Age, occupation, that sort of thing. Just the usual background stuff that you did before. Nothing heavy."

My mother would never forgive me. She'd never liked me working for the paper in the first place and would much prefer I was working for her in the salon where she could 'keep her eye on me' (her words not mine, obviously).

Besides, there was also that look in Will's eyes as he'd accused me of using Tanya's murder to further my career. Not that he was right, you understand. But I just didn't want him giving me another lecture.

"Mike," I said, aware of the fact that I was probably kissing goodbye to my career in local journalism. Such as it was. "I'm sorry. But I can't do that, I'm afraid."

"Not even like the one you did for Margot?" He sounded

put out.

"Especially not like the one I did for Margot," I said, hanging up.

Prescott and the pub tabby were still engaging in eyeball to eyeball confrontation. I gave his lead a sharp tug and headed back to Elsie's.

***

After dropping Prescott off and apologising once again to Elsie for her broken fridge door and baked beans shortfall, I set off for home, hoping that by the time I got there Mum would be back.

As I got closer to the house I was relieved to see her car parked in her usual space. But before I could go in, I heard someone calling my name and turned to see Doris Yarcombe, our elderly neighbour, beckoning me frantically.

"What's wrong, Mrs Yarcombe?" The poor soul looked really worried.

"Oh, my dear, I've done such a terrible thing, but I was so upset and confused I didn't know what I was saying." Her words tumbled over themselves in her anxiety to get them out. "I really didn't mean... Now I feel so bad. I don't know what to do. And your poor dear mother, who's always been so kind to me, will never speak to me again."

"Slow down and tell me what's wrong. I'm sure it can't be that bad."

"Oh but it is, my dear. It is. And now your mother's going to be arrested and it'll be all my fault."

"Nobody's going to be arrested. Just calm down and tell me what's wrong." I was worried she was going to have a heart attack. "What are you talking about?"

"I – I told the police that I heard your mother threaten to kill that poor woman. Don't you remember? The time I got the wrong date for my hair appointment? I told that nice young policeman what I'd heard, and now he's going to arrest her. And it's all my fault."

Chapter Seventeen

I froze as I tried to recall Mum's exact words.

"You remember, dear," Doris went on, gently. "It was Friday afternoon. I got in a muddle over the date and when I went into the salon, there was no one there. Then I heard voices. So I followed the sound and found myself in your kitchen. And there was your mother, in such a state. I told the police that she's normally very quiet and calm, but this was something..." she broke off as she struggled to find the right words. "Something totally out of character."

"And you told the police what, exactly?" I asked.

"Oh dear," her hand fluttered to her mouth again. "Well, my dear, I'm afraid I told them the truth. Because, well, let's face it, that's what you have to do, don't you?"

"And what was that? What did you tell them?" I repeated the question as quietly and calmly as I could. But my heart was thudding. I had a bad feeling I knew where this conversation was going.

"I told them I heard your mother say quite clearly that she would kill... whoever it was she was shouting at," she whispered. "And I then saw the lady who'd been staying with you – the one who wore all those jingling bracelets and skin-tight trousers – walking past your kitchen window. So I realised Cheryl must have been shouting at her. And now she's dead. But, oh my life, I wish I hadn't said anything to that young policeman. I didn't mean to. It just came out when he asked me if I'd seen or heard anything. And now I think poor Cheryl is in serious trouble, and it's all my fault."

I took the old lady's papery hand and gave it a gentle squeeze. "No, Mrs Yarcombe. It is not your fault. The fault lies with whoever did that awful thing to my aunt. And it was not my mother, I promise you. So you needn't worry."

Her face cleared and she gripped my hand. "Are you sure?"

"I am absolutely one hundred per cent certain."

"Oh, my dear, that's such a relief. You have no idea how worried I've been. I've been standing here wondering if it would be better to go and see Cheryl and warn her about what I did. But now I know there's no need. I'm so glad I saw you."

"So am I," I smiled. "Now you go on back indoors and make yourself a nice cup of tea."

"I will, dear. And thank you. My son's always telling me I worry over nothing. I suppose that's what he'll say this time."

He might, I thought ruefully as I watched her shuffle back into her house. But I wished I really believed it when I'd told her that it was nothing to worry about. Because I was worried. A lot.

Mum was poking around in the fridge when I went into the kitchen.

"Where are those soba noodles from Saturday?" she said. "Have you and your father eaten them all?"

"I think Dad must have had the last of them," I said, which wasn't exactly a lie. I didn't, after all, say that he'd eaten them, and hoped he'd had the sense not to leave them in the kitchen bin where she'd see them.

"It's really good to see you, Mum," I went on. "I've been so worried."

She gave me a hug. "I didn't mean to worry you, sweetheart. I thought you'd realise I'd gone to Grandma's. After all, where else would I go?"

Before I could say anything, there was a rap on the back door. It was the same rap Dad and I had heard that morning.

"That'll be the police," I said quickly. "Mum, they're going to want to know where you were at four o'clock yesterday afternoon. I'm going to have to let them in."

"Well, yes, of course you are," she said.

Her face cleared when she saw Ben Watkins come into the room. But it darkened again, when she saw he was not alone.

Ben introduced the man with him as Detective Sergeant Miller. He was a short, dapper little man, who looked more like a bank manager than a policeman. The sort of bank manager who would take great pleasure in calling in your overdraft.

"Sit down, Mrs Latcham," he said brusquely. "You, too, Miss."

Mum and I obediently sat on one side of the kitchen table, Ben on the other. DS Miller remained standing.

Ben took out his notebook and cleared his throat. "We're asking everyone who had contact with your sister-in-law when they last saw her. You weren't here when I spoke to your husband and daughter this morning. So, perhaps you'd be kind enough to tell us now?"

"The last time I saw Tanya was on Friday," Mum said. "I was preparing lunch and she came in to say she'd be moving in to the pub. She'd been staying here for a couple of days, you see, while she and her husband..." she paused.

"They'd been having a few problems," I put in. "In fact, Tanya told Richard she wanted a divorce. Have you managed to trace him yet?"

Ben opened his mouth to answer, but DS Miller got in first.

"Can you tell us where you were at four o'clock yesterday afternoon, Mrs Latcham?"

"Four o'clock?" Mum look flustered, even though I'd warned her they were going to be asking her this very question. "Well, let me see... yesterday afternoon... Well, I went to see my mother. She, um, she lives just outside Taunton."

"What time was that?" asked DS Miller.

"I'm not really sure. I suppose I left here about half past three."

"We'll need your mother's name and address. So we can check the time you arrived with her."

Mum's face drained of colour. I shifted my chair closer, worried she was going to keel over.

"Well, to be honest..." she began.

"Honesty is always best, Mrs Latcham," DS Miller said, and there was more than a hint of a threat behind his words.

"I – I didn't go straight to Mum's," she said in a low voice. "It was a nice afternoon so I thought I'd stop off at the RSPB bird reserve at Greylake. It's lovely down there and, if you're lucky, you'll see the cranes. The birds, I mean," she added with a laugh that didn't sound at all like hers. "Not the things you see on building sites."

"Can anyone confirm that?" DS Miller asked, his tone getting more abrasive by the minute. "Did you meet anyone while you were…" he paused. "Looking for the cranes?"

Mum flushed. The significance of his pause was not lost on her. "No. There were only a couple of cars in the car park but no-one was in them. I assume they were in one of the hides. I – I sat in the car for a bit, thinking, and then realised time was getting on. So I drove to Mum's. I must have got there about six."

"What were relations like between you and your sister-in-law, Tanya Latcham? Did you get on? Had you quarrelled?"

I really admired Mum for the way she kept her cool. If he'd been barking questions at me like that, I'd have barked back.

Instead she didn't rush to answer but thought for a moment. "I've known Tanya for years. We used to be friends, but over time we'd drifted apart, as you do. In fact, if we hadn't married brothers, I dare say we'd have lost touch completely."

"Have you managed to trace Uncle Richard?" I asked Ben before DS Barking Mad Miller could get in any more questions. Ben looked towards his sergeant who gave a quick nod.

"We have," Ben said. "He's on his way back now."

"On his way back from where?" I asked.

At another nod from the sergeant, Ben went on: "Yorkshire. He was staying overnight in a very remote part of the Dales where there was no phone signal."

Mum and I exchanged puzzled glances. "Yorkshire?" I echoed. "But what was he doing up there? He didn't say anything about going to Yorkshire when we saw him yesterday."

When it looked obvious that neither of them were going to answer my question, I tried another tack, if only to keep them away from Mum's 'relationship' with Tanya: "Did you know Tanya was about to buy a cottage in the village?"

"What?" Mum looked startled. "Why would she do that? She always said how much she hated this place."

I was about to tell her about Tanya's plans to open up a rival hair and beauty salon, but checked myself in time. I didn't want Ben or his hatchet-faced sergeant to get the wrong idea about Mum and Tanya being business rivals. Or rivals of any sort, come to that.

"You know what Aunty Tanya was like. Always buying things on a whim. And, of course, she and Uncle Richard were divorcing, so I suppose she was looking for somewhere to downsize."

Yeah, right. Tanya's idea of downsizing would be moving from their present five bedroom detached house in a smart area of Bristol to a four bedroom detached house in an only slightly less smart area of Bristol. I never for a moment thought she'd settle in Much Winchmoor, and was quite sure she'd only told me she was going to in the hope that I'd tell Mum.

But the police didn't need to know that. Particularly DS Barking Mad Miller, who had no right to bully my mother the way he had been.

Neither, I decided, did he need to know what Mary had told me about Tanya taking a phone call from someone she was planning to meet. He probably knew that anyway, if they'd found her phone.

"Please make yourself available for further questioning, Mrs Latcham," DS Miller said. "Our enquiries into your sister-in-law's death are still very much ongoing."

As he and Ben turned to the door, I gave a silent sigh of relief. He was obviously not going to say anything about the row between Mum and Tanya. I could see Mum start to relax too.

"Oh yes, just one more thing, Mrs Latcham," he said, pausing with his hand on the door handle. "I've had it from several sources now that you and Mrs Tanya Latcham had a violent disagreement on Saturday afternoon. Would you care to tell us what that was about?"

Mum gave a short, breathy laugh. "Oh, that. It wasn't a

disagreement, as such. It's just, well, Tanya is – sorry, was – a fussy eater. Nothing was ever quite to her taste. And I'd be the first to admit, I'm not the greatest cook in the world. But I'd worked really hard to make a wholesome, vegetarian meal for Saturday lunch. Lots of lovely tofu and noodles, really tasty and nourishing. But she looked at it, then at me and, very rudely I thought, demanded to know if I was trying to kill her? By starvation. Said my food was inedible and disgusting and the next thing I knew, she'd taken herself off to the pub. Hardly the most polite way of saying thanks for your hospitality, I have to say."

Until that moment, I had never known my mum to lie. But I had to hand it to her, if I hadn't been there at the time of the falling out, I'd have believed her. Ben, who knew Mum's cooking of old, bought in to her story wholesale. DS Miller, maybe not so much.

Nevertheless, they left and this time both Mum and I breathed a genuine sigh of relief as I closed the door behind them.

"Ok then, Mum," I said as I turned towards her. "What's going on?"

She checked her watch. "I've texted your dad. He should be home any moment. I'd rather tell you both at the same time, if you don't mind."

As if on cue, we heard the sound of Dad's car pulling up outside and the slam of the door.

He stood framed in the doorway, looking at Mum. His hands were shoved deep in his coat pocket.

"I saw a police car as I was coming down the road," he said. "Had they been here?"

Mum nodded. "They wanted to know where I was yesterday afternoon. At the time of Tanya's… accident."

"It was no accident," Dad grunted.

"I know," Mum said. "It's just – just such a horrible word."

"It's a horrible act," Dad said shortly as he took his coat off and hung it up. He looked across at Mum, his face grim. "So, where have you been? And why didn't you call? Katie and I have been worried sick about you."

"I know. And I'm sorry. I – I had some thinking to do. So I went to Mum's."

"Oh really?" Dad's voice dripped with sarcasm. "And, of course, your mother's place is just perfect if you've got a bit of thinking to do, isn't it? She doesn't give anyone time to draw breath, let alone think."

"I'd done my thinking before I got to Mum's," she said. "I – I was just buying myself a bit of time."

"Ok." He sat down in the chair at the far end of the table, leaned back and folded his arms. "So, what were you thinking about? Are you going to share it with us?"

"Of course."

"And is this the bit where you say you're very sorry but you realise now what you've always suspected? That you married the wrong brother and that you and Richard…"

"For God's sake, Terry, don't talk such bloody rubbish!" Mum's angry voice rang across the kitchen and stopped Dad in mid sentence. Mum hardly ever shouted (she didn't have to, one of her looks was usually enough) and she certainly didn't swear. Right now she was doing both.

I figured they needed some space and made to leave the room.

"Stay where you are, Katie," she said. "You might as well hear this too. I should have told you ages ago. If I had—" she stopped and shook her head. Her anger seemed to fade as suddenly as it had arisen.

"If I had," she went on in a quiet voice, "Then maybe none of this would have happened."

"Go on then," said Dad. "We're listening."

"Would you like some tea?" I asked.

"No," they both said in unison. At least they could agree on that, which was something I supposed.

"Do you remember when Tanya suddenly invited me to spend a weekend with her at Bournemouth?" Mum asked.

Dad nodded. "Of course. She'd got some complimentary tickets for some spa hotel or something."

"Well, I thought it was a bit strange, because Tanya and I hadn't been getting along, particularly not since there was all

166

that upset between the four of us over Gran Latcham's cottage."

"What was all that about?" I was still at college when Gran died and was surprised when the cottage had been sold, because it had always been planned that it would be kept in the family.

"Dad and I wanted to keep the cottage," Mum told me. "Your dad had great plans for doing it up. I was going to have my salon downstairs and we were going to turn the upstairs into a flat. Richard, who was going to get the income from the flat, was all for it, right until the last moment when Tanya suddenly decided she wanted to go on a world cruise or something. So Richard, who could never say no to her, changed his mind and said to sell it. He offered to let us buy him out, but of course we couldn't afford to."

"And now it's one of Margot's holiday cottages," I said.

Dad sighed. "Mum would have hated to see that."

"Anyway," Mum went on, "Tanya and I fell out over that and hadn't really spoken since. Until a couple of years ago – you were still in Bristol, Katie – she suddenly rang me out of the blue and asked if I wanted a weekend in Bournemouth with her. I wasn't keen. But your dad persuaded me to go. I'd had that bad bout of flu, if you remember, and he thought the sea air would do me good."

Dad sniffed. "Much good it did. You came back worse than before you went away. Said you'd caught a chill."

Mum took a deep breath. "Yes, well, I lied. I'm sorry. I should have told you back then what really happened. But I was ashamed."

"Go on." Dad's face was grim.

I shifted in my chair. "Look, I think I'd better…"

"No, Katie. Stay. Please." Mum said firmly. "When we got to Bournemouth, I realised that the whole point of the weekend was so that Tanya could spend time with this guy she was having an affair with. And I was to be her cover. I got really upset and wanted to come home there and then. But Tanya was driving and she said we'd go home in the morning. So, against my better judgement, I agreed to make up a foursome for the evening. This guy that Tanya had been seeing had brought a friend along."

She flicked an anxious look at Dad. Then she cleared her throat and went on. "He seemed a decent enough man. A bit awkward about the whole thing, same as I was. We were a pair of gooseberries together, I thought. So we sat and chatted about our families while Tanya and her guy – well, you know. Anyway," she swallowed. "I hardly drink at all, as you know, and was sticking to soft drinks. But then Tanya bought a bottle of Prosecco and insisted I had some – and well, it went completely to my head. I'm afraid I don't remember much else of the evening."

A hint of a smile tugged at the corner of Dad's mouth. "And is that it? Your terrible confession? You went out in a foursome and got drunk?"

"No," Mum looked down at her hands, clasping and unclasping them in her lap. "No, that's not all. I woke up in the morning with the hangover from hell. And Tanya flew at me. Accused me of being a hypocrite, criticising her for having an affair while I'd been happy enough to have a – a one night stand. She also advised me to find a chemist and ask for the morning after pill."

Dad gave a sharp intake of breath. He stared at her, stunned.

"I don't remember any of it," Mum said miserably. "No, I tell a lie. I have vague memories of the man – God help me, I can't even remember his name – helping me to my room. But nothing after that. Tanya, however, did remember, and was more than happy to fill me in on all the graphic details. I suppose I should be thankful she didn't take pictures and plaster them all over Facebook."

"So that's why she kept going on about Bournemouth?" I said.

Mum nodded. "She's been blackmailing me about it ever since. Oh, not in the financial sense. Mostly she wanted me to cover for her, say I'd been with her if Richard asked. Until last week, of course. When she just turned up on the doorstep, looking for somewhere to stay. And knowing I wouldn't be able to turn her away."

There was a long, deep silence. Inside, the whirring of the fridge, the ticking of a clock. Outside, a dog barked and somewhere a child laughed.

"I should have told you before," Mum said. "I'm sorry. To you both."

Dad stood up and, without saying a word, picked up his coat and left.

Mum stayed at the table, her head bent, eyes fixed intently on her hands, as she twisted her wedding ring round and round her finger.

Chapter Eighteen

"Mum?" I said after a few minutes when it seemed she was going to sit staring down at her hands for ever. "You've got to go after him."

"There's no point," she said without lifting her head. "You saw the way he looked at me. He hates me. And I can't say I blame him."

"He was shocked, that was all. He'll come round."

"I don't think so."

"Look, are you sure you can't remember anything?"

Her head snapped up and a bit of the Mum I knew re-emerged. "For goodness sake, Katie, you're not expecting all the graphic details, are you?"

"What?" The thought of Mum and her graphic details sent a shudder down my spine. "Of course not. I just wondered what exactly you did remember?"

"Just what I told you and your dad. Now, if you don't mind, I don't want to talk about it any more."

"But you must. Not to me, of course," I added hastily, in case she decided to launch into the graphic details after all. "But to Dad. You can't let him go off like that. Go after him."

"Like I said, there's no point."

"There's every point." Jeez, doing marriage guidance stuff for my parents was the pits. But I forced myself on. "That thing he said about Uncle Richard. Do you really want him to go on believing you married him on the rebound? That you're only staying with him until a decent interval has elapsed and you and Richard can be together again?"

Her head shot up. "What do you mean? Again?"

"I know you were once engaged to Richard. That he broke it off when Tanya came along. And that you then took up with Dad."

"Who told you that? No, don't answer that. As if I can't guess. It was Elsie, wasn't it?" She shook her head. "Honestly, that woman. She wasn't even living around here at the time."

"No, but Gran Latcham and Elsie were great friends. And, for the record, Elsie reckoned you got the best of the two brothers. And so, if you want to know, do I."

I thought that this time I'd gone too far because Mum looked like she was trying to decide whether to send me to the naughty step or not. Then she gave a little smile.

"And so, if you must know, do I," she said softly. "That's one thing I have to thank Tanya for, at least. Taking Richard and leaving Terry for me. I did indeed get the best of the two brothers."

"Then tell him," I urged. "Believe me, Mum, he doesn't think you did."

This was so wrong. On so many levels. She should have been giving me relationship advice, not the other way round. Goodness knows, I could have done with it after my recent encounters with Will.

"It won't do any good," she said. "You know what your father's like when he makes up his mind about something. I think I'll…"

She broke off at the sound of a car pulling up outside. She stood up and went across to the window, then pulled back out of sight with a groan.

My heart sank. "Not the police again? What do they want now?"

"No. Not the police. It's Richard. I can't face him at the moment. I'll go out the back way. Sorry, love. Go and let him in the front door so he doesn't see me, will you?"

***

I opened the front door as Richard was getting out of his top of the range BMW. He looked grey and utterly drained.

"Come on in," I said, as I ushered him through the salon and into the kitchen. "I'll make you a cup of tea – unless you want something stronger?"

He shook his head. "Tea will be fine, thanks, love. Is your mum or dad in?"

"Neither, I'm afraid. Have you just driven down from Yorkshire? You look all in."

He shook his head and sank into the chair with a long sigh. "No. I drove back this morning. I've just come from the mortuary. I had to – to identify my... wife. It was... difficult. And I really didn't fancy going home to an empty house. Not after that."

I swallowed. "No. I guess not. I'm so sorry." The words seemed so inadequate.

"The police say she was murdered," he went on, still in the same weary voice of a man who's had one shock too many. "Did you know that?"

"I'd heard they were treating her death as suspicious. Have they told you what happened?"

"They said there'd been some attempt to make it look like an accident, but the post mortem showed she'd died from a blow to the head which wasn't caused by the car going into the rhine. It had been deliberately driven in there."

I shivered. "That's awful. Who'd do such a terrible thing? And why?"

"I have no idea." He sighed. "I – I know we had our problems. I came down here yesterday to ask her to give our marriage another go. But she was adamant it was over. That the only thing she wanted from me was a quick divorce."

An image of Tanya, the last time I'd seen her, came into my head. She was laughing, excited. 'Like a teenager rushing off for a first date,' I remembered thinking at the time.

But I couldn't tell Uncle Richard that.

"And – and there's something else, Katie," Uncle Richard went on. "I – I thought I'd best let your Mum know. I didn't mean to. But I'm afraid it slipped out."

"What?"

"I told the police that Tanya and your mum had had a big falling-out."

"Uncle Richard! You surely don't think Mum would do something like that? How could you?"

172

"For pity's sake, of course I don't. I feel really bad about it now. It's just… well, they asked."

"They asked what? If you knew who'd want to kill your wife? And you suggested Mum?"

"Of course not. Although Tanya did say how very aggressive Cheryl had become. That she'd moved into the pub because she was frightened of what your mother would do to her if she stayed."

I'd have got pretty aggressive, too, if Tanya had been blackmailing me. Now that I knew the full story of Bournemouth, I could only admire my mother's restraint.

"I was there at the time," I said sharply. "And Tanya was really winding Mum up, goading her…"

"Goading her about what?"

I could have bitten my tongue. The last thing I wanted was for it to get back to the police that Mum had reason to want Tanya out of her life.

"It was nothing. Just a little spat about Mum's cooking," I said, figuring it was better to stick to the story Mum told DS Barking Mad Miller. "Tanya was very rude about it and Mum objected. It was nothing more than that. As for threatening her, you know what a drama queen Tanya is. And I'll tell you why…"

"Was," he corrected me bleakly. "She was a drama queen."

"I'm sorry. It still doesn't seem real."

"It does to me," he said quietly. "But go on. You started to say you'll tell me why – what?"

"I was just going to say why she moved to the pub. It was because the WiFi signal's rubbish down this end of the village and it's ok in the pub."

He nodded. "A good signal would count for a lot with Tanya. She lived most of her life on line. Never off her bloody phone."

"Did the police say if they'd found it?"

He shook his head. "Not to me, they didn't. They were more interested in asking me where I was at the time of the…" he paused. "At the time she died."

"And what did you say?"

"The truth, of course," he said huffily. "I told them I was on my way home. Now, where's that cup of tea? I could really do with something warm inside me. Since I left the mortuary I've felt chilled from the inside out."

As I put the kettle on, I asked: "Did you know Tanya was thinking of buying a property in Much Winchmoor? That she had plans to open a hair and beauty salon?"

He shook his head. "That's the first I've heard of it, but then, she didn't confide in me."

"She didn't ask you for money to help her buy it?" I asked as I placed a mug of tea in front of him.

He gave a short, bitter laugh. "Hardly. I'm broke."

"You're kidding?"

He gave me a stern look. "That is hardly the sort of thing I would joke about, Katie."

"No, I'm sorry. I'm just – surprised, that's all."

"The reason I'm broke," he began, then paused to wrap his long, thin fingers around the mug and inhale the steam. "Is my inability to say no to Tanya. We've been living a millionaire lifestyle on a non-millionaire income for years, and you don't have to be a financial genius to realise that's unsustainable. The house is about to be repossessed and my accountancy practice is up the Swanee after I lost two major clients last year."

"Did Tanya know?"

"Oh yes, that was one of the reasons she wanted a divorce. None of this for richer, for poorer nonsense for her," he added bitterly. "She was going to take every last penny I had, and even that wouldn't have been enough."

A sudden thought struck me. *If Uncle Richard wasn't Tanya's pot of gold at the end of the rainbow, then who was?*

"What are you going to do now?" I asked.

He relaxed back into his chair and took a sip of the tea. A hint of a smile tugged at the corners of his thin mouth. "You're never going to believe this."

"Try me."

"I've bought a pig farm with the little money I have left, after the mortgage company and the bank have had their

174

pound and a half of flesh."

"A pig farm?" If he'd said he was going to limbo naked down Dintscombe High Street on market day, I couldn't have been more surprised.

"Why not? I've always loved pigs and farming's been something I've wanted to do since I was a kid. I hate accountancy and was only doing it for the money. Anyway, I had a client in Yorkshire who was selling up and that's where I've just been. I put in an offer to buy it and he accepted." His eyes shone and, for the moment at least, he lost that careworn, defeated look. "It really is in the most stunning location, deep in this beautiful but very remote dale."

"Which was why you couldn't be reached."

He nodded. "It wasn't until I was driving home that my phone came back to life and I found I had all these missed calls."

"Poor you. That must have been tough."

"It was a shock. Yes."

"Tell me, did Aunty Tanya know about your pig farming ambition?" I asked.

He looked up quickly. "What do you think?" he said with an unexpected grin. "She'd have had a fit. But once I accepted that our marriage was well and truly over, well, there was nothing to stop me going ahead with realising my boyhood dream, was there?"

"I suppose not. We should all follow our dreams," I added, as I thought wistfully of the dream I'd had to give up on. I was about to go on to say something like, 'life's too short,' then realised that that would have sounded a tad insensitive, given the circumstances.

"Look, Uncle Richard, I'm sorry I have to ask you this. But, do you know the name of the man Tanya was having an affair with?"

For a moment, he looked as if he was going to tell me to mind my own damn business. But he didn't.

"It was never mentioned. As for his wife, now there was someone who looked as if she could do Tanya harm. I thought when she turned up at our house that night she was going to

175

strike her. I've never seen someone so angry."

"Did you tell the police this?"

He shook his head. "I couldn't see how it was relevant."

And yet he thought that Mum having a few words with Tanya was *relevant?*

"Are you sure you don't remember her name? Or his?"

He shook his head. "I'd have remembered, had she mentioned it."

"And you say she struck Tanya?"

"No, but I thought she was going to. And when I remonstrated with her, she rounded on me and had the nerve to tell me to keep better control of my wife, if you ever heard anything so outrageous. Like Tanya was a badly behaved poodle."

I thought that, actually, it was a pretty good description of Tanya, but figured this wasn't the time to say so.

"Why do you want to know?" he went on.

"Just trying to piece a few things together."

"You surely don't think either of them had anything to do with Tanya's death, do you?" he said sharply.

"Of course not." I was beginning to wish I hadn't said anything now. Because I certainly didn't want to have to tell him about Mum's weekend in Bournemouth.

"Then why?" The look he gave me was challenging, verging on the hostile.

"Because the police are asking my mother all sorts of horrible questions," I said. "Not helped by the fact that you told them about the spat she and Tanya had."

"I couldn't lie to the police," he said stiffly.

"No. But did you tell them about the row you'd had with Tanya? In the pub? I heard it got so heated, the barman was getting ready to ask you to leave. So where exactly were you at the time Tanya was killed?"

He glared at me. "On my way back to Bristol, of course."

"And do you have proof of that?"

"For heaven's sake, Katie, you're being ridiculous. And, if I may say so, extremely insensitive." His voice shook with barely suppressed anger as he pushed his half-finished cup of tea to one side and stood up. There was a hardness in his eyes I'd never seen before. "This isn't a game of Cluedo, you know, young lady."

I flushed at his patronising tone.

"Of course I know. My mother's just been interrogated by an extremely unpleasant detective," I said, my voice as sharp as his.

We stood and glared at each other for what seemed like ages. He was the first to look away.

"Thank you for the tea," he said stiffly. "I'll be off now. I just wanted to let your parents know how things stood."

Suddenly, I felt bad about letting him go off like that. The poor guy had, after all, just lost his wife in horrific circumstances. And here I was, making him feel even worse. *Nice one, Kat.*

"Look, I'm sorry, Uncle Richard, I didn't mean to offend you," I said, my voice conciliatory. "Of course I don't think you could have done it, any more than I think Mum did. I just wanted to point out to you that, as things stand, you and Mum are in a similar position. You both had rows with Tanya and you were both in your cars driving at the time of the murder. With, I'm assuming, no witnesses. And of course I don't see this as a game. I'm as upset and shaken by the whole thing as anyone else."

His face softened. "Yes, you're right. It's a sorry mess, isn't it?"

"It certainly it. So what are you going to do now? Are you going back to Bristol?"

"Good Lord, no. I've never really thought of that place as home. Even less so, now. And I will tell the police about that woman, threatening Tanya the way she did. Even though it's going to bring all that nastiness about her affair out in the open. Well, thank you for the tea."

"But you didn't finish it."

He gave a wintry smile. "I think a tot of Mary's best malt will go down better at the moment."

"I'm sure if they were here, Mum and Dad would say for you to stay here. You can have my room and I'll have the spare room. It's what we did when Tanya was staying."

"I don't think that would work, do you? Terry and I didn't exactly part the best of friends the last time we saw each other."

"He's calmed down now," I said, crossing my fingers against the lie.

"Don't worry, I've already made arrangements. I'm going to stay in the pub overnight and see what's what in the morning. I wish now I'd never let Tanya talk me into selling Mum's cottage."

Don't we all, I thought, as I saw him to the door. But I kept it to myself. I'd upset him enough for one day.

Yet, as he drove away, I couldn't help thinking that Tanya's death had come at the right time for him. If he was as broke as he said he was, there'd have been precious little left for his beloved pig farm once Tanya had dragged him through the divorce courts.

And if they'd decided to give their marriage another go, there was no way on earth Tanya would have agreed to become the wife of a pig farmer in the depths of a Yorkshire dale, particularly one where there was no mobile phone signal.

So, when you sat down and thought about it, my Uncle Richard had more to gain from his wife's death than anyone else I could think of. And wasn't that what the police did in a murder investigation? Look to see who had the most to gain?

***

I sat for ages after Richard had left, staring at his half-empty cup and thinking about the man Tanya had been having an affair with. And his fiery-tempered wife. Was it him Tanya had been going to meet that afternoon? Or her?

But no, it wouldn't have been a woman. Tanya had looked excited – as if she was going to meet her lover.

She'd said something about her personal trainer the day she'd first arrived. I racked my brain, trying to remember if she'd said his name or where he worked. But it was no good. It wouldn't come.

178

"Has Richard gone, then?" Mum asked as she came back a few minutes later.

"He's staying in the pub for the night. Did you see Dad?"

"I didn't try. I just went to the church and sat there quietly for a bit while I tried to sort my head out." She took her coat off. "Not that it did any good. I'd best get dinner going. Although I don't suppose any of us have much of an appetite."

"Mum, what was the name of Tanya's guy, do you remember?"

She flushed. "Are you going to keep dragging that up every five minutes?"

"No. But I should have told the police that I saw Tanya on Sunday afternoon, after Richard had left. She was arranging to meet someone. And she looked like a woman going to meet her lover."

Mum stared at me, her eyes wide. "And you think…?"

"I don't know. Richard said the affair was over, that the guy's wife made him break it off. But you never know. Perhaps Tanya didn't want to break it off and was blackmailing him. Like she was blackmailing you."

Mum thought for a moment. "You could be right," she said slowly. "To be honest, I didn't see that much of him. He only had eyes for Tanya. But I think his name was Adam."

"Did she mention his surname?"

Mum shook her head. "Definitely not."

"I suppose if I started with all the gyms within reach of their house in Bristol…"

"No, Katie. No. I absolutely forbid it," Mum said fiercely. "I will not have you chasing around, tracking down someone who may or may not be a murderer. Look what happened last time you did that. Goodness knows, if Will hadn't come along when he did…"

"I'd have been fine. I had everything under control," I said.

"So you say. Even so, just tell the police and let them handle it. They'll not thank you for interfering. Now, what do you want for dinner? I thought I'd make your dad something really special. What do you think?"

"Steak and kidney pie is his favourite," I said, without

much hope.

"I care about the state of his arteries even if he doesn't," Mum said dismissively. "I'm going to have a cup of tea before I start on dinner. Do you want one?"

"I'll take it up to my room with me, if that's ok?" I said. "I've got some work to do for *The Chronicle*."

Mum frowned. "You're not going to be writing anything about Tanya, are you?"

"Of course not." I didn't tell her that, after the exchange with Mike earlier, there probably wouldn't be any more jobs from the paper coming my way. "Just a parish council meeting. The usual boring stuff."

Only, of course, I didn't have any meetings, boring or otherwise, to write up. Once I was in my room and away from her all-seeing eyes, I started trawling the Internet looking for leisure clubs in and around Richard and Tanya's part of Bristol.

The people of Bristol must be incredibly health conscious as there were hundreds of them. Or that's how it felt as I tried one number after another. But eventually I struck it lucky.

Yes, they did have a personal trainer called Adam. But no, he was not on duty until tomorrow. And no, they could not give out his number, 'data protection and all that,' but if I cared to leave my number and a message, they'd be happy to give it to him.

Could it be him? There was only one way to find out.

I left a message, asking him to call me. I said it was personal and urgent but didn't go into details, except to say that it concerned Tanya. I finished the call, and, feeling I was getting somewhere at last, punched the air. As I did so, my hand caught the mug of tea which sat untouched on my bedside table.

Before I could stop it, the entire contents of the mug spread across my bedclothes, soaking everything right through to the bottom sheet.

I cursed. There was nothing for it. I'd have to change the lot. As I tugged at the fitted sheet, the mattress lifted a little and there was a slithering sound as something fell down between the bed and the wall.

I scrabbled around among the dust bunnies under the bed, looking for whatever it was. Eventually, the torch on my phone picked out a small, bright pink, spiral-bound notebook that certainly wasn't mine.

It had to be Tanya's. My heart leapt. Was it a diary? Would I find an entry that would maybe tell us who she was going to meet yesterday afternoon?

Chapter Nineteen

My hand shook with excitement as I blew the dust off the notebook, sneezed and made a silent promise to Mum that I'd clean my room properly next time.

Most of it was deadly dull. Page after page of what she'd eaten. For heaven's sake, who eats half a banana? And, if they do, what happens to the other half? Then she'd listed how many calories she'd burned, her daily weight gain or loss (recorded to three decimal points of an ounce) and so on. It was all very *Bridget Jones's Diary,* but without the funny bits. And there was no mention at all of Colin Firth, or any other man's name as far as I could see, which was disappointing.

However, towards the end of the book, things changed. Instead of the neatly written pages, these were filled with scribbled notes and rough sketches. It was obviously plans for her beauty salon. *Heaven Scents Spa and Beauty Salon*, in big fancy letters at the top of one page, was a bit of a giveaway. Very ambitious plans they were, too, by the look of it. The rough sketches included labels like reception, nail bar, treatment room, spa, all with arrows pointing to the morning room, drawing room, orangery and even library.

Orangery? I didn't even know what an orangery was. *And library?* Tanya must have been indulging in a bit of day-dreaming when she wrote this. Our maybe she was writing a cosmic wish list. But then I remembered the way she'd laughed when I'd joked about putting the spa in the old stone shed at the bottom of The Old Forge's garden.

What if she wasn't talking about the Old Forge at all? As far as I knew, there was hardly room on the ground floor for a book shelf, much less a library.

My brain was reeling as one *what if* followed another, swirling around inside my head like leaves in an autumn gale.

What if the business partner Tanya had been hinting at, the day she'd first told me about her plans, had been Margot?

What if Heaven Scents Spa and Beauty Salon wasn't in The Old Forge at all, but in Winchmoor Manor? *What if* Margot saw it as a good fit for her upmarket holidaymakers, in her trendy Farrow & Ball cottages?

What if the reason Tanya had been skulking around the entrance to the Manor, after Margot's death, was because she'd been taking one last look at what might have been? No wonder she'd been so upset by the news of Margot's murder.

I looked more closely at her notes. There were a few numbers jotted around. Big numbers, with lots of zeros after them. As well as cryptic notes like... 'car park? Old barn? Swimming pool? Stable block?'

Then came the *what if* that chilled me to the bone. *What if* both women were killed by the same person? *What if* Tanya hadn't made a mistake when she'd thought she'd recognised Margot, that day in the salon, and the two women were connected in some way?

She'd told Mary about finding the pot of gold at the end of the rainbow. So where was this pot of gold coming from? Could it be Richard? Yet, according to him, she knew he was almost broke. It was, he'd said, the reason she'd wanted a divorce.

And yet, although Richard said he was broke, he had enough money left in the kitty to buy a farm. Now I've never gone shopping for a farm, but I'm willing to bet you won't find one in the 'tenner and under' section in *The Chronicle*'s classified ads.

At least now there was no chance of Tanya getting her grasping little hands on Richard's pig farm fund.

So, what if she'd been she blackmailing him as well? I only had his word about the fall-out with this personal trainer Adam and his wife. From the way she'd treated Mum, I knew Tanya wouldn't hesitate to use a bit of blackmail to get what she wanted.

I called Jules, to see if she'd heard Margot talking about plans for a beauty salon. It rang and rang and I was about to give up when she answered. She sounded totally stressed and out of breath.

"Sorry, Jules. Is this a bad time?"

"Just a bit," she said. "Kylie's having a total meltdown because I said she couldn't wear her new pink sparkly shoes to school tomorrow. And now the baby's joining in."

I could hardly hear what she was saying above what sounded like a dozen screaming children, not just two. "Don't worry. I'll call tomorrow. Ok?"

"Thanks. Catch you later."

As she rang off I made a silent vow to myself that I would never, ever have children.

It sounded like hell on earth.

***

Having said that, there was a time later on that evening when I'd have gladly changed places with Jules. The atmosphere between Mum and Dad was so frosty it would have had penguins queuing up for hot water bottles.

Then there was the soya mince 'moussaka' she served up. Dad took one mouthful, pushed it away and got his coat.

"Where are you going?" Mum asked.

"To the pub."

"You do know Richard's staying there, don't you?" Mum said.

Dad paused, his coat half on. "I'll take that chance," he said curtly. "I'll go in the public bar. I dare say he won't lower himself to drink in there."

"Dad, please..." I started, but I was talking to a closed door.

Mum sighed and looked down at the unappetising mess in front of us.

"Do you know, Katie, I think I might have been better off taking your advice and serving up steak and kidney pie? If he doesn't care about his arteries, why should I?"

I was almost tempted to join him at the pub. Mary didn't do cooked food on a Monday night but a packet of cheese and onion crisps and a pickled egg would taste a whole load better than Mum's pretend moussaka.

But then I remembered the promise I made to myself when I'd realised the body in the rhine wasn't Mum.

"It's very nice, Mum," I lied as I began to eat it.

A couple of times during the evening, I picked up the phone to speak to Will. But put it down again because I just couldn't think what to say to him and, to be honest, I was still smarting from the fact that he thought I would exploit Tanya's death by writing about it. And at his 'out of my league' comment.

Eventually, I gave up and went to bed early. Mum followed soon after.

We hadn't been in bed very long when Dad came back but, instead of going into the room he shared with Mum, he went into the spare room. Of all the stubborn idiots, I thought. How on earth were they going to put things right between them when they were in different rooms? I felt like going in and having a go at him but I knew that would probably only make things worse.

But one good thing might come from his self-imposed banishment to the spare room. At least now, I hoped, he'd finally get around to mending the legs on that bed, after spending the night in it.

In the morning, things between them were no better. No surprise there. Dad took himself off to work and Mum opened up the salon as usual.

I phoned Mike to see if there were any jobs going, but he was not very encouraging.

"I'm sorry, Kat," he said. "There's not much at the moment. I've got to leave plenty of space for the murders so everything else is getting squeezed out. But there's a meeting over at Little Chantling tomorrow evening which the organisers would like us to cover. A developer wants to demolish the village pub and build a housing estate on the site. And the locals are getting together and talking of forming a co-operative to buy it."

"Sounds a good story."

"Sure. But that's ten miles or so away from you, isn't it?"

"I'm afraid so."

He sighed. "How are you getting on with fixing up some transport? You said the other day you were getting closer?"

"I'm working on it." I figured he didn't need to know that in my mother's current mood, there was no way she'd even let me clean her precious car, least of all drive it. And that the balance of my savings account was £2.51p.

"Pity. But I accept your reasons for not wanting to work on your aunt's story. I've got one of the staff reporters to cover it. I've given her your number and said you'd be happy to help with any background stuff. It's all covered. So you don't have to worry."

The thought of a staff reporter nosing around on my patch wasn't just worrying, it was infuriating.

***

Elsie was even crankier than usual that morning. Her bunions, she complained before I was even through the door, were 'giving her gyp' and when something gave Elsie 'gyp,' she believed in sharing the misery with those around her.

And, moreover, she grumbled on, there was a new 'chirrupist' coming this afternoon and it was a woman. Elsie didn't hold with 'women chirrupists,' and what had happened to Clint, who'd had such a magic touch with a callus file, she wanted to know?

I could have told her he'd hopped off to Torquay with Sandra, but that it had all ended in tears and Sandra was now back in the salon, a sadder and wiser woman. Fickle Clint had found other toes to tickle and was staying on in Torquay, leaving poor Sandra to limp back to her husband and to Chez Cheryl. But I was my mother's daughter and didn't pass on gossip – at least, not always.

In the mood Elsie was in, it wouldn't have made any difference anyway. Everything I did that morning was wrong and, even when I made a pretty good job (though I say it myself) of mending her fridge door, she grumpily reminded me that it was my fault it had got broken in the first place.

As for Prescott, he, too, was even stroppier than usual, and I was heartily glad to be shot of the pair of them when I took him back after his walk.

I was on my way home past the pub when I heard someone calling after me. It was Shane Freeman.

"Katie, hang on," he called.

I sighed. My bad day was about to get a whole heap worse. Uncle Richard's car was still in the car park and Shane probably wanted to know the full story.

"Blimey, girl, where's the fire?' he panted as he hurried after me.

"Sorry, Shane. I didn't hear you," I said, which wasn't quite true. The incumbents of the church graveyard had probably heard him bellowing after me. "What did you want?"

"I've got some good news for you," he announced, a beaming smile on his large round face. "At least, I may well have."

"Jeez, I could sure as hell do with some of that. What is it?"

"First off, I've got a deal you won't want to miss."

"Want to bet?" I knew from past experience that Shane's unmissable deals could turn out very costly to the unwary.

"You know how you were admiring my scooter the other day?"

Admiring it was one way of putting it. Wondering how on earth he managed to balance his huge body on that tiny thing was another.

"Y-e-e-e-s," I said, slowly and carefully.

"Well, it's for sale and I'm letting you have first refusal, knowing how you need wheels. And this is as cheap a means of transport as you can get."

"You're kidding?" For the first time in I don't know how long, I felt my spirits lift. Just slightly. I remained cautious though because, knowing Shane as I did, there was usually a catch. "And what is it going to cost me?"

He named a sum that was way beyond my reach. Nevertheless, it might be worth asking Mum or Dad for a loan. And it would mean that I could get myself to Little Chantling tomorrow night.

"But what about you?" I asked. "Don't you need it? Or," I

added as I realised this could well be the catch. "Have you broken it?"

"Of course I haven't. I wouldn't be offering it to you if I had, would I?"

I shrugged. "Maybe not."

He beamed. "I'm getting rid of it because I don't need it any more. Because that's the other bit of good news. I've got me a job. A proper job that pays proper money. And wheels to go with it."

"Oh, wow, that's brilliant." I felt genuinely pleased for him. "Good for you. A company car, eh?"

"Well, not so much a company car as a van. But that's the other thing I wanted to tell you. I'm giving up my shifts in the pub. I shan't need the extra money now and I've recommended you to Mary. And she wants to see you. As soon as you can."

I could have hugged him, only I didn't want to give him the wrong idea. But a tiny little scooter and regular weekend shifts at the pub could change everything for me.

At one time I'd have turned my nose up at both. But not now. Now I couldn't wait to grab them with open arms.

"Well, are you interested?"

"Course I am. You're a star. I owe you one."

He grinned. "You sure do. I'll have to give that some thought. Anyway, do you want to give the scooter a try?"

"What, now?"

"Later on this afternoon. My sister has a helmet that will fit you. Hardly been worn. And I can put you on my insurance temporarily, until you can sort your own out. Go and see Mary, and then come round to mine."

***

Fast forward a couple of hours and I was not only the new weekend barmaid at the Winchmoor Arms, starting at 11.30am Saturday prompt with a 'don't you dare be late, young lady!' but also the owner of a set of very small wheels. Plus a pair of L-plates and an extremely pink and glittery helmet that would have gone very well with young Kylie's pink sparkly shoes and could probably be seen from space.

Shane's sister had never really grown out of the Disney Princess stage, but I supposed I should be thankful it didn't have a unicorn horn sticking out of the top of it.

Of course, in the interests of accuracy, I'd better point out that my mum was the owner of the scooter, seeing as she was the one who'd agreed, somewhat grudgingly, to lend me the money.

Shane showed me how everything worked and asked if I'd like to drive it around for a bit, just to get the feel of it.

I would like – and I knew exactly where I wanted to go for my first outing.

I was a bit wobbly going down the lane but I soon got into the hang of it and took the narrow road known as Long Moor Drove that led out of the village across the moors.

I was intrigued by the scribbled comment in Tanya's notebook. *'Old barn?'* she had written. There were lots of old barns around the village, quite a few of them on Will's farm. But the one out on Long Moor Drove was the nearest to Winchmoor Manor land. In fact, when I checked it out on the ordnance survey map, I could see that Longmoor Drove actually went along the estate's boundary, which was clearly delineated by an old but freshly-painted black metal fence.

As I drove along the narrow road I had a bit of a wobble when I passed the spot where Tanya's car had gone into the rhine. It was hard to miss. The narrow grass verge was churned up, no doubt from the wheels of the recovery vehicle. I gripped the handlebars fiercely and drove on, not daring to look down into the steep-sided rhine, filled almost to the brim with brackish water and looking horribly close to the road.

A bit further on down the lane, I saw the barn. It was, as Elsie had said, in a very sorry state. The roofline dipped like an overstretched washing line and a buddleia bush grew from one of the upper windows. A large wooden door sagged on broken hinges.

I parked the scooter in the gateway and made my way along the stony track that led to the front of the barn. I pulled the door and it shifted enough for me to peer inside.

At first, it was difficult to see anything. The only window was almost completely blocked by the bush. But as my eyes gradually became accustomed to the dim interior, I could just about make out that the barn was empty.

Of course it was. What was I expecting? Architects' drawings pinned to the walls? More of Tanya's scribbled notes? Wherever she had been planning to create her Heaven Scents Spa and Beauty Salon, it certainly couldn't have been in this run-down old ruin, where the scents were anything but heavenly.

As I turned to go, something struck me. Obviously it had been used as shelter by various animals, but there was something else. An odour I couldn't quite identify, although I was pretty sure I'd smelt it somewhere before.

It certainly wasn't the cannabis from the barn's previous owner. The police would have cleared every last trace of that. But there was something tantalisingly familiar. Something...

I turned round at the sound of a car pulling up. It was a highly-polished dark blue car with those blacked-out windows that always made me think there was a posse of gangsters hiding inside. The driver got out and stood by the gate.

"What are you doing?" he called across to me. "This place is private. Didn't you see the sign?"

"What? No, I'm sorry, I'm afraid I didn't. I was – I was just looking for somewhere to... um... to..." I looked wildly around me, at the flat open fields that stretched towards Glastonbury Tor in the distance. And I said the first thing that came into my head.

"I was looking for somewhere quiet to meditate." I waved my hand in the direction of the Tor. "This whole place has such wonderful vibes. Ley lines and all that. And round here they are especially strong. The energy force is amazing."

He made no attempt to hide his scorn. "You bloody hippies and your damn stupid nonsense," he growled. "There are no vibes around here. And this is private land. So clear off."

"No worries. That's cool. Peace, brother," I said, playing the part for all I was worth. "Peace and harmony to you."

I got back on my scooter. He was watching me, with arms folded, a forbidding expression on his face. So instead of heading back to the village, I drove towards Glastonbury.

He may not have recognised me as coming from the village, especially in my Disney Princess helmet. But I'd recognised him. It was John Duckett-Trimble's gardener-cum-handyman-cum-driver. I remembered Jules saying he was a surly so-and-so, by the name of Jenkins.

What was he doing still around? Wouldn't he have left the area when John had?

Perhaps John had retained him as caretaker until the sale went through, which would explain why he was so edgy about me being on Winchmoor Manor land. Now I came to think of it, this was the most likely explanation.

I didn't fancy going all the way in to Glastonbury so, when I thought I'd gone far enough for Jenkins to have left, I turned round and drove back across the moor. But, to my dismay, as I approached the barn, I could see his car was still parked in the gateway to the barn.

And Jenkins was just getting into it.

He scowled, and I hoped he wouldn't recognise me. But how many people drive around in a pink, glittery helmet? I could see from the way he was frowning that he'd clocked me.

I gave him a cheery wave and drove past. A few minutes later, I heard the car start up and come in my direction. He got closer and closer. I pulled in as far as I could to let him pass, but he made no attempt to do so. Instead, if anything, he got even closer.

I speeded up. He speeded up. I slowed down. He slowed down. I was beginning to panic. I looked back – which was a mistake. I went into such a wobble that I was waiting for the splash as I toppled into the dark, brackish water of the rhine.

But somehow, the scooter and I remained upright and on the road – a triumph of hope over gravity. I hung on tighter than ever and kept going. Jaw clenched. Hands in a death grip on the handlebars.

He was still there. I could hear him. Feel him. So close now that I could have reached back and touched the front bumper of his car. Or I could have, if my balance had been better.

I tried to think if there were any gateways up ahead so that I could pull in. There were none. But then, if I stopped and got off, what would he do? I didn't fancy finding out. My only thought now was just to keep going.

I glanced back again. He was so close that I could see his black-gloved hands gripping the steering wheel, his expression grim. Threatening, even.

I speeded up. He moved closer. I glanced from one side of the road to the other. To the black sludgy rhines. The steep sides. The narrow verge.

Ahead, an empty road. Behind me, the car which kept on coming.

Then, to my relief, I saw a vehicle coming along the ruler-straight road towards me. Jenkins stopped and began to reverse back to the closest passing place which was, in fact, the barn.

I stopped and manoeuvred myself and the scooter off onto the verge, to allow the car to pass me. He tooted his horn in thanks. But I should have been the one to thank him.

As soon as the car had gone, I got back on the scooter and headed for the village. My pulse rate didn't return to normal until I pulled up outside my parents' home.

***

"For pity's sake, Katie," Mum shouted up the stairs. "Will you answer your wretched phone? It's been ringing for ages."

"Sorry, I was in the shower." I'd come back after the encounter with Jenkins, shaken and anxious. But after a long hot shower and a change of clothes, I was beginning to feel a little foolish, and had come to the conclusion that I'd imagined the whole thing. Or at least blown it into something it clearly was not.

I picked up my phone and didn't recognise the number on the screen.

"This is Olive Shrewton here." She spoke in a very formal, half-shouting way that reminded me of Gran Latcham. "Is that you, Katie?"

"Olive? Is something wrong?"

"It's Elsie. She's gone missing – and that dog of hers is going mad in there. I'd go in and sort him out but you've got the only spare key. I remember Elsie saying she'd let you have it."

"But what makes you think she's gone missing? She's probably just gone out for the afternoon."

"She wouldn't do that. Not with the chir – not with the foot lady coming. She's a really nice girl, by all accounts. Elsie would never miss that. Not with her bunions."

"Which have been giving her gyp," I completed the sentence for her.

"Then there was this shifty-looking bloke hanging around. I didn't like the look of him. Neither did Prescott."

"Prescott doesn't like the look of anyone," I tried to sound reassuring even though, like Olive, I was worried. "I'll be round straight away."

"Would you, dear?" Olive sounded relieved. "What with those horrible murders, and now poor Elsie going missing. It makes you wonder who's going to be next, doesn't it?"

Chapter Twenty

As I let myself into Elsie's bungalow, Prescott's manic barking rose to ear-perforating levels. He'd been shut in the kitchen and, by the sound of it, was intent on demolishing the door that stood between him and freedom.

"It's all right, Prescott," I called out in my most soothing voice. "You know me, don't you? It's Kat."

But that sent him into warp drive. "Ok, ok," I called through the door. "I'm sorry. I shouldn't have mentioned the c-a-t word in your hearing. Let's start again. It's Katie, Prescott. You know me, I'm the one who takes you for walkies."

But far from being soothed by that, his barking reached a crescendo so I tried a new tactic.

"Prescott! You little hooligan!" I yelled as loudly as Elsie had the first time we'd met. "Stop that now. I'm coming in."

What do you know? It worked. The barking subsided to a muted grumble and I began to see a whole new career ahead of me. If not exactly as a Dog Whisperer then maybe a Dog Bellower.

I pushed open the door with difficulty and stared in horror at the wreckage of Elsie's kitchen. Everything that could have been trashed had been. The floor was ankle-deep in debris and in the middle of it all stood Prescott, the tattered remnants of Elsie's favourite tea towel dangling from his mouth like spaghetti.

I started to clear up the mess. I was on my third trip to the dustbin with the sad remains of two of her favourite bone china cups, a Busy Lizzie and the tea towel which was now reduced to '....eetings fro.... Super-Mare,' when Olive appeared.

"Oh, my life! What's been going on here?"

"Prescott was shut in the kitchen and he's been on the

rampage."

"So I see. Well, at least you've managed to quieten him, that's something. But what to do with him now? I can't have him. My poor Jasper would leave home permanently if that dog set foot over the threshold. I'm due up our Millie's, I said I'd be there half an hour ago. But we can't leave him here." She rubbed her face wearily. "Millie's taken to her bed with the worry of everything and you know what? For two pins and a ha'penny, I'd join her."

"But surely Abe isn't still helping the police with their enquiries?" I said, as I picked up a black bin bag and scooped into it the wreckage of a wooden spoon, a mangled egg whisk and a heap of shredded twigs which was all that remained of a wicker basket.

"No, they've let him go," Olive said. "The old fool finally admitted where he was the night Lady Duckface was killed."

"And where was that?"

"Ferret racing with a load of his no-good mates, who vouched for him."

"Then why on earth didn't he come out and say that straight away?" I asked. "Ferret racing's a pretty weird thing to do, but it's hardly a criminal offence."

"Not as far as the police are concerned, no. But our Millie's another matter. Because it's not the actual racing that's the problem. It's the gambling that goes on at the same time."

"Gambling on ferret racing? You're kidding."

"That man would gamble on two raindrops running down a window pane," she sniffed, dropping a piece of pink plastic that was so well chewed it was impossible to guess what it had once been into the almost-full bin bag. "He'd promised her he wouldn't do it any more, not after he lost the money she'd put by for the Women's Institute's outing to Wookey Hole Caves last year."

"Well, at least Millie doesn't have to worry about him being arrested any more."

Olive tutted. "That's as maybe, but now he reckons he's going to claim compensation. Says he's the victim of a crime."

"How does he work that one out?"

"He reckons he's lost a complete vat of cider, half his entire stock, and it were going to be a vintage year, or so he says. His best yet. He was even thinking of approaching poor Mr Duckett-Trimble for it, if you ever heard anything so terrible. I tell you, Katie, he's driving my poor sister – and me – mad with his nonsense."

"Well, at least I can put your mind at rest on one thing. Elsie's coat's missing from the hallstand and her Homer Simpsons are in the sitting room."

Olive looked bewildered. "Her home whats?"

"Those slippers she always wears, in the shape of Homer Simpson's head." Olive looked at me so blankly that I decided against trying to explain any further. "She's obviously off on a jaunt somewhere – shoes, best coat and all. Her grandson, Danny was here on Friday. Chances are she's with him."

Her face cleared. "Happen you're right, lovely. I don't know, all these murders have got me jumping at shadows. Even so, it's not like her to miss her appointment with the new foot lady. Not with…"

"Her bunions," I couldn't resist a smirk as I finished the sentence for her.

"And that's where you're wrong, Miss Clever-Clogs," she said archly. "*Not without telling someone* was what I was actually going to say."

I was relieved to see a smile replace the worry lines on her face. I promised to take Prescott with me when I'd cleared up as much as I could.

"If Elsie's not back in time for *Countdown*, I'll phone her son," I reassured her.

I left Elsie a note, explaining what I'd done, then took Prescott away from the scene of his crime before he could do any more damage.

***

As I walked in with Prescott, our cat Cedric, who made a sloth look hyper-active, arched his back, hissed a few of his most colourful cat curses then rocketed up the stairs.

"What on earth is that dog doing here?" Mum asked, as she came in from the salon to see what all the noise was about.

I explained about Elsie going AWOL and how I'd brought Prescott with me to save the neighbours getting up a dog-lynching party.

"Well, you're not keeping him," she said. "I know the vet said Cedric needs more exercise, but that was a bit extreme. I've never seen him move like that before. Cats can sense things, you know, and that dog…"

"Is a psycho, who's going back the minute Elsie gets home. But don't worry. I'll take him out again in a minute. That always calms him down. But I just want to make a couple of quick phone calls before I go."

The first was to Mike, to tell him I could cover the Let's Buy a Pub meeting in Little Chantling after all. The next was to Jules.

"Is it safe to talk?" I asked.

"Sorry about last night." She sighed. "My daughter can be a right little madam when the mood takes her. I don't know where she gets it from."

I laughed. "I can't think. Anyway, all I wanted was to ask you was something about Winchmoor Manor."

"Why do you want to know?" Her tone sharpened. "This isn't for *The Chronicle*, is it?"

"Of course it's not. If you must know, it's about my aunt Tanya."

"Jeez, Kat, I was really sorry to hear about that," her voice softened now. "Your mum and dad must be really cut up."

"It's been a shock for the whole family," I said, which was nothing less than the truth.

"But what's the Manor got to do with your aunt?" Jules asked. "It's not like she even knew the Duckfaces. Or did she?"

I wasn't ready to tell anyone about Tanya's notebook yet. At least not until I'd thought it through.

"I don't suppose you heard anything about Margot taking on a business partner in some new venture she was planning?" I asked Jules.

197

"Margot discuss her plans with me? You've got to be kidding. We weren't exactly into girly chats over morning coffee. She was very much the sort who believed in keeping the staff firmly in their place."

"Talking of which, I was nearly run off the road by the Duckett-Trimbles' driver just now. I thought he'd have left when John did."

"Jenkins? The guy gives me the creeps. I did hear that he was staying on to look after the place until the new owners move in."

"The Manor's definitely been sold then? That was all a bit quick, wasn't it? Who's bought it, do you know?"

"Some mega-rich foreigner. He's bought not only the Manor but all Margot's holiday cottages as well, I heard. I'll tell you something else I heard, if you're interested?"

"About Margot?"

"Only indirectly. It's about Gerald Crabshaw. Apparently, he's been going around the village asking anyone who looks over eighteen if they'd be prepared to stand for the parish council."

"Against his wife, you mean?"

"He doesn't think she'll have the time to spare from their business to attend council meetings. He even asked my dad, which shows how desperate he must be. He'll be asking Abe Compton next."

"Now that really would be scraping the barrel."

"Now I think about it," she went on, "He's probably the one who persuaded Margot to stand. I bet that's what they were discussing that time I saw them together."

"Knowing Gruesome Gerald, he's probably worried he'll actually have to get on and do some work at the guest house if Fiona gets elected."

"Exactly," Jules said. "Was that what you wanted to ask me about?"

"No. It was about the layout of the Manor. This might sound a weird question, but what did Margot call the rooms on the ground floor?"

Jules laughed. "You should have heard her. Talk about lady

of the Manor. It was like Winchmoor Manor was Somerset's answer to Downton Abbey and had been in her family for centuries. She would insist on calling the rooms the drawing room, the orangery (that's a conservatory to you and me), the morning room – she even called one room the library, although there were precious few books in it."

I had to stop myself from punching the air and shouting, "Yay!" I'd been right. The business partner Tanya had been talking about had to be Margot. Tanya's notebook proved it. There really was a connection between the two women.

"That's great. I'll…"

I got no further as Prescott, who I'd left having a drink in the kitchen while I made the calls, launched yet another volley of hysterical barking. I promised to catch Jules later and hurried down to shut him up. I decided to go for the Dog Bellower approach seeing as it had worked last time.

He was standing on the kitchen window sill. Mum's precious pots of basil and coriander that she'd been cosseting for months were scattered on the floor, while Prescott made threatening noises through the window to Cedric, who was watching him with disdain from the safety of the roof of the garden shed.

"Prescott!" I bellowed. "Be quiet and get down."

He ignored me. Mum, unfortunately, did not. She came in from the salon, took one look at the floor and then at Prescott, who was still dancing about on the window sill, his claws clicking on the tiles like he was a little four-legged Fred Astaire.

"Get down from there this minute, you horrible little creature," she said without raising her voice. But Prescott was no fool. He knew when he'd met his match. He jumped down and sat obediently at her feet, trying to pretend that it was some other dog – or maybe even the cat – who'd caused all the damage, and not him. All he'd been doing was trying to raise the alarm.

Mum rounded on me. "And I'll thank you to remember I have customers in the salon. Poor Mrs Sweetman thought something had gone wrong with her hearing aid and is still in a state of shock. So when you've cleared up that mess, you can make her a cup of tea and then get that creature out of my house. And don't bring him back."

***

So, for the second time in as many hours, I was clearing up Prescott's trail of destruction. I'd just finished when my phone rang again. It was a number I didn't recognise.

But I didn't dare hang around in the kitchen to answer it in case Prescott kicked off again, so I hurriedly clipped on his lead, opened the door and didn't answer the call until I was safely out of the house.

"Hello?" I said once I was sure Prescott could no longer see Cedric.

"Hi, it's Adam Wickham here. You left a message for me to call you."

For a moment, I couldn't think who he was or what he was on about. Then I remembered. I was talking to the man Tanya had been having an affair with.

He'd actually called me back. My mouth went dry.

"You mentioned Tanya," he said, his voice wary.

"Yes. I did, didn't I?" I said, desperately playing for time while I tried to work out what on earth I was going to say to him. Particularly as I wasn't sure if he knew about Tanya.

"Who is this, please?" he demanded.

"I'm – I'm Tanya's niece," I said. "I'm not sure… I mean, I don't know—"

"If you're trying to ask me if I know about her death, then, yes I do," he said briskly. "My wife and I have already had a visit from the police."

"Oh, good. No, sorry. I don't mean good that you've had a visit from the police, of course. I mean, good that you know and…"

"Look, what's this all about?" he cut in. "Only I've got a class in five minutes."

Go for it. That's what they say when you're dithering on the edge, wondering whether to dive in, isn't it? So I went for it.

"I understand you went to Bournemouth last year with Tanya and – and a friend of hers," I said.

His voice rose. "What the devil has this got to do with you? Was it you who put the police on to me and my wife? Because if so, I have nothing more to say to you and what's more, my wife and I have watertight alibis for the time of Tanya's death. We were at a rugby match in Bath with ten thousand other people. And, if you'd care to check, the match was televised and we were caught on camera. Just before half time."

"No, no, please believe me. This has nothing to do with Tanya's death. It's just…" I took a deep breath and got ready to dive in again, head first this time. "Look, I'm going to come straight out and say this. Do you remember Tanya's friend?"

There was such a long pause that I didn't think he was going to answer. Eventually he said, "Vaguely. She was very shy so we didn't speak much. I think she said her name was Shirley, or something like that."

"It's Cheryl. And Tanya's been blackmailing Cheryl ever since that weekend."

I heard his sudden intake of breath. "That sounds like Tanya. She liked a bit of blackmail," he said bitterly. "Threatened me with it when I broke things off with her. But I told my wife before she could. I don't get it, what on earth would she find to blackmail little Shirley with?"

"Cheryl."

"Sorry, Cheryl. Surely not over the fact that she'd just had a bit too much to drink that night?"

Another deep breath. I was in too deep to back out now. Although to continue the swimming analogy, I was floundering and beginning to sink. And also wishing I'd never started this.

"I wondered if you would give me the number of your friend?"

"So that you can continue your aunt's career as a blackmailer? I most certainly will not," he snapped. "Furthermore, if you continue to harass me in this way, I'll report this conversation to the police."

"No. You don't understand. I'm not looking to blackmail

anyone. I'm Cheryl's daughter. And she and my dad aren't talking and – and it's all a horrible mess."

"She was blackmailing Cheryl over the fact that she'd had a few drinks? Is your dad some sort of diehard teetotaller?"

"Of course not. It wasn't the drink – although it's not like my mum to do that. It's – it's what happened after."

"Nothing happened after. I wasn't there but my friend told me that he was worried about her so helped her to her room and left her there."

"Nothing happened? But Tanya told Mum that she and your friend had – had spent the night together."

"No way," he said forcefully. "My mate's a happily married man who went home to his wife at the end of the evening. To be honest, I'm afraid I sort of conned him into coming, to give me an alibi. He gave me a right dressing down about it when he realised. But are you saying Tanya let your mother believe…?"

"That she'd slept with your friend. And Mum was so drunk, she couldn't remember and so she did believe her."

He swore. "She was a piece of work, wasn't she? I mean, I'm sorry she's dead. But jeez – do you know, I always thought it was weird the way Shirley – I mean, Cheryl – suddenly went. One minute she was drinking mineral water, the next Tanya had ordered a bottle of fizz and that was it. My mate said he wondered if she was on some pills of some sort that reacted badly to alcohol. Hello? Are you still there?"

I was still there. Still trying to take it in. It made more sense. But would Tanya have actually sunk so low as to spike Mum's drink? Why?

Would it have been to keep Mum quiet? I found it hard to believe that even Tanya could have been so cold and calculating. And yet, it was the only explanation.

Adam was actually very nice in the end. He offered to talk to his friend and get him to confirm what he'd just told me. I was dying to go back and tell Mum, but I didn't dare return to the house until I'd got rid of Prescott.

I called Elsie's landline – none of these nasty 'mobility phones that fry your brains' for her, thank you very much – to

202

see if she was back yet, but there was no answer. There was no way of leaving a message, either, so I carried on with my plan to walk Prescott as far as the Manor and back. Having a dog with me would give me a good excuse if I was caught nosing around.

***

He'd already peed on every lamppost and barked at every leaf, cat and squirrel during our morning walk, so for a change of scenery I took the longer route to the Manor, which led up past Winchmoor Mill.

I thought about knocking on the door and asking Fiona if she and Gerald had got their alibis sorted out yet, just for the fun of it. But Prescott began digging up their tulips, so I decided it would be better to keep him moving.

Winchmoor Manor is right on the edge of the village. I'd just reached it and was about to turn round and go and see if Elsie was back, when I saw Fiona. She was walking up the long tree-lined drive that led up to the Manor. What was she doing? On impulse, I decided to follow her.

But have you ever tried following someone unobtrusively when you're with a lunatic dog who barks hysterically at every bird or insect that comes within six feet of him? I had no chance.

The look on Fiona's face as she watched me approach suggested she'd not yet forgiven me for Saturday's grilling at the restaurant.

"Do you have business at the Manor?" she asked icily.

"Sort of." I scrabbled in my pocket and took out one of Mum's appointment cards I'd used for a shopping list. "I'm delivering a condolence card."

I waved it about and hoped she wouldn't notice. Unfortunately, she did.

"When are you going to grow up?" Her voice had been at freezing point before, now it was fifty degrees below and her strange eyes glittered like silver-green icicles. "I've had enough of your childish games. I'm going to tell the police you've been harassing me."

"And will you also tell them about the row you had with Margot?" I flashed back. "And how you stand to gain, twofold, by Margot's death?"

"You ridiculous girl. How do you make that out?"

"First there's the parish council election. And, second, the damage Margot was doing to your business."

"That's nonsense." She stepped towards me, her fists clenched. "For your information, I've decided not to stand for election to the parish council anyway. My husband's convinced me that our business needs me to focus on it one hundred per cent if we are to survive."

"Has he now? And did you know your husband was the one who encouraged Margot to stand against you? To stop you being elected? And that now she's dead, he's going around asking anyone in the village who can write their name to put themselves forward for election?"

"How dare you spread lies like that?" Her voice was a cross between a hiss and a growl, and reminded me strongly of Cedric's reaction to Prescott earlier. "You've always had it in for Gerald, haven't you? What has he ever done to you?"

How long have you got? I wanted to ask her. But there was no point.

"So what are you really doing here?" I said, "Knowing John Duckett-Trimble is away and the house is all shut up?"

"Unlike you, I really was going to deliver this," she held out an envelope. "I was going to see if Mr Jenkins is around and ask him to forward it for me. But I've changed my mind." She advanced towards me, the envelope crumpled in her tightly-clenched fist. "And now I'm warning you, Katie, take your unpleasant little dog and go home before you find yourself seriously out of your depth."

I took a step back, my heart hammering. Had I just been threatened by Fiona wouldn't't-say-boo-to-a-goose Crabshaw?

Chapter Twenty-One

As she stalked off I looked around for my 'unpleasant little dog' (she'd got that right, at least) and realised he was no longer with me. He must have slipped his lead while I was scratching around for my fake condolence card.

"Prescott!" I yelled, but my Dog Bellower strategy was obviously not working any more. I didn't dare call again in case Jenkins heard me, so I walked on up the drive, looking and listening all the time. I was just working out how I was going to break it to Elsie that I'd lost Prescott, when I heard a familiar snarling sound. It was coming from a building to the left that was screened from the main house by a thick laurel hedge.

Could this be the old stables Tanya had mentioned in her notebook? Fetching Prescott would give me a perfect excuse to go and have a nose around the place if Jenkins challenged me.

"Cheers, Prescott," I whispered as I crept towards the half-timber, half-brick building. As I got closer I could see it was indeed an old stable block, although it must have been a long time since any horses were stabled here.

Half a dozen loose boxes, each with a split stable door, stood around three sides of a courtyard, where a fine crop of thistles grew up among the cobblestones. An old stone shed that was probably once the tack room made up the fourth side.

The stables, like the barn I'd looked in earlier, were in a very poor state of repair. There were missing roof tiles, rotting door frames and grime-encrusted, cracked or broken windows. These buildings, like the barn, had obviously not been included in the extensive repairs John Duckett-Trimble had made when he'd renovated the Manor.

The door to a loose box in the far corner was open, and I

could hear Prescott's distinctive snarling coming from inside, which meant I'd got the little ratbag cornered. My plan was to creep up on him and snap the lead on while he was still snuffling about. That done, I could then have a good look around.

But as I went into the loose box to get him, a stomach-churning smell hit me. A combination of raw, rough cider, rotting vegetation and engine oil, I recognised it immediately.

When Will and I were fourteen and fifteen respectively, we'd broken into Abe Compton's cider barn one summer evening and helped ourselves to a drop or ten of Abe's legendary HeadBender cider. We'd heard so much about it and were anxious to try it out for ourselves.

It did more than bend my head. It bent my legs, arms, lips and tongue and turned most of my internal organs inside out. I have never felt so ill or been so sick, either before or since.

Never, ever, ever again, I'd vowed then, and I've had no difficulty keeping that promise. Anything remotely cider-like still sends my stomach into its super-spin cycle.

And yet I'd smelt it somewhere else. And recently. Not just the cider, but the whole thing, even down to the engine oil. I couldn't believe I hadn't been able to identify it at the time.

It was in the old barn. And now, it was here. But why? Why would the inside of this tumble-down stable smell like the inside of Abe Compton's cider barn? I took a deep breath and tried not to inhale again as I went in after Prescott.

There was a pile of old rags in the far corner and he was burrowing so deeply into it that the only bit of him still visible was his stubby little tail, which was going like a supercharged windscreen wiper.

Still holding my breath, I crept towards him, intending to grab him before he saw me. But before I could do so, my phone rang.

"Dog-napper!" an angry voice shrieked. "Where are you? And, more to the point, where's Prescott?"

"It's all right, Elsie, he's with me. I'm up at the Manor. But where have you been? I've been—"

"Never you mind about me, you dog-napper. I got your

ransom note but I'll tell you now I'm not paying you a single penny. And if you harm one hair of his little head…"

"But I told you in my note," I began, but at that moment Prescott backed away from the rags and started barking. Elsie screeched, "Dog-napper!" again and slammed the phone down.

I was in the middle of calling her back when the sound of footsteps made me whirl round.

"Are you going to shut that bloody dog up, or am I going to have to shoot it?" asked a voice behind me.

I expected to see hatchet-faced Jenkins scowling at me. But it wasn't Jenkins. Only it took my confused brain a little while to compute that.

It was John Duckett-Trimble.

He was standing in the doorway, the loaded shotgun in his hand pointing straight at me. He looked every inch the genial English country gentleman, out for an afternoon's sport.

Except his expression wasn't terribly genial. In fact, his face was cold. Unsmiling.

"H-hi," I stammered, trying really hard to keep my voice from drying up completely under that icy stare. "I bet you're wondering what I'm doing in here, aren't you? And yes, I know that technically I am trespassing. But, you see, the thing is the – the dog slipped his lead. He does that quite often, the little hooligan, and he – he came in here. I was just getting him. I'm really, really sorry."

"Well?" he demanded and turned the gun from me to Prescott. "Shut him up or I shoot him. Your call. I can't bear yapping dogs."

Neither could I. We had that much in common, at least. I grabbed Prescott by the collar and went to pick him up. But as I did so, he made a lunge for the pile of rags and, as I lifted him up, he had what looked like an old green fleecy jacket clamped between his jaws. I took it out of his mouth but quickly dropped it, as it was obviously the source of the foul smell.

I held him so close I could feel his little heart hammering. Or was that mine? Amazingly, for once in his life, he didn't wriggle or snarl but lay there, in my arms, as the truth of what that jacket was doing here hit me. I couldn't believe it had taken me so long to work it out.

"He's all quiet now," I said, praying he would stay that way. "But would you mind moving your gun? I'm sure you're very safe with it but I have a thing about guns. I'm afraid I have something to tell you that's going to come as a shock. And I'd prefer you weren't pointing that in my direction when I do."

"And what would that be?" he asked as, to my enormous relief, he lowered the gun.

"It's about Jenkins. I-I think… look, I'm sorry to have to tell you this, but I think he killed your wife."

"How do you work that one out?"

"It was the smell. It's on this old jacket. I smelt it earlier in the old barn on Longmoor Drove and I think Jenkins put it there."

He frowned. "I don't follow you. How does that connect with my wife's death?"

"It can only have come from Abe Compton's barn. Believe me, once you've smelt the inside of that place, you never forget it. I'm afraid Jenkins must have been wearing this jacket when he killed her. And then he hid it in the barn. Only when he saw me there this morning, he panicked and moved it to here. He tried to kill me as well, you know. He almost forced me off the road and into the rhine. If a car hadn't come along when it did, I probably wouldn't be standing here now."

"Jenkins told me someone had been nosing around in the barn. That was you?"

"Well, I wouldn't say I was nosing around…"

"And what would you call it? You see, I call it trespassing. Like you're doing now."

"Yes, I know. And I'm sorry. But I explained that, didn't I? I really think you should call the police. And put that in a safe place until they get here." I pointed at the jacket. "They'll need it as evidence."

"But first, tell me, what were you doing in here? And don't give me that nonsense about trying to find the dog."

I decided it was better to tell him the truth. "Tanya had

written something about the stables in her notebook and I was curious to follow it up."

"Tanya?" He frowned.

"My aunt. You probably don't know this because you've been away. But she was murdered as well. But the thing is, I think there's a link between your wife's death and hers. I can only think that Jenkins killed them both."

"Why?"

That was the bit I hadn't thought through.

"I don't know." My brain was racing as things were beginning to fall into place. "What I do know is that Tanya and your wife were planning on going into business together. But, of course, you probably knew that. But what I don't get is why Jenkins would want to stop that? I thought maybe he had something illegal going on in the barn, or maybe these old stables – both places that they'd considered for their spa. But both are almost derelict. There's no way either could be used as an upmarket beauty salon. Which only leaves…"

I stopped.

"Go on." His face looked as if it had been set in stone. His eyes cold.

"Which only leaves your house." As soon as the words were out, I regretted them, as his stony expression turned to full-on granite. I went into a bit of rapid verbal back-pedalling: "Only I expect that was just Tanya doing a bit of wishful thinking. She was very big on wishful thinking."

But then I thought of the way she'd looked when she'd hurried off to meet someone that Sunday afternoon, just before she died. She wouldn't have primped and giggled like that for Jenkins.

It was him. She was going to meet John Duckett-Trimble. Which could only mean…

Chapter Twenty-Two

OMG. Time for a quick exit.

"Anyhow," I said brightly, holding Prescott tightly and beginning to sidle towards the door. "I'll let you get on. I can see you're busy. I'll – I'll just head off now and leave you to it."

"You're going nowhere," he snapped as he levelled the gun. He nodded towards an old wooden tack box in the far corner. "Over there. Sit down."

"But I won't tell anyone, I promise," I said, horribly conscious of his finger hovering over the trigger. Conscious, too, that I was beginning to babble. Because that's what I do when I'm frightened. Words come tumbling out of my mouth before I even know I'm saying them. Words that have completely by-passed my brain. At least, the sensible part of my brain.

Because, while that part was frozen with fear at the sight of the gun, the other part was clicking away, as the cogs began to fall into place.

"Tell anyone what?" he asked quietly. "What is there to tell?"

To my horror I heard myself say, "It was you, wasn't it? Tanya was going to meet you on Sunday afternoon." *Click. Click.* "There's no way she'd have rushed off like that to meet Jenkins."

"Go on."

"Then there's the smell." *Click. Click.* "You must have got cider and oil on your clothes when you were in Abe's barn." *Click.* "At first you hid them in the old barn, but now you've moved them here, because Jenkins told you I was nosing around this morning and may have seen them. Which I hadn't. But I smelt them. And recognised the smell. Although I couldn't make the connection. Until now."

Click. Click. Click, went the only part of my brain that was working. The other part, the bit that covers self-preservation, had shut down the moment he pointed that gun at me.

"And that is?" His voice was dead quiet. And calm. Like we were standing here, discussing the increase in the price of potatoes.

But still that didn't stop me. In fact, it made me worse.

"That it wasn't Jenkins who killed Margot. It was you. Then you dumped her body in the cider vat."

"Clever little thing, aren't you?"

No. No. Nooooo. Not clever at all, a voice inside my head screamed as the self-preservation part of my brain finally woke up. Too late. *Very, very stupid.*

"I won't tell a soul," I whimpered. "I promise."

"Damn right you won't." He was still speaking in this dead ordinary voice, which somehow made it all a million times more scary. "I came out here to burn down this stable block. A nice little insurance claim, plus I get rid of the clothes which, as you so rightly surmise, I wore when I killed my wife. She made a bigger splash than I'd anticipated. Damn cider went everywhere."

"T-terrible stuff," I stammered, hanging on to Prescott like he was a lifebelt and I'd just abandoned ship.

"So on the bonfire they go," he went on, still in the same quiet voice. "You, too. When they search the rubble, they'll find the char-grilled remains of you and your annoying little dog, who were both trespassing and got trapped inside. Maybe it was you who started it? Do you smoke?"

"No. Please..." I whispered, as I prepared to grovel.

"So isn't this the bit where you tell me why I did it, and I say it's a fair cop and come quietly?"

I should have made out I didn't have a clue what he was talking about. Instead, I said: "Because she was having an affair?"

He shook his head. "She could have had every man in the village for all I cared. She wasn't really my wife. I've got more sense than to tie myself down, particularly to someone like her. I needed someone who could play the part of the lady of the manor for a while, which she did to a tee."

I thought of the conversation Jules had overheard when Margot had talked about wanting everything out in the open. She hadn't been talking to Gruesome Gerald. But to John, her supposed husband.

"How do you mean, play a part?" I asked.

"This country squire thing was a good cover for a while but it's time to move on. Particularly now I've got a buyer for the place."

"Good cover? You mean you're not…?"

"John Duckett-Trimble? Something big in the City?" he laughed. "Dear old Maggie, that's Margot to you. She loved pulling that one, didn't she? Of course my name isn't John Duckett-Trimble. That was just something I made up. And sure I'm big in the city, only the city's Bristol and I'm big in betting shops and massage parlours, among other things. The country manor pose was a cover for a nice little money-laundering scam I had going on which, I'm glad to say, has just come to a very successful conclusion. I've just sold the entire Much Winchmoor Estate, as we liked to call it, to a very rich Albanian who thinks he's buying in to a little bit of English aristocracy. Which is why it's time to move on. Only Maggie didn't want to."

"You killed her because she didn't want to move?"

"I killed her because she thought she could get what she wanted by threatening to shop me," he snapped. "Nobody does that."

"No, of course not," I agreed feverishly.

"She was a good actress, was Maggie, which was why I picked her in the first place. But, the problem was, she began to believe this lady of the manor nonsense. It all came to a head during a dinner we were hosting to sell the whole country estate thing to the Albanians." His face darkened. "The silly mare only announced, in the middle of the main course, that while I'd been away setting the deal up, she'd actually agreed to stand for the parish council in this little rat-hole of a place. I was livid. There was no way I was going to let her do that."

"Chances are, she wouldn't have been elected," I said.

"Couldn't take that chance, could I? Even when I explained to her that the first thing that would happen, in the unlikely event of her getting elected, was that she – and that meant me as well – would have to complete the Register of Members' Interests. Every busybody from the local council would go over her finances, and mine, with a magnifying glass. And I couldn't have that happen, not while the Albanian deal was so finely balanced. Once they'd signed on the dotted line, I'd be out of here, and out of this bloody country, faster than a rat down a drain pipe. But in the meantime, I told her she had to withdraw from the election. Then she refused. Said she was in too deep to do so."

"But you didn't have to kill her," I said.

He shrugged. "Course I did." He gave a laugh which I didn't feel like joining in with. "And she wasn't the only one who was good at putting on an accent. 'This be Abe Compton speakin', Mrs Duckett-Trimble,'" he drawled. "Not a bad Somerset accent, don't you think?"

It was a pretty rubbish one, actually. But that's not something you tell a guy who's waving a shotgun at you, is it?

"She'd been droning on for ages about this yokel's cider-making and how she was going to 'introduce him to the basic elements of hygiene'. So, I put on this accent, pretended to be him and left a message on the landline asking if she'd come up to the barn later that evening, 'to tell I where I be goin' wrong.' I said for her to be there by 7 o'clock and got Jenkins, who, you may have noticed, can look remarkably like me given the right clothes, to travel to Spain, using the passport in my John Duckett-Trimble name. The perfect alibi, eh? Not only that, I made sure her phone was dead when she set off that evening. She never did remember to check it and the battery was always going on her. I didn't want her shining a light on me and spoiling everything. Not when I'd planned it so carefully."

I shuddered as I realised I was stuck in this smelly old stable with a shivering dog and a cold-blooded, calculating killer.

"It all went exactly to plan. I knew she couldn't resist that message from the yokel, any more than I could resist creeping up behind her in the dark (my eyesight was always better than hers), banging her on the head and heaving her into the vat of cider. And do you want to know why I chose to do that?"

I shook my head. I really, really didn't want to know. But I had a horrible feeling he was going to tell me.

"When she was showing off to my Albanian guests that night at the dinner party, she told us how someone had offered her some of the cider for her guests, and she had retorted that she wouldn't be seen dead drinking the stuff. Really proud of herself, she was. So I thought it was a fitting end for her. What you might call rough justice. Get it? Rough cider? Rough justice? Rough and deadly, more like."

I felt sick and pulled Prescott closer to me. He couldn't have been feeling himself either, because he turned and licked my face.

"I'm sorry they found her so quickly, though," he went on. "That was the only bit that didn't go quite to plan. The regulars in the Winchmoor Arms were saying one night how rough cider would strip the meat off anything. Margot didn't have much flesh on her. It would have been interesting to see how long it took. But now we'll never know. Pity about that. Still, enough chat. I'm going to tie you up, bang the dog on the head, then stand back and enjoy the bonfire."

"But what about Jenkins?" I was grasping at straws now. "He saw me come up here."

He laughed. "Nice try. But Jenkins is on his way to Spain once more, as we speak, with the passport in the name of John Duckett-Trimble. Only this time he's not coming back. I've paid him off. He doesn't have the stomach for this kind of thing."

This kind of thing? Jenkins had seemed to me to have the stomach for a bit of grievous bodily harm. I remembered the way he'd driven behind me, edging me closer and closer to the rhine where Tanya's body was found.

And that was when the last of the pieces clicked into place. But this time, I didn't blurt it out. This time I thought I could use it to buy me and Prescott a bit of a chance.

"I have evidence linking you to the murder," I said.

"Nice try, but I know what you're doing."

"You do?" I said, though I thought it was pretty obvious what I was doing. I was shaking in my shoes.

"You're trying to keep me talking, thinking that if we stay here long enough, the cavalry will come charging in to the rescue. Well, sorry, sweetheart. That only works in the movies."

"You also killed Tanya, my aunt. She was going to go into business with Margot. You killed them both, didn't you?"

"I said the time for talking is over," he snapped. "I've got things to do and you're beginning to get on my nerves."

"But you won't get away with it. Tanya kept a notebook where she wrote it all down. All about meeting you on Sunday afternoon. And about the business plan she and Margot had put together. And, before you ask, it's already with the police. I handed it over this morning when I found it."

For the first time, there was a flicker of doubt in his eyes. Then it cleared.

"I don't believe you. Anyway, one of the advantages of living under an assumed name is that I don't exist. I can disappear in an instant, and I have some very good friends on standby to help me do just that, as soon as I've finished here."

"You might as well tell me. You owe me that, at least. Why did you kill Tanya? What did she ever do to you?"

"Now there was another really, really stupid woman. She threatened me and, as Maggie found to her cost, no one does that and lives to tell the tale. As you're about to find out, too."

"But I'm not threatening you."

He gave a short laugh. "You reckon? You're the biggest threat of the lot. What is it with you women that you can't leave well alone?"

What indeed? I thought with a gulp. A few years ago Tanya had worked in a busy city centre hairdressing salon in Bristol which, I imagined, was where she'd remembered 'Margot' from – only of course she hadn't been Margot then, but Maggie.

215

Once she discovered that 'Margot' was living here under a false name, she obviously began to see the potential in hanging around Much Winchmoor for a while, particularly once she found out how rich John Duckett-Trimble was. That would have been at about the same time that she decided Margot was a potential business partner. Did she blackmail Margot into agreeing to it? I wouldn't have put it past her.

"So what was it Tanya wouldn't leave well alone?" I asked. "You might as well tell me."

"She claimed Margot had agreed to go in to business with her, some stupid story about how they were going to turn part of the Manor into a beauty salon, or some such nonsense. Told me the partnership could still go ahead, in spite of 'darling Margot's tragic death,' was how she put it. Said it was what Margot would have wanted and the place would be a tribute to her. Oh yes, and she also said we would both make a fortune."

"But you didn't want that."

"Own a bloody beauty salon? Too damn right I didn't. I've spent a lot of money, not to say time, transferring funds from my various businesses to the Winchmoor Estate Limited, then setting up this deal with the Albanians. Why on earth would I throw that away? I've got enough money out of this deal to leave this damned country and go to a place with no extradition treaties."

"But you didn't have to kill her."

He shrugged. "She wouldn't take no for an answer. That was when she turned nasty. Said she knew who Maggie really was. How she'd recognised her because she used to work in the salon that Maggie used sometimes. Then she threatened to blow the whistle, unless I agreed to go ahead with Maggie's plan for her stupid beauty salon."

"Heaven Scents Spa and Beauty," I murmured.

He shook his head. "Bloody nonsense. Anyway, I agreed to meet her to discuss location. I said it wouldn't work in the Manor itself but that I had an old barn that could work very well, if she'd like to meet me there. Which she did."

"It was you she was going to see that Sunday afternoon, wasn't it?" I thought how excited she'd been when I'd seen

216

her getting into her car.

"I made sure the barn door was open, then hid inside. I'd told her to wait outside for me but I knew she wouldn't be able to resist having a nose around. And so she did."

"You killed her in the barn? Like you did with Maggie."

He nodded. "Different barn. Same MO. I whacked her over the head with the baseball bat I used on Maggie. That one over there, look. That'll do for the dog. I'd rather not waste a shotgun cartridge on him. Nor you. I'd prefer they didn't find traces of it among your remains. Although I will if I have to. It's just the baseball bat will be so much more convenient, and will burn along with everything else."

I shuddered. "But why did you dump Tanya's body in the rhine? Why not leave it in the barn?"

"She put the idea of staging an accident into my head. Made a big thing of telling me how she didn't think the barn would be suitable for her precious salon because of the state of the road. How she'd skidded on her way to meet me and almost ended up in the rhine. It seemed a shame to waste those skid marks. So I put her in her car, drove it to where the skid marks were, heaved her across to the driver's seat and pushed the car into the rhine. With a bit of luck, the local plod would have put it down as an accident."

"But they didn't," I said.

He shrugged. "It doesn't matter now. Like I said, just need to do this last bit of tidying up, then I'm out of here. Now," he picked up with baseball bat with his free hand and came towards me. "Bedtime story is over."

***

I'd like to say I resisted him. That I remembered the judo I'd learnt at college and hurled him to the floor.

Only I didn't. I froze. And whimpered. And cried when he tied Prescott to the doorpost. I cried, too, when the baler twine cut into my wrists and ankles. And when he poured petrol everywhere.

I thought of Will, the way I felt when he kissed me, how his eyes crinkled up when he laughed and of the future we'd never have together. Because, of course, I'd always known we'd end up together. Deep in my heart. I was never going to leave Much Winchmoor as long as he was there, no matter how much I talked about doing so. Because he was all I needed. All I'd ever wanted. The man I'd thought I'd grow old with.

But now, I'd never get the chance to tell him that. Never get the chance to tell him that I was sorry that the last words I'd exchanged with him had been harsh ones (even though he'd been the one in the wrong).

And that he was, and always would be, the love of my life.

I thought of my mum and dad and the big cartwheel wedding hat Mum would never get to wear, the over-the-top meringue wedding dress she'd never force me into. The grandchildren they'd never cluck and fuss over. I thought of poor little Prescott and how Elsie would miss him.

Then I heard Prescott yelp and something inside me snapped. I jumped to my feet, screamed at John to leave him alone, and took a step towards him.

Pain ripped through my body.

I was falling. Falling.

More pain. Searing. Blinding. Then everything went black.

Chapter Twenty-Three

When I opened my eyes, I was on one of those fairground rides where the floor suddenly starts to buck and weave beneath your feet. I hate those things and couldn't work out what on earth I was doing on one. Any more than I could work out what the noise was. It was unlike any fairground music I'd ever heard.

Lots of yelling, cursing, growling.

Growling?

I shook my head to try and shake down the cotton wool that was filling it. Growling meant dog. Dog meant Prescott. Growling dog meant Prescott was alive.

And so was I.

With a sudden whoosh the cotton wool disappeared as it all came rushing back. You wouldn't think it was possible to forget you're tied up, would you? And yet, when I'd thought John was hurting poor little Prescott, I was so desperate to defend him, that's exactly what had happened.

I'd pitched forward like a sack of King Edwards and, unable to use my hands to save myself, cracked my knees, shoulder and head on the stable's concrete floor. Blood was oozing down my face from the cut on my temple.

'Poor little Prescott,' on the other hand, was doing just fine on his own. He'd slipped his lead again and his jaws were clamped so firmly around John's lower leg, it was like he was welded on. And the more John struggled and cursed, the deeper Prescott's razor-sharp teeth sank into John's fleshy calf. He was screaming with rage and, hopefully, lots and lots of pain.

I struggled to free my hands so I could call the police. But John might be rubbish at disentangling himself from a very cross, determined little terrier but he was sure good at tying people up.

Then, like John Wayne leading the cavalry down into the canyon, the police arrived anyway.

"Will someone deal with that blasted dog?" they yelled.

***

"So, my little Prescott was the hero of the hour, was he?" Elsie said as she, her grandson Danny and I crowded into her wrecked kitchen and watched as Prescott tucked into a dish of his favourite sherry trifle.

"He certainly was," I smiled fondly and, without thinking, reached down to pat him. Big mistake. Prescott was back to his usual snapping, snarling self. "But if the police hadn't arrived when they did…" I shivered and didn't complete the sentence.

"And that was all thanks to me," Elsie preened. "I knew they wouldn't turn out for a dog so I made out it was you being held against your will at the Manor, thinking that when they showed up, you'd realise the game was up and let Prescott go."

Actually I'd heard the police say that Jenkins had been arrested at Bristol airport with John's passport and they were on their way to the Manor to check it out when they got the call. But when they got there, there was no answer from the house, so they had a look around, and that's when they heard John shouting at the dog and decided to go and investigate.

But I let Elsie have her moment. It was her dog, after all, who'd saved me.

"But why on earth did you think I'd dog-napped Prescott?" I asked. "Didn't you see the note I left for you?"

Elsie flushed. "Your writing's terrible," she muttered. "I don't know what they teach you youngsters in schools these days. It's certainly not how to write properly. Nor to respect their elders and betters."

"What Gran's trying to say, in her sweet old-fashioned way, is that she didn't have the right glasses on so she didn't read your note properly," said Danny. "She'd phoned you and then the police while I was parking the car. By the time I came in, it was too late to stop her. Thank goodness," he added with a slow, lazy smile that gave me the same warm, fuzzy feeling I get when I drink a mug of hot chocolate – with marshmallows.

I smiled back at him, enjoying the warmth and fuzziness. Until I remembered he was a rat. My smile faded abruptly.

"So where've you been?" I asked Elsie. "Olive thought you'd been abducted, seeing as it was chiropodist day."

She gave me an indignant look. "My life doesn't revolve around my bunions. As it happens, I had better things to do. My son Mark, that's Danny's dad, took me shopping at Cribbs Causeway. I've had lunch in John Lewis, tea in Marks and Sparks and I've bought a new fridge. Top of the range. And now," she said, looking around the wreckage of her kitchen and beaming. "Now, it looks like I'm going to have to get a new kitchen to go with it."

"But I thought you were—" I stopped, not wanting them to know I'd accidentally overheard their conversation the other day.

"Thought I was what? Broke?" She frowned at me. "Yes, Danny told me that's what you thought. Where did you get that idea from? I might not be rolling in money. But I'm not broke."

"I'm not sure exactly..." I mumbled. Well, I wasn't going to say 'from inside your broom cupboard,' was I?

"Certainly I've been a bit strapped for cash recently," she said. "But that's all sorted now, thanks to young Danny here. When he was here last week he asked about the plot of land I've bought in the village and came up with this great idea to persuade Mark to release some of my capital. I think that was how you put it, Danny, wasn't it?"

Danny nodded. "I told Dad Gran was thinking of selling her plot as she needed the cash. And Dad, who has a thing about rising land values and capitalising your assets, came here at the weekend. He saw the plot of land by the church and got very excited. Reckoned it could well be worth a small fortune in a few years."

"He begged me not to sell," Elsie chuckled. "Said he'd let

221

me have all the money I needed and promised to transfer my money from his high interest don't-touch-for-years account back into my current account."

"She even got him to take her to the Mall at Cribbs Causeway," laughed Danny, giving his grandmother a look of pure admiration. "Absolutely priceless. Dad hates shopping."

"Good for you. But still, that piece of land down by the church," I said. "It would be such a shame if that was built on. The apple trees…"

"Are quite safe," Danny said, with that smile again. "Go on, Gran, don't tease her. Tell her where your plot of land really is."

"It is near the church, like I said. Row K, Plot twenty-nine."

I stared at her blankly, so she went on: "I bought a burial plot in the churchyard. Very nice it is, too, with a lovely view of the church clock. Only I haven't quite got round to telling Mark that yet. He still thinks I've bought a building plot."

She was still cackling as I left. I started the walk home, wondering how on earth I was going to explain the big, sterile dressing that the paramedic had insisted on sticking on my forehead to Mum and Dad. Not to mention how much of what went on in John Duckett-Trimble's stables to tell them. Then I heard someone call my name.

"Katie?" It was Danny. "Look, for some reason we seem to have got off on the wrong foot. How about we start again? Like tonight, over dinner?"

I looked at his Johnny Depp smile and chocolate brown eyes. He was still the best-looking thing to appear in Much Winchmoor since the church weather vane got a shiny new brass cockerel for the millennium. And I was tempted.

Then I remembered Will, who's more John Wayne than Johnny Depp – except he didn't come charging into the canyon with the rest of the cavalry back there in the stables. But I know he would have done so without a moment's hesitation, if I'd asked. Although he'd have moaned and grumbled at me for getting into the mess in the first place.

Will's one of the good guys. Solid and dependable. I remembered how I'd felt when I thought I'd never see him again. I tried to imagine what life would be like without him teasing me, bullying me and generally getting on my nerves. And I couldn't.

"Sorry, Danny," I said, with genuine regret. "I'm spoken for. And so, according to your grandmother, are you."

Three months later

Not much has changed in Not Much Winchmoor, except that spring has finally given way to summer, the apple trees near the church have blossomed and Elsie has got not only a new fridge but a new cooker as well. She's also got a new coffee machine – that she has no idea how to work – even though she thinks coffee is the drink of the devil and it gives her 'paltry-patians'.

Her ankle is now completely healed, which means I don't have a job with her any more. But I still walk Prescott every day. For free. He saved my life and I owe the little monster. Also, it means I get to see Elsie every day. And although I get on her nerves and she gets on mine, we both kind of like it that way.

Mum and Dad are speaking to each other again. And that wasn't because of what Adam told me about the way Tanya had set Mum up in Bournemouth. They'd already made up before I got the chance to tell them that. What really brought them together was when they learnt what happened between me and John Duckett-Trimble. I'd been hoping they need never find out. No chance. This is Much Winchmoor, after all.

They were both furious with me and said it was a pity I wasn't a few years younger as they'd have grounded me for life for behaving so irresponsibly. As for Will, he was worse than the pair of them put together and says I shouldn't be allowed out on my own.

I told him he was not my mother and he said, no, thank goodness.

On a more positive note, my finances are slowly improving. Shane's little scooter has made a mega difference and Mike at *The Chronicle* has extended my patch to villages within a fifteen mile radius. And I get to claim mileage allowance and now have several meetings a week to cover, while my weekends are taken up working in the pub.

Even my secondary career as a dog walker is beginning to work out, and I now walk Shane's Labrador, Rosie, while he's out at work. And only last week, someone in the bar was moaning about the cost of doggy day care, which has got me thinking...

Fiona Crabshaw took my advice and tackled Gerald about his efforts to get someone to stand against her in the parish council elections. After Margot's death, she'd been going to withdraw, but once Gerald admitted what he'd done, she changed her mind and got herself elected unopposed. And at last month's meeting she volunteered herself onto the sub-committee responsible for the parish's potholes. She is now often to be seen around the village with her clipboard and ruler, measuring and charting the potholes. Rumour has it that Gerald can be found most mornings in the kitchen of Winchmoor Mill guest house, cooking up sausages and bacon for the guests' full English breakfasts.

Jules is a lot happier since the baby started sleeping through the night and Ed got himself a half-decent job with a regular wage.

On a less pleasant note, John Duckett-Trimble has been remanded in custody, awaiting trial for double murder. Jenkins is being called as a witness for the prosecution and has already provided the police with enough information about John's shady business dealings to keep him in prison for a long, long time. The sale of the Manor fell through, as the purchasers weren't as gullible as he'd thought and pulled out before anything was signed.

The talk among the regulars at the pub is of the Manor being sold as a hotel. Or becoming headquarters of some hi-tech company that's going to turn Much Winchmoor into Somerset's own Silicon Valley. Or a rehab centre for injured footballers. Or maybe even a combination of all three. That's the thing about the regulars of the Winchmoor Arms – if they don't know something, they'll make it up.

Like the stuff they've been making up about me and Will. They all think we're getting married – cartwheel hats, meringue wedding dresses, the lot – and are already planning Will's stag do down to the last detail.

And yes, I know what I said back there in the stable when John Duckett-Trimble was waving that shotgun in my face. About Will being my soul mate. The guy who I want to spend the rest of my life with. And, he is. Of course, he is.

But. And it's a big one.

He's as much a part of Much Winchmoor as the village pond. And his family have been here since forever. Whereas I'm – well, I don't know what I'm part of, if I'm completely honest. For the first time since I was forced to come back here, more broke than broken-hearted, I am completely debt free and the bank owe me money rather than the other way around. It's not a fortune. But it's growing steadily and it's already enough for my ticket out of here.

I'm sitting here, on the bench by the pond. A solitary white duck is swimming towards me in the mistaken belief that I'm going to feed it.

It's Saturday afternoon. I've finished my lunchtime shift at the pub and I'm enjoying the sunshine while I'm waiting for Will. We're going to the village Flower and Produce Show together. He and his dad are presenting the Sally Manning Cup for the best baker, in memory of Will's mum, who made the best meat and potato pies on the planet.

I'm covering the show for *The Chronicle* and am hoping there will be a bit of a showdown between Olive Shrewton, who has won the Victoria sponge class for the last twenty-eight years, and Jane Bixton, a newcomer to the village who thinks she's in with a chance just because Mary Berry once told her that her rock cakes 'showed promise.'

When my phone rings, I groan, thinking it's Will, standing me up again. He does this on a regular basis.

Only it's not Will.

"Hello there," says this lovely Irish voice. You know, the sort of soft, sexy lilt that can make a shopping list sound like a poem. "Would I be talking to the Miss Marple of Much

Winchmoor?"

"Liam? What do you want?" I asked, warily. The last time I'd had dealings with this smooth-talking, ruthlessly ambitious journo, he'd called me an amateur. Among other things. And we hadn't parted on the best of terms.

"I might have some freelance work I could put your way, if you're interested? NUJ rates and a by-line. This could be your big break, Kat Latcham, so it could."

THE END

Read *Murder Served Cold*
the first in the series.

Fantastic Books
Great Authors

CROOKED
CAT

Meet our authors and discover
our exciting range:

- Gripping Thrillers
- Cosy Mysteries
- Romantic Chick-Lit
- Fascinating Historicals
- Exciting Fantasy
- Young Adult and Children's
  Adventures
- Non-Fiction

Visit us at:
www.crookedcatbooks.com

Join us on facebook:
www.facebook.com/crookedcatbooks

39665999R00139

Printed in Poland
by Amazon Fulfillment
Poland Sp. z o.o., Wrocław